ILONA BANNISTER
FIVE

Juniper

Juniper
An imprint of HarperCollins*Publishers* Ltd
1 London Bridge Street
London SE1 9GF

www.harpercollins.co.uk

HarperCollins*Publishers*
Macken House, 39/40 Mayor Street Upper,
Dublin 1, D01 C9W8, Ireland

This edition 2026
1
First published in Great Britain by Juniper,
an imprint of HarperCollins*Publishers* Ltd 2026

Copyright © Ilona Bannister 2026

Ilona Bannister asserts the moral right to be identified as the author of this work.
A catalogue record for this book is available from the British Library.

ISBN: HB: 978-0-00-877056-3
TPB: 978-0-00-877057-0

This book is set in 10.7/15.5 pt. Sabon by Type-it AS, Norway

This novel is entirely a work of fiction. The names, characters and incidents portrayed in it are the work of the author's imagination. Any resemblance to actual persons, living or dead, events or localities is entirely coincidental.

All rights reserved. No part of this publication may be reproduced, stored in a retrieval system, or transmitted, in any form or by any means, electronic, mechanical, photocopying, recording or otherwise, without the prior permission of the publishers.

Without limiting the exclusive rights of any author, contributor or the publisher of this publication, any unauthorised use of this publication to train generative artificial intelligence (AI) technologies is expressly prohibited. HarperCollins also exercise their rights under Article 4(3) of the Digital Single Market Directive 2019/790 and expressly reserve this publication from the text and data mining exception.

Printed and bound in the UK using 100% Renewable
Electricity by CPI Group (UK) Ltd

'Ridiculously good. Razor-sharp, wickedly funny, and darkly thrilling. *Five* is a gripping, chilling story that asks difficult questions about judgement, forgiveness, and the notion of cause and effect. Unforgettable'
Chris Whitaker, *Sunday Times* **bestselling author of** *All the Colours of the Dark*

'Original. Urgent. Disturbing. Brilliant. Quite unlike anything I've ever read. Don't miss this one – Ilona Bannister is a major talent'
Shari Lapena, *Sunday Times* **bestselling author of**
The Couple Next Door

'Viscerally insightful, emotionally punchy, wryly observed, and with scalpel-precision writing . . . I read it in one sitting'
Sarah Pinborough, *Sunday Times* **bestselling author of** *Behind Her Eyes*

'Ilona Bannister has written a riveting, ticking time bomb of a novel. *Five* is brilliant: a gripping tour de force about destiny and choice . . . I devoured it. You will, too'
Chris Bohjalian, Number One *New York Times* **bestselling author**

'I came for the hook but I stayed for the absolutely beautiful storytelling . . . A masterpiece'
Laura Pearson, author of *The Last List of Mabel Beaumont*

'Propulsive, sharp, and ferociously addictive, *Five* is one of the most original novels I've read in years . . . I can't stop thinking about this story. Ilona Bannister is such a talent'
Alafair Burke, *New York Times* **bestselling author of** *The Note*

'Addictive. Bannister's writing waltzes between the tantalising and the profound, leaving you desperate for the outcome whilst deeply conflicted about how you judge people'
Natalie Gregory, author of *Mother Ghost Mango Seed*

'A child, a mother, a businessman, an old woman and a gambler. You'll fall in love with them, you'll pity them, and you'll judge them. But most importantly, you won't want any of them to die'
Stylist

'Clever and incisive . . . the unique format makes readers participants in the action and complicit in weighing the characters' worthiness . . . Unsettling and immersive'
Kirkus Reviews, **starred review**

ILONA BANNISTER is a New Yorker who has lived in the UK for many years with her husband and sons. She is a dual qualified US lawyer and UK solicitor and practised immigration law in the UK before she started writing fiction. Her family's history of migration to the US, her experience as an American mother raising children in the UK, and her work as a lawyer have led her to write stories about otherness, belonging, and what it means to be on the outside of a place looking in. Her first book *When I Ran Away* was longlisted for the First Novel Prize in 2021.

Also by Ilona Bannister

When I Ran Away
Little Prisons

For Tim, Leo, and Rex, always, everything

Time	Destination	Expected
1st 7:06	London Victoria	5 min
South London Service formed of 8 coaches.		
2nd 7:13	Bedford	12 min

07:01

Someone will die here this morning, at this suburban train station. It will happen in the next five minutes when the 7:06 to London Victoria arrives.

Four others have died here previously. In 1861, an alcoholic mourning his dead wife and child in a stupor of grief. In 1923, a World War I veteran, suffering from shell shock, bombs exploding in his head until his last breath. In 1972, a teenage girl, unmarried and pregnant, forced to leave home by her parents. In 1994, a seeing-eye dog who gave its life to save its owner when he stumbled perilously close to the tracks at just the wrong moment.

At least two of these deaths were accidental, one was intentional, and one seemed intentional but wasn't, but they will not be described here in detail because we have only a few minutes before the train arrives. And there is a great deal yet to discuss. And a fifth death to witness that may or may not be deliberate. It will be hard to tell when it happens.

Turn your attention now to the stairs descending to the platform. A small child struggles out of his mother's grasp. He shrieks. He bolts towards the tracks.

He looks over his shoulder and sees his stricken mother, running. He laughs and trots to the edge of the platform. He turns around to face her, his back to the platform edge and the tracks beneath it. He does not realise that he has crossed the yellow caution line. Even if he does realise it, he is too young to understand the yellow line's warning that another step back will be too far. He steps.

He loses his footing and the platform disappears underneath him. He looks at his mother. As he begins to fall, he meets her eyes and in them he sees something he does not yet have the words to name. It is not anger or fear.

It is hesitation. *It would be easier if I lost him,* is the thought she thinks for a sliver of a moment, a granule of time, thirty-nine hundredths of a second, to be precise.

Pause here for a moment.

Please do not judge this mother for having this thought. Thoughts like these come to all mothers. They are involuntary. Sometimes they appear precisely because they are the opposite of what the mother truly thinks. The mother's anxious, exhausted brain plays a sinister game with her. It makes her think that she will say and do things that she would never, ever say or do.

For example, a mother does not really want to throw her baby out of the third-storey window to perish on the pavement below, although she may think this every time the window catches her eye when she passes it, holding her crying infant to her chest and swaying in her reflection in the glass. A mother does not want to push her baby buggy in front of

FIVE

a bus, although the thought flickers across her mind every time she stands at the bus stop, her toddler whining and struggling against the straps of the seat.

A mother's brain, knowing how much she loves her child, tortures her with that love, inverts her love, turns it inside out with horrible, haunting thoughts of terrible things that she would never do and that will never happen to her child. So please, do not think badly of this mother for having this thought in this moment.

It is her thoughts that come after it that should concern you.

They'll say it's a shame if he falls, she thinks, the next step she takes imperceptibly slower than the last.

They'll say it was an accident, she thinks, reaching out, but not quite reaching him.

'Oi!' a man shouts on the platform, at 7:01 and seventeen seconds. He is a businessman. A man's man, a macho man, a family man, a self-made man, *whatta man, whatta man, whatta man, whatta might*—

'Oi!' the man shouts as he runs up to the mother and grabs her by the elbow, helping her regain her balance as she in turn grabs her son by the shoulders of his coat. The man pulls the mother with her child from the platform edge. 'Careful now,' he says.

The boy, Gideon, does not say anything. His mother, Emma, thinks, *Fuck,* and says, 'What are you doing here?' quietly. She does not look him in the eye. Breathless, she puts a protective arm around her son's shoulders, adjusts her bag with her other hand, bends to hoist him onto her hip, and struggles because of their bulky coats and because he is six years old and too big for her to carry. The skin on the knuckles of her ungloved hand is cracked and bleeding. From the cold grey air of this morning. From the mother's work that she does.

Emma says, softly, seriously, 'Why are you here?' as Gideon pulls the hat off her head and throws it on the ground and screams. He kicks away from her. She puts him down but grasps his arm tightly, forcefully. 'Gideon,' she says sharply through clenched teeth.

'Here you go,' the man says, picking up the hat. 'One of those mornings, eh?' he says, and he shrugs with a friendly smile.

Emma says nothing. He is speaking to her like they're friends, like colleagues on good terms, and not each other's downfall. How much simpler, better, her life would have been if she had never met, never known this man.

'Did you follow me?' she asks.

'Should I have a little chat with 'im?' the businessman says to her in a lower voice, ignoring her question. 'Tell the boy to give 'is mum a break—'

Emma grabs the hat, briefly looking the man in the eye, and says, 'No. I'm trying to do what you want. I need time.'

The businessman steps back. 'Look, forget about yesterday. Just hear me out,' he says. 'And you,' he crouches down to be on Gideon's eye level, 'you be good for your mum.' Standing he says to Emma, 'He's just like my others, full of beans.'

Except that Gideon is nothing like his 'others', the other six children of the businessman. The two youngest of whom

FIVE

are boys, a little older than Gideon, the result of his third marriage to a much younger woman who will be dropping them off at school about twenty-five minutes after the death in their brand-new G-Wagon. They are well adjusted and rosy cheeked, and the young wife will tell them that she loves them when she leaves them and then drives away to start her day with Pilates, then the PTA fundraiser meeting, then walking the dog and shopping online before she picks them up from after-school football or drama or how-to-grow-up-to-be-just-like-your-asshole-rich-dad training. Emma would like to tell his wife to fuck off and die. She would like to tell all the wives like the businessman's wife to fuck off and die.

She would like to get away from the businessman now, she would like for him not to look at her and her son and make assumptions.

'I'm working on your brother,' she says to the businessman. 'But I can't talk about it now.'

Emma then turns abruptly with Gideon and moves to a bench further down the platform. She doesn't care if the businessman thinks she's a bitch. Their exchange lasts twenty-seven seconds.

Bitch, the businessman thinks for sixteen hundredths of a second as she leaves. He watches Emma and her son walk down the platform. He considers his next move. Emma is skittish and he had hoped she'd behave herself in a public place. He scared her yesterday. He shouldn't have done that. He just wants her to smooth it over with his brother. Then put their pooled money into the start-up he's funding today – a project with lifesaving potential on a world-changing scale – and forget all of this when they're rolling in it. That's all. Money fixes everything. Which is why the businessman is confused by Emma's reaction because usually women listen to him. Usually women love him. Well, perhaps not all women.

For example, the slender, elderly white woman with the short white hair who is watching him and Emma right now would definitely not love him if she met him. The businessman, admittedly, does not do well with her demographic, as he is only interested in women who are fuckable, so he has not noticed her this morning. And this is just as well because the old woman, Mrs Worth, does not want to be noticed. And she certainly doesn't want to be fucked. Not this morning. She is standing in her long black coat, collar up against the wind, at the far end of the platform where the sign warns, PASSENGERS MUST NOT PASS THIS POINT OR CROSS THE LINE.

During the twenty-seven seconds of the businessman and Emma's conversation, Mrs Worth was lighting a surreptitious cigarette. She knows no one is watching her because it is early in the morning and no one cares about the activities of old women, and she also doesn't give a goddamn if they do. She is nervous. It is an important day.

Mrs Worth takes her second drag and enjoys judging Emma, who is now on a bench furiously taking things out of her bag, looking for something.

Emma's every emotion is betrayed by her skin. Red blotches of rage and embarrassment creep up her neck as Mrs Worth watches her shove things into her bag, empty her coat pockets,

FIVE

and swear when she can't find her phone. Mrs Worth notices the small bandage on Emma's eyebrow. Emma once had a golden complexion, sparkling eyes and enviable blonde tresses. But she has been so drained by Gideon's difficult birth and subsequent difficult life that her eyes have lost their colour and her hair has faded from gold to gossamer. Her skin is as pale as the butter of post office walls. Only when she feels shame or self-consciousness does her pallor change, the red patches pulsing under her translucence like neon hotel signs on postcards of Las Vegas.

Good Lord, Mrs Worth thinks, watching her, referring to Emma but also by extension to all women born after 1975 who have careers and children but constantly complain about how difficult the 'balance' is, and take pride in not being able to cook as though being negligent about a child's diet is a feminist statement while they pay other women to be their cleaners and nannies and assistants and still, with all that support, can't manage the behaviour of their children on a public outing when women like her did it all alone, all the time, with no one's help. *Useless,* she thinks. She looks at Gideon, swinging his legs, shouting something incoherent, and thinks, *Probably hyperactive or transgender or allergic to nuts like all of them these days.*

Emma feels Mrs Worth's eyes on her, she looks up. There is a flicker of eye contact that lasts thirty-one-hundredths of a second. *Old crone,* Emma thinks, familiar with the disapproving glares of mean old women.

Incompetent bint, Mrs Worth thinks and sniffs with

satisfaction, now that she knows that Emma knows she disapproves of her. If more people disapproved of things – social media, self-checkout machines at the supermarket, vegetarians, fat children, those disgraceful leggings that all the women round here wear – the world would be a better place for Mrs Worth. She is perceptive, though. Gideon is indeed allergic to nuts.

Mrs Worth turns her attention away from Emma and watches a small bird alight on the platform. She looks for the train down the track as she puffs on her cigarette. She checks her watch, not long now until the train gets here and takes her to London to see her grandsons. The last time she saw them the little one was four and the big one was six. The little one is nine now and the big one is eleven, and she reckons they have only a vague memory of her, if they have one at all. And God knows what her daughter-in-law put into their heads about her over all these years. But they are her son's sons, and the invitation to her daughter-in-law's funeral feels like a step in the right direction. For all of them. Especially her daughter-in-law.

And then, Mrs Worth finds herself lying on the concrete floor of the platform. She tries to get her bearings, but she is too light-headed. She does not know how she came to be there. But the others do.

At 7:02 and thirteen seconds they heard Emma shout, 'Gideon!' They saw Emma and Gideon struggle over her phone, Gideon clutching his mother's wrist and pushing her arm, the phone flying from Emma's grasp with surprising velocity as she

FIVE

wrestled her bag and her child. They saw the phone shoot past Mrs Worth's head, surprising her and throwing her off balance. As the phone slid off the platform edge and onto the tracks, Mrs Worth fell, due to the hit of nicotine, the cold, the fact she'd had no breakfast, her nerves, and her advanced age – Mrs Worth will be seventy-eight this year – which combined to trigger a cardiac event. She feels a sudden shooting pain from her chest to her jaw to her arm.

From her position Mrs Worth doesn't know the others are looking over the platform edge to see where the phone fell; she can't see Emma running to the edge, Gideon running to the stairs. She doesn't register Emma yelling, 'Goddamn it!'

She only notices the pin-striped burgundy knee of the stranger kneeling beside her. The brown skin of the hand put out towards her, a memory from a long time ago of a hand put out to help her, and then she looks at his face.

'Um,' the stranger says, 'are you all right?'

Despite her disorientation, she manages to give a Mrs Worthian answer: 'Of course I am, don't be ridiculous,' she says, although she thinks she is having a heart attack and she finds it most inconvenient.

'OK,' he says, unsure. 'Are you here with someone?'

'Do I know you?' she asks in a tone that makes him feel as though his question was too personal.

'Uh, no, sorry, look, do you think you can get up? Maybe you shouldn't get up, actually. Did you hit your head?' he says, looking down at her, then up at the digital information display. It says the time is 7:02. *Four minutes,* he thinks.

'I need to get there. I just need to get there,' Mrs Worth says, finding the words hard to say because a fist is tightening around her heart and it won't let go.

'Um, yes, OK, but first we need to make sure you're all right. Can I call someone for you? Do you have a mobile?'

The Good Samaritan is Sonny, a young man of twenty-seven. He grew up in this affluent London suburb, attended a private school nearby, and has been living here since coming home from university to save money and work out his next steps in life. Except that his homecoming was almost six years ago, and he should have made more progress by now. But a few things got in the way. They always do.

Sonny makes excellent first impressions. He is attractive and instantly likeable. He is tall with a slim, athletic, runner's build, and handsome, with a unique sense of style. He relies on his looks, his dress, his racially ambiguous features, as a kind of sleight of hand, a misdirection. There is so much to look at when one meets Sonny – his face, his clothes, his eyes, his way of being – that people often don't actually see him. And he knows it, and this is how he prefers it.

He is wearing an outfit this morning that is very Sonny. A burgundy pin-striped suit with slim-fit flared trousers. To guard against the cold, he's not wearing a coat but an oversized, chunky-knit claret and orange bohemian scarf that is completely inappropriate with a suit, except when Sonny wears it.

The hem of his trousers hits well above his ankles, drawing attention to his white patent wingtips, which he wears

FIVE

without socks, despite the cold day. He is wearing a black shirt with a thin black satin tie. His nails are carefully manicured, painted white. The manicure is feminine but on Sonny's hands also unexpectedly masculine, as is the suit, which he found in the women's section of his favourite vintage clothing shop. His head is shaved but for the crop of copper-brown curls with bleached streaks, which he sometimes ties back to look serious but today put up in a topknot that falls forward just so, allowing one or two of his spiral curls to escape and fall charmingly just in front of his left eye, which is brown, drawing attention to his right eye, which is green.

His green-eyed mother said the green eye was from her Colombian father and the brown eye from her Jamaican mother, and though they had both passed, they loved him so much they came back to see the world with their grandson. Sonny's pale and freckled, copper-haired, blue-eyed Scottish father, whom his wife's parents had never trusted, said his son's different eyes were the result of his mother drinking when she was pregnant, and people laughed when he said this, because they knew that a woman like her would do no such thing.

If you were his friend you would say to your other friend, 'Only Sonny,' and both of you would shake your heads and smile and know you meant that only he could pull off this outfit. You are, and always will be, a little bit in love with him, but you tell your friends that you would never date him because he's *soooo* amazing but he has capital I *Issues*. Although, if you were honest with yourself, you know the reason you are not dating him is that he has never shown the least bit of interest in you. Not in that way. Oh – you think longingly, in secret – but if he did, you could *definitely* be the one to save him. Definitely.

Except you couldn't, because one of his issues is that he is £32,000 in debt due to an online gambling addiction, and even his closest friends don't know. His girlfriend – who isn't as good looking as he is, which you and the other girls find annoying because you're all better looking than her – knows about the gambling. But she doesn't know that he's at this station today.

He has lost all of the money from his trust and sold the vintage Rolex left by his Colombian grandfather, which he mourns every day as it was the most meaningful object he owned. And the £32,000 debt would have been £27,000, except that instead of paying it off, as he had told himself he would, he lost half the money he got for the watch on his favourite poker site.

If he could just get a better job and start earning more, he could pay off the debt, put this behind him, or work two jobs, bring down the debt, pay the debt, or he could play a game right now, because you never know, he might win, he could win enough for it all to go away, or it could all end now, this morning, and he could do what he planned to do and just go to the edge of the platform, just there, and at the right moment, at the right time, imagine it, the relief, he could just jump in front of the—

'Oi, you can't do that!' the voice of the businessman suddenly cuts through Sonny's conversation with Mrs Worth and

FIVE

the constant monologue of the debt, the debt, the debt flowing under his every thought and action.

Emma yells, 'Just watch me!' as she jumps down onto the tracks, so overtaken by adrenaline and anger and frustration that she just barely registers her son mimicking her somewhere, 'Just watch me, watch me!'

'Oi!' the businessman shouts again, as he jumps down onto the tracks after Emma.

Perhaps now is the time to introduce him properly. His name is Liam. He is tall and broad, conventionally handsome, the alpha male in every room he enters. He wears exactly too much expensive cologne. He has a Mediterranean complexion, always tan in defiance of the sunless English winter. His smile, charmingly imperfect with that slight gap between his two front teeth, is a small gift he bestows upon women. When they deserve it.

He is in his mid-fifties, but age has only made him more attractive, adding salt, pepper and distinction to his close-cut beard, which matches the dark stubble of his close-cut shaved head. Even Liam cannot make hair grow where nature has determined it no longer will, but he has turned his hair loss to his advantage. He is ruggedly handsome, his male pattern baldness a credit to his virility, as though his hair simply could not survive his potent masculinity and so surrendered, defeated, leaving his scalp as a shining emblem of his vigour.

Liam gets up at five every morning to run and work out in the very expensive gym in the finished basement of his enormous suburban house, and it shows. No potbelly of middle age for him. He has the abs of a much younger man. And the bank account of a very rich one.

Liam usually drives to his office in London. He's only at the station today because he was hoping to catch Emma. He hates taking the train with all of its sad, ordinary people. Having been ordinary himself once, he prefers not to be reminded of those days. Although when doing business, he does like to bring a touch of the common man into the room. It's a useful tool that makes men born into affluence uncomfortable and deferential. Especially in today's climate. It is why he still thickens his accent when he speaks to men of greater education and higher birth. He knows it stings when his dropped *h*s and double negatives remind them of his lesser beginnings but his bespoke Italian shoes remind them of his greater wealth.

If he survives and gets to his meeting, Liam will make an investment in an opportunity presented to him by two young people from the generation that people Liam's age have little respect for because they're sensitive, self-centred and politically self-righteous. But these two are onto something, he can feel it. And if he is right, as he usually is, it will have global implications. And if he can get Emma to get his brother on board, all his problems would be solved.

So it really would be a shame if Liam died before making today's investment. Perhaps even a greater shame than if Gideon, the child, died. Gideon, after all, has nothing to invest. Neither does Emma, who is in debt, having invested all she has in Gideon. Liam knows this. That's why he follows her onto the tracks.

FIVE

Now, pause here.

Take note of their positions.

The child, the mother, the businessman, the old woman and the gambler.

Consider these five in relation to one another.

Consider them in relation to themselves.

Leave them here and meet the others, the witnesses to this morning's events. But please don't hang about. We don't have much time.

In the middle of the platform stand two middle-class, middle-aged, middle-management commuters who are slightly hungover from last night's midweek, mid-priced, mid-range red wine.

The first, whom we'll refer to as Bad Back for reasons that will soon reveal themselves, is tired from training for the charity 10k he was pressured into signing up for and for which he has collected no donations, planning to just give £500 himself at the end and be done with it.

The second, To Do List, is trying to finish her online shopping order on her phone before the train gets here, but she forgot her reading glasses and cannot see the screen clearly and consequently orders Royal Gala apples instead of Pink Ladies.

When her food delivery arrives tomorrow, To Do List will argue with the delivery person and say, 'I didn't order these.' He will show her his handheld device, where it will demonstrate clearly that she ordered Royal Galas, but she will insist that this is impossible, even in the face of hard evidence. To Do List often misdirects her difficult emotions, and the supermarket delivery person will bear the brunt of her reaction to witnessing a death at the train station the day before, not knowing that the Royal Galas represent her new certitude about the futility of her own existence.

But that is tomorrow. On a day like today, a physical description of Bad Back and To Do List would ordinarily follow here. Clever observations about their modes of dress and thinning hair. The matronly bosom of To Do List, for example. Or the paunch of Bad Back and the small tufts of hair in his ears, which suggest a dying marriage because his wife has not noticed as she no longer sees him when she looks at him and/or she does not have the energy to raise the topic of ear hair in a way that will not drive the final nail into the coffin of their union. There are many other mundane but poignant details we could explore in the lives of these ordinary commuters, but we have time constraints. Let's just say that you've seen them before, on some other train platform in some other suburb, weighed down by bags and coats and unmet goals and unrealised dreams.

You might be looking at one of them right now as you wait for your train. Or maybe you're avoiding looking at the unseemly ear hair or mature bust you have noticed in the one sitting next to you by keeping your head down in this book, reading it for book club during your commute, asking yourself why you always put off reading the book until the day before book club.

In any case, Emma and Liam shout at each other, but Bad Back and To Do List can't quite hear what they're saying.

FIVE

They look up from their phones for a moment to roll their eyes privately and sigh heavily. They try to ascertain what roles, if any, they will have in this situation.

Bad Back knows it is never a good idea to get involved when abnormal behaviour is on display in public and returns to looking at his phone.

But To Do List feels uneasy. She's not sure if she added regular or fat-free Greek yogurt to her basket. She'll have to check the order when she gets to the office. Then she turns her attention to the scene.

This isn't good, she thinks, looking at Gideon bouncing by the stairs, and Emma and Liam on the tracks, and Mrs Worth still on the ground. *Someone will have to do something,* she thinks. She pulls out her phone. She leaves herself a voice memo, 'Order Archie's shin guards.'

There is another witness here as well, a young man descending the steps, walking onto the platform. He is a home health aide who has finally finished the night shift at one of the old, large, unrenovated homes in this area that have high but crumbling ceilings and beautiful rooms with peeling brocade wallpaper, where important men once smoked cigars in dinner jackets and velvet slippers but that now house their forgotten elderly owners who both fear and long for the quiet of death.

This young man, whom we will know as Medical Student, is newly arrived in this country. He left his home country in Eastern Africa to study medicine in a country in Eastern Europe, but his training was interrupted there by a homicidal psychotic dictator's egomaniacal war.

He entered the UK on a student visa, intending to start again from scratch. But to pay his university fees and to live, he must work more than the allotted twenty hours permitted, which leaves little time for his studies. So he takes the night shifts to catch up on his reading while occasionally checking to make sure the old rich people are still breathing. Medical Student is tired but will soon spring into action. Unfortunately, he will be just a little too late. Or maybe, depending on how things go, he'll be right on time.

Right now, as he walks down the last few steps to the platform, he is taking in the scene and looking around for anyone with whom he could make eye contact and share a laugh of disbelief at Emma and the incomprehensible behaviour of pale British women when he spots Mrs Worth on the ground. He runs to her side.

Those are the witnesses.

Now, observe that Gideon is crying, or is it laughing? It is hard to know. He rocks on his feet, wraps his arms around himself, makes an aeroplane noise and runs in a circle. 'Watch me!' he echoes his mother and then sits down on the platform edge, his legs dangling over the side, arms crossed. Emma calls to him, 'Stay right there!'

Liam yells at Emma, 'Are you mad?'

Bad Back looks up at them and thinks, *Best not to get involved*. He looks at the digital information display. It says 7:02. He hopes Emma and Liam will wrap this up soon. He has to get to the office. He texts his assistant, just in case he's late.

FIVE

> Nutters on the tracks. Hopefully no delays but will let you know

'C'mon, love, be sensible—' Liam says, walking slowly towards Emma, the phone lying on the tracks between them. Liam's arms are tensed, his knees bent, he approaches her slowly, as though she's a wild animal or a hostage taker or about to jump off a ledge.

But Emma is a mother standing on train tracks. And she has had enough.

They both lunge for the phone, but Liam overpowers her, grabs it, and holds it in the air above her head, out of her reach, as he takes a step backward towards the platform.

'Careful, the third rail!' he warns her.

'What are you doing?' she shrieks, pulling at his jacket, jumping up to grab his arm.

He easily holds her back with his other arm and says, 'I just want to talk.'

To Do List, watching them, feels a surge in her gut, as much as one can feel a surge when wearing very tight tummy control undergarments, and knows that tragedy is upon them. She says into her voice memo app, 'Call window cleaner,' as she hurries up the stairs to find a staff member.

'I'm trying to do what you want, just fuck off!' Emma says, angrily, pushing at Liam.

Liam says, urgently, 'Think about the boy,' gesturing towards Gideon, as he takes careful steps back to the platform.

To this, Emma gives a response, but everyone present hears

her words differently, imbues them with meaning based on their own beliefs about who she is and how women – mothers – should behave. We cannot explore each interpretation in depth, as the clock is ticking and the train has just arrived at the station before this one and opened its doors and will soon be doing the same here. And there is much that still needs to be accomplished before the death.

In summary, Sonny hears her say, 'Don't be a hero, don't try to play me.'

Mrs Worth hears, 'I can't change him, don't try to save me.'

Bad Back hears, 'Don't go changin' to try and please me,' and is momentarily distracted by a brief memory of dancing with his wife on holiday last year to Billy Joel's 'Just the Way You Are', of which this is the first line.

It is at this point, at 7:02 and forty-three seconds, that Gideon shrieks, 'Mama!' his arms outstretched, his eyes fixed on the back of Liam's head and his mother's phone in the air.

'That's Mama's!' Gideon yells, as he leaps from the platform onto Liam's back, eleven seconds before 7:03.

People who experience tragic events often say that they happened in a flash, out of the blue, in the blink of an eye. The average adult blinks fifteen to twenty times a minute. In twenty blinks of an eye, think of all that can happen, and a minute becomes a very long time.

'That's Mama's!' Gideon charges and grapples for the phone, wrapping his legs around the stunned Liam's waist, digging his child's fingers into Liam's collar, scratching the flesh of his neck, reaching up to his arm with surprising strength.

FIVE

The one thing no one hears next is Emma saying, 'He never calls me Mama.'

'Well, it's Daddy's now!' Liam taunts Gideon, waving the phone in the air, the child flailing on his back.

'You bastard!' Emma yells.

'Bastardo!' Gideon exclaims in an Italian accent for a reason known only to him.

'Takes one to know one!' Liam retorts as Gideon bites into his neck.

'Harder!' Emma encourages her son, and Liam finally drops the phone.

One station away, at 7:03 and nine seconds, the passengers board, the train closes its doors. And the driver releases the brake.

Emma

Emma didn't get the ring or the wedding. She never was The One and she never got The One. Now, if Emma was a different kind of girl this would have depressed her and made her journal and gain a lot of weight and then lose it all while documenting her #unfiltered #journey to #self-love on her social media accounts, where she would receive fire emojis in the comments declaring her beautiful at any size but, of course, most fire-emoji-worthy in the size 6 tiny gold bikini.

Or it would have hardened her and driven her to drink heavily, to lose her job, and to be disinvited to her friends' weddings, where she would show up anyway and make inappropriate, slurring, bitter toasts and then fuck a groomsman in full hearing of the bride's grandmother in the neighbouring stall in the luxury, heated port-a-loos, followed by mornings of horrific, consuming regret.

Or it would have led her to a quiet life of work, Pilates, home decor, veganism, remembering the birthdays of all her friends' children, and community volunteering. And really, honestly, being OK with being alone, until one day she would

FIVE

finally meet him at the primary school where she was a literacy mentor for underprivileged children and he was a teacher. They would have a small wedding because by that time many of their friends would already be divorced, with new awkward partners and shitty teenage children and stepkids, and they'd be happy for Emma because God knows, after all the money she'd spent on their weddings and babies all these years she deserved it, so woo-fucking-hoo, but there'd better an open bar at this wedding because her guests would be over love.

However, Emma's single status at age thirty-four and thirty-five and thirty-six did not lead her down any of these paths. And she doesn't mind being the last one standing, even at thirty-seven, because she doesn't feel things the way other people do. And she loves this about herself. The freedom that comes with not feeling. Some have described Emma as a sociopath or a narcissist. But she prefers to think of herself as a winner.

In her peak fertility years, instead of posing for engagement photos, buying a pug, enforcing a mandatory matching Christmas pyjamas post including fiancé/boyfriend with said pug, choosing kitchen cupboard doors, and researching ovulation kits and school districts like her peers and their men, Emma works, and works, and works, and, undistracted by wifedom and motherhood, she makes a lot of money and becomes a Rich Bitch.

She accomplishes this in the male-dominated world of finance. Offended by nothing, she views the inevitable workplace harassment from her male peers as a challenge and accepts their salacious, disgusting offers. She surprises them by appearing in their hotel rooms in full dominatrix attire and laughs at them when they're inevitably too scared of the electrodes and the whip and her mace to get it up. Then she takes photos of them in compromising positions, which she texts to their wives from their own phones with a winking-face emoji.

She does this three times: once with the head of derivatives, once with the head of European equities, and finally with her boss. She blackmails each of them out of their jobs and then does their jobs better than them, and now no one fucks with Emma. At least not in business. In the world of women and wives and mothers, however, Emma does not enjoy the same success.

For example, observe her at her grandmother's ninetieth birthday party. The whole extended family is present. Emma is wearing her signature black, high-necked sheath, cut from fine crepe. It's conservative, not sexy or revealing, but it cannot help itself on Emma and clings to her like liquid latex. She is not conventionally beautiful or voluptuous. She is angular and sharp, slim and severe, with a face like a Byzantine saint. And somehow she wears her plain dress like a scandal. She is not pretty. She doesn't want to be. She is powerful instead.

Her sister, her cousins, and the wives of other relations put effort into their outfits for the party, but they deflate inside their fuchsia cashmere Boden cardigans and redden with shame at their deliberations over their hopelessly middle-aged leopard-print belts, and despair at their sadly maternal metallic

FIVE

trainers with the utterly style-less star motifs that were so cute this morning but that mortify them to their core when they see Emma. And worse, when Emma sees them.

Emma has arrived just in time to see her pretty, good-hearted, normal, boring sister Anne stand hand in hand at the front of the room with the nice and bland Ollie, who compensates for his mediocrity with a handlebar moustache, a T-shirt with a stupidly deep V-neck, and a conspicuously placed, ironic tattoo.

'And so, Nanna, and everyone,' Anne says to the silent room, with a tremulous voice, champagne glass raised, 'Ollie and I would like to announce . . .'

'Yawn,' Emma says loudly, rolling her eyes. She takes no notice of her aunts and cousins directing raised eyebrows and darting glances at her as she flips her very tight, very high, very blonde and glossy ponytail during Anne's long pause for effect.

'We're engaged!' and everyone but Emma and Nanna cheers and applauds. Emma leans down to her grandmother and speaks into her ear.

'Are you all right, Nan?' she asks.

'I thought this was my party,' the old woman says.

'It is your party, Nan. She thinks it's a present for you,' Emma explains.

'Well, no thank you. Ridiculous moustache. For God's sake, he looks like my father,' Nanna says, 'and he's been dead for seventy-five years.' She looks at Ollie and knocks back the rest of her neat whisky. 'Get me another one of these, would you? And tell that boy to park his penny farthing somewhere else,' she says.

Emma weaves through the happy crowd and dodges her cousins and aunts and their exclamations of wonder at *lovely* Anne's *lovely* news on her way to the kitchen. Her mother stops her.

'Emma,' she says, curtly, by way of greeting, her own once-blonde hair framing her face in a perfectly straight precision bob, like a silver Anna Wintour.

'Mother,' Emma responds, coldly.

'It's lovely, isn't it?' her mother says, in a way that isn't lovely, locking eyes with her. 'Don't ruin it for her,' she says, coming close to her daughter's face.

'It's so dull, Mother, I couldn't possibly make it any worse,' Emma says. 'I need to congratulate her, Mumsy, excuse me,' and as Emma moves past her, her mother grabs her arm. 'Let go of me,' Emma says quietly, sharply.

'Do the right thing for once,' her mother says through gritted teeth.

'Or what? I won't be your favourite any more?' Emma says, and pulls away forcefully, downing her plastic flute of champagne on the way to the kitchen. Any interaction with her mother requires alcohol. She pretends to herself it is instant anger her mother provokes, and she ignores the hurt beneath the fury, the pain only a mother can inflict that never goes away.

Emma stops in the doorway of her grandmother's kitchen, Anne's back to her, and as she eyes the bottles she listens in on the hushed feminine tones.

FIVE

'I hope Emma can be happy for me. I mean, I know this can't be easy for her,' Anne says to their married, frumpy cousin Phoebe, mother of three, who is pulling self-consciously at her cold-shoulder blouse. She'd thought it was slimming this morning when she finally decided on it after she'd tried on, then thrown on the floor, every other blouse in her wardrobe, but when Emma arrived she wished she'd worn anything else. Phoebe refills Anne's glass.

'It's so true, it must be tough when everyone around you is getting engaged and you don't even have someone you're serious about,' says Phoebe.

'I know,' says Anne, unbuttoning the top button of her denim shirt dress, then thinking better of it and buttoning it again.

'I mean, I know she's got her career or whatever, but when was the last time she even had a boyfriend?' asks Phoebe.

'It was before the baby slowed your metabolism and your husband started cycling every weekend, Phoebs,' Emma says, picking up a platter of pigs in blankets and holding it out to her. 'His name was Nicholas. Huge penis. It was good while it lasted. Sausage?' she offers.

'God, Emma, why are you always like this?' Phoebe says, pretending not to look at the sausages, a flush rising up her neck.

'What do you mean, Phoebs? You look great by the way. That blouse is so clever. So, like, they cut out the shoulders, is that the look? Cute,' Emma says, as Phoebe dies inside.

'Anyway, *soooo* happy for you and Ollie, sis. *Really*,' Emma says, turning to Anne. 'It's adorable.' She puts the platter down on the counter and pulls her sister into a stiff hug. Over Anne's shoulder Emma watches Phoebe sneak a sausage, catches her eye, and winks.

What Anne and Phoebe don't know is that Emma is already working on it. Having dominated the world of men in her career, far surpassing every woman she knows in her ambition, and having earned more money than any sad, little flaccid husband of every woman she knows, Emma is bored. She is looking for another way to win and so has now turned her attention to finding the best-looking, richest man she can, someone whose very presence shrivels lesser penises and causes marital discord when he walks into the room, so that wives will never see their husbands the same way again.

She finds a selective dating website that caters to high-achieving, wealthy narcissists. She meets the first man but quickly realises that this may not be as easy as she thinks.

'Oh, nothing,' he says. 'It's just I'm surprised, you don't really look like your profile.'

'Um, in a good way, I mean,' he corrects himself, after a pause, a slight question mark in his voice.

Emma gives him a long, deliberate appraisal, from his shoes to his hairline. 'Well, you look poor,' she says, downing her drink, 'and like a wanker.' Then she pays the bill and leaves.

'I don't usually date older women,' says the second man.

'We're both thirty-seven,' she says.

'You know what I mean,' he says.

'You mean you fuck little girls?!' she says, standing up,

FIVE

throwing her napkin down dramatically, and marching away, faux-crying, making sure everyone in the restaurant has turned to stop and stare. She pays the bill and leaves.

'My cat needs hydrotherapy, you know, for feline arthritis. I'm so stressed,' says the last. 'You wouldn't believe how hard it is to find a good alternative veterinarian.'

She downs her drink in one, says, 'Actually, I hate pussies,' pays the bill, and leaves.

She decides a different strategy is necessary. She notices that a new wave of unsolicited, misplaced pity is starting to crest over her as female peers and relatives begin speaking to her with their heads tilted sympathetically to the side.

'So do you think you'll freeze your eggs,' asks one, 'just in case?'

'Your priorities change, you'll see, things that matter to you now will seem so trivial,' says another.

'What do you do on Saturday mornings, Emma? It must be divine. I mean, I can't actually remember the last time I had a Saturday morning on my own,' says the last.

'I usually fuck until noon,' Emma says to the boring, the married, the second- or third-time pregnant, the maternal. 'Then I drink margaritas in the bath for the rest of the day.' And she smiles while they burn inside with jealousy.

Emma does not pay much attention to these women or their unattractive, ordinary progeny. And it drives them crazy. Because they know their men are boring and their children are average. But they followed the rules, they got those men and children, like they were supposed to, and they desperately want her to want what they have and to not be able to have it. But Emma knows that their condescension is wrapped in envy that they can never speak aloud for the sake of self-preservation. They must convince themselves that they have made the right choices by comparing them to her choices, which, deep down, they know are the better choices, the choices they wish they'd made. The choices they would have made if they weren't so scared of everything, if they were brave enough not to believe what they were taught about being women. If they really believed they were the equals of men.

But these wives and mothers are formidable opponents, she'll give them that. They are not easy to knock off their pedestals of gynaeco-normative righteousness. They stubbornly appear so sure of the safety of their life paths, smugly bestowing their sympathy cloaked as advice to relieve the ennui of their ordinariness, while they chomp on more than the recommended dose of antacids to help neutralise their regret and anxiety.

But then, a couple of years later, Emma discovers a weakness in one married, would-be mother, and she gets an idea. An idea that is better than a boyfriend. A much bigger prize.

'We've been trying for almost two years now. I mean, I've been off the pill since we got engaged, but it's just not happening, nothing's happening,' Emma hears an anguished Anne say to Phoebe, this time at their grandmother's ninety-second birthday party.

'Sausage?' Emma says, coming up behind them, holding out the platter of pigs in blankets, noticing the fragile slimness of her sister's figure and the fuller fullness of Phoebe's.

FIVE

'God, Emma, can't you see we're in the middle of a conversation?' Anne says tearfully as Phoebe places a protective, maternal arm around her.

Emma looks at one woman, then the other. And then it clicks.

'Sorry, girls, it's just Mum put honey on these, and I didn't want Phoebe to miss out,' Emma says. Placing the platter in front of her cousin, she adds, 'I know how much you love them.' Then she grabs a glass of wine and her mobile, retreats into one of her grandmother's guest rooms, and composes a message.

`I have a proposal for you. I think you'll like it` 😉, she texts her boss, Liam, a very handsome, very fit, very rich man with a shiny bald head. When he smiled at her with that slight gap between his teeth that first day in the office, she understood it meant that he would always be open to her ideas. Whenever she might have them. Whatever they might be. There was also something he had that the others she'd met didn't. Drive, ambition, pulsing physicality. Something she wanted not to crack or break, not to tame like she did in other men, but to consume. Whole.

`I like it already,` he texts back.

Message sent, she rejoins the party, sits down next to her grandmother, and holds her hand.

'Hello, dear,' the old woman says, and adds with a wink, 'Have you tried the finger sandwiches, or has Phoebe got to those too?'

Emma smiles. 'Nanna,' she says, 'I have excellent news. I'm going to have a baby.'

'Tremendous!' Nanna says. 'Who's the fellow, then?'

'No, Nan, it's just going to be me. On my own,' Emma says.

The old woman looks across the room at the childless Anne, whom she has always thought too big for her britches, announcing her engagement on her ninetieth birthday like that, getting married on the anniversary of her late husband's death. He was a war hero, for God's sake; the child has no respect. And then at Phoebe, so matronly and dull, with that figure, good heavens, she has no self-control, that one.

Then she looks at Emma, whom she has always loved the most of all her grandchildren because she knows how it feels to be hard to love. Then, looking back at the others for just a moment, she says, 'Now that's the spirit, Emmy. You go give them what for.'

Emma doesn't need to make an announcement to the family, she just shows up at Nanna's ninety-third, seven months pregnant, stunning in a pair of Louboutins and her same signature black sheath, which now hugs her perfect bump.

'Why didn't you tell me?' says Anne, pale, shocked, still not pregnant, red blotches crawling across her breastbone at her sister's betrayal.

'Oh,' says Emma, stroking Anne's arm, 'I hope you can be happy for me. I mean, I know this can't be easy for you, when everyone around you is getting pregnant and you're still—'

'Who's the father?' Emma's mother says, voice shaking, spitting the words, taking a step towards her daughter. She asked this once before, when Emma was sixteen, when her mother should have protected her but blamed her instead.

FIVE

'C'mon now, Mum, you know me better than that. What do I need him for? I mean, except for the fucking, ladies, am I right?' Emma says, with a smile like a dagger.

'What is *wrong* with you, Emma? It's an actual person! A real baby. Why did you do this?' Anne half-shouts, with trembling hands, clenched teeth.

'Well,' Emma says, after a pause, 'because I *can*,' throwing *can* at Anne's empty womb like a grenade.

And that is how Emma wins. Or thinks she wins. Because soon she will know what the Annes and Phoebes all around her know, about the primal love for one's child, the wonder and the terror of motherhood that even Emma will have to feel. But in this moment, all the women in the room, in their lightning-bolt earrings and DISCO MAMA tees and faux-leather leggings that bunch at the knees, hate her for everything she can and will do without a man. And hate themselves more for everything they do, and will do, forever, because of one.

'You've outdone yourself, Emma,' Phoebe says, contemptuously, but also hurt that no relatives at the party noticed her own five-month gestational belly, except for the cousin who assumed she'd gained weight again and tried to sell her some Herbalife.

Emma cradles her bump, kicking up one leg behind her like a forties pin-up girl. 'Guess I have, Phoebs. This really isn't as hard as you lot have made it out to be, you know.'

'Just you wait,' Phoebe says, as she locks eyes with Emma, pops a tiny sausage in her mouth, and swallows it. Whole.

■ ■ ■ ■ ■

'Gideon?' she asks the air of his empty room.

'Gideon?' she asks the line of her shoes, placed in precise single file, every toe touching each heel, each left shoe followed by a right shoe of a different pair – Chelsea boots, court shoes, stilettos, platform heels – marching through the hallway down the stairs.

'Gideon,' she says, following the line, bleary eyed, fumbling for her glasses in the pocket of her dressing gown, a familiar clench squeezing her stomach.

'Gideon,' she whispers to herself, rubbing her forehead, trying to wake up, looking for him room by room downstairs. She checks the kitchen, the under-stairs cupboard. She checks under the dining table, behind the sofa in the living room, her heart pounding louder, her breath coming faster.

He is curled up in a ball behind the armchair. She smells him first, ammonia and wet flannel. After consulting with the doctor, they abandoned the night-time disposable pull-ups. It would not have been her choice, but the doctor said they were a crutch, he needed to feel the consequences to understand. But she knows he understands the consequences very well. Too well.

She gets down on her hands and knees, swallows hard, steadies her voice, moves in close to him, and says, reaching out her hand to the small, pyjama-covered dome of his back, 'Gideon, darling, Mummy isn't cross, it's just it's the middle of the night and I didn't know—'

FIVE

'Knock, knock,' he says, lifting his head out of his folded arms, not looking at her.

'Gideon!' she says, exasperated.

'Knock, knock!' he shouts.

But by the time she says, 'All right, who's there?' she is already bleeding.

'Gideon!' she screams, one hand over the eye he stabbed with the heel of her stiletto, and one hand on his wrist, shaking it until he drops the shoe.

'Ow, you're hurting me,' he whines as he squirms out of her grasp. She lets him go, and he runs upstairs, crying, or imitating crying. She hears the TV flick on in his bedroom, the volume turned high, the crying over as soon as his show comes on. He likes cartoons after violence.

She tastes the blood that has dribbled in a tiny stream from her eyebrow to her lip. *'Meet him with love no matter how hard that may be,'* she hears the child psychologist saying – the second, the third, or the fourth psychologist. She takes a scatter cushion from the sofa, puts it over her face, and screams.

Then she gets up. She goes to the kitchen. She opens the cupboard to get a teabag but moves deftly sideways and steps back as she opens the door in case he's rigged it, a new trick he has. The rolling pin comes crashing down onto the kitchen counter, intended to knock her in the head or crush her fingers.

She picks it up, feels the weight of it in her hand. She bought it at the upscale kitchen shop outside the clinic after her twelve-week scan. She had pictured herself rolling out dough with a cherubic child by her side standing on a stool, flour dusting his curly hair, and posting a video of the scene, sending it to her family WhatsApp group, showing them how good she was at this. A fleeting thought she did not allow that they might even be proud of her.

You're such a stupid bitch, she thinks now, pouring hot water and regret over the teabag in her cup. She has thought this every day of Gideon's life. From the very first one.

It was a torturous, terrifying birth that left her with a ragged scar across a numb, gelatinous field of flesh, left her sitting in a haze of grief and outrage and pain, unable to hold her baby boy, who was underweight and fragile, lying in a heated plastic box, oblivious to her presence. He came too early. And Emma, who had never lost control over anything ever, stubbornly refused to understand the signs of his distress in her pulsing abdomen. She took the pain because she arrogantly insisted that life and death were her decisions to make, until she lay in a pool of blood on her bathroom floor, alone, until it was almost too late and she finally understood that she had made a terrible mistake. She'd thought she could never feel what other people did, until now. And what she felt was fear.

Then there were other feelings too – worry when Gideon rejected her milk; disappointment that he never smiled when he saw her; heartbreak when she left him with the day nanny on her first day back at work; and worse heartbreak when she came home and he didn't reach for her. Dismay that nothing was within her control any more.

And another feeling, one she had been ignoring, although she knew its name. Or his name – Liam. Her offer to him

FIVE

had been simple: Have fun with her, get her pregnant, no strings attached after that. She would have the baby, he would relinquish his parental rights, a clean break. She didn't need his money; she had her own. He obliged. It sounded like a great deal to him, so he gave her what she wanted, but now she wished he hadn't. Because now she wished he was here. And he wasn't. She had to put that feeling away, though, for another time and place. She had to put her son before herself now, and she would for the foreseeable future out of love for her child. Or terror. It was hard for her to tell the difference.

'How often does he do this?' the doctor asked her when Gideon was seventeen months old.

'I try to catch him whenever I hear the thumping, but sometimes he's done it and I won't know until he's crying or I see the bump,' she said, worried about how often – how hard – Gideon banged his head against the bars of his crib.

'Or it will wake the night nanny,' she said.

'Night nanny?' the doctor asked with naked judgement as she checked Gideon's pupils with the tiny flashlight.

'I'm a single mum, I work, I can't stay up all night with him,' Emma said, a faint glimmer of her former self in her voice.

'No, it's not that, it's that he shouldn't be up all night, he should be well past that by now,' the doctor said. 'Have you tried . . .'

But Emma stopped listening. She had tried everything.

In the car on the way home Gideon mimicked the doctor: 'Have you tried change his naps?'

'Very good, Gideon,' Emma said. He was an early talker,

speaking in full sentences by the time he was thirteen months old. An expert impressionist, he copied adult speech and had an unusually advanced vocabulary. He was already deciphering basic written words.

'What a clever boy,' she said, absently. But being smart didn't help this, whatever this was. His intelligence only made it worse as time went on and Gideon grew and grew but did not outgrow the thing she knew was inside him.

'But, Michelle, you can't just not show up. I have to get to work, you can't just—' Emma pleaded with the day nanny as she scrubbed Gideon's faeces off the kitchen wall where he'd thrown them after breakfast.

'Look, I know, but it's just a phase, and it's hard for some kids, especially boys, he's only three,' she said, trying to sound level and patient so that Michelle wouldn't quit. She had threatened many times to leave, but Gideon's toilet training had pushed her beyond her limits. Michelle was the only nanny who had stayed more than a few weeks. Who had actually tried to help Emma. She couldn't lose her.

'He needs professional help, Emma,' Michelle said, firmly, honestly.

'But *you're* a professional,' Emma tried not to beg.

'He shat in my shoes. That's not a phase, that's intent. I'm sorry, I feel for you, Emma, I do, but I can't work for you any more,' Michelle said, and hung up.

'This isn't happening,' Emma said to herself. Then she called, 'Gideon!', trying to modulate her voice. Her panic was not about missing another day of work. She was far past caring

FIVE

about that. She understood she wouldn't be going back to her job anytime soon because she wouldn't find another Michelle. Her panic was instead focused on her son and what he had done. And what he would do next.

'Gideon?' she called to him. He was on the living room sofa staring at the TV. He pressed all the buttons on the remote control and landed on a plastic surgery reality show where doctors were siphoning yellow fat from a headless, naked torso.

'Look at me,' Emma said, turning his face gently with her hand to face her as she sat on the coffee table in front of him. He flinched out of her grasp.

'Yes, Emma,' he said, flatly, trying to watch the surgery over her shoulder.

'Did you do that to Michelle's shoes on purpose? Did you mean to do that?'

'I wanted Cheerios. She didn't listen,' he said, looking past her at a different body flayed open now on the screen.

'Good riddance to bad rubbish, Emma,' he said in a deep voice, repeating some TV show he had seen. 'Now say to me, "Clever boy."'

'Clever boy,' she said, absently. *Stupid, stupid bitch,* she thought then.

She thinks it again now with a gash over her eye she can't bear to look at in a mirror, with her hands curved around her mug of tea. But she tries to push the thought away, along with the job she was forced to leave, and the collection of Cartier she sold, and the Porsche that was repossessed when she could not make her payments because she could not work, because Gideon needed her. Being needed. Another feeling she had never known before. As the first sip of tea scalds her tongue she is thankful for the sliver of burn, relieved that she is not completely numb. She is still here. He has not made her into a ghost. Not yet.

She waits and listens. She can hear the TV blaring in Gideon's room. She walks upstairs quietly. She looks at him from the doorway of his bedroom, his soft profile, his golden, flawless skin of childhood, his rounded chin, his precious elfin nose, slightly upturned, his lips gently parted in wonder as he stares, unblinking, into the animated ocean and listens to a starfish talk.

He is beautiful, she thinks. *He should change his pyjamas,* she thinks, *but . . .*

She gently closes the bedroom door. She secures the bolt she had installed at the top of the door on the outside. And the one on the bottom. It will be a while before he tries to get out.

■ ■ ■ ■ ■

She makes another cup of tea. She hears a thump on the floor above and waits in silence. She freezes for a moment, hand suspended holding the milk, tilted, ready to pour. She hears nothing further, pours the milk, takes a sip.

At the kitchen table, she sits down to make a list: *Balloons, cake, candles, pizza, party bags.* Gideon's birthday is next week. She browses on Amazon on her phone with one hand as she drinks her tea with the other and plays a game with herself that she calls Normal Mother.

FIVE

She orders a set of ten Batman plastic party bags with matching paper plates, cups, napkins and table cover. She buys marbles, those small, super bouncy balls, individual tins of slime, gummy sweets, bottles of bubbles. They come in packs of ten or twenty. But she only needs one of each of these items, of course. No, two. She'll make herself a party bag as well, to match his. She'll set the table, blow up the balloons, she will make it special. It's his birthday, after all, he shouldn't miss out just because of last year. Just because she knows his classmates' parents would all decline if she invited their children this time. She briefly touches the gash on her forehead. She still hasn't looked at it. But she can feel the blood has dried.

'Now Mama needs a new pair of shoes,' she says to herself, as swipe, swipe, she switches to Net-A-Porter. She clicks and buys and clicks and buys beautiful things that she has no reason to wear. Rich Bitch clothes she would have worn before motherhood. New clothes for an old life.

She buys an asymmetric, silver, long-sleeved, form-fitting maxi dress. She buys white leather disco boots and a clutch shaped like pouting red lips, more artwork than accessory. Click, click, click. She exhales deeply when she gets the order confirmation by email. It is better than chocolate, better than wine, better than sex. Of course, she will return all of it after it arrives, she must. But it's worth this moment of bliss.

'Emma, what about self-care? Have you tried yoga, meditation, journalling, a bath, a book club?' asked her therapist, the last therapist or the one before that.

That was when Emma stopped seeing him or her because

they hadn't been listening. They had not heard her say that Gideon needs to be supervised every second that he is awake, and also when he is asleep, and that anyone she has ever hired to help her has quit. So reading and bath taking and tree poses are not options. Nor is journalling, the most shocking suggestion. As if she would ever document her days with her son, as if she would ever make a record for social services or police or lawyers or true crime documentary filmmakers to use someday when she knows that they, inevitably, will be involved.

Instead, she buys designer clothes she cannot afford, then puts them on and forgets, for just a few minutes, about Gideon and his play therapist and his occupational therapist and his learning needs specialist and the paediatric urologist and the educational psychologist and his private prescriptions and the neurodiversity nutritionist and private school fees. The night nannies, the day nannies, the sleep nannies, the sleep specialist, and all the money she has spent on tests, assessments, evaluations, scans, treatments, special diets, medications, herbal remedies, holistic therapies, traditional therapies, counselling for herself, for him, family counselling for them both together, therapeutic toys and games, a therapy swing, a sensory room that he destroyed within minutes. Private tutors because he was missing too many days at his private school where she also paid for a part-time classroom assistant to get him through the day. She is running out of money, and it's been so much money, for every expert and nanny and teacher and specialist too afraid to tell her the thing that all of them saw in him but

FIVE

could not bring themselves to name because he was so young. And that they didn't want to believe was true.

Self-care complete, Emma peels a tangerine. She lays the pieces out on a paper plate, alternating raisins in between each segment. Gideon loves symmetry. In the centre she places a piece of precut, dinosaur-shaped cheddar. She spends a moment admiring her creation. She really could have been a great mother if she had just had the chance.

She hears a thump from upstairs, then another, and then a series in quick succession. It is a familiar sound, her son throwing himself against the barricaded bedroom door.

'Just a second, darling,' she says to the empty kitchen, like a normal mother.

■ ■ ■ ■ ■

She puts the snack on the hallway floor. She unlocks the bolts and says, 'Gideon, stop.'

She opens the door carefully. He stands in front of her. The smear of dried blood across his cheek is hers.

'Why did I lock you in?' she asks him, steadily, authoritatively.

'I'm hungry,' he says.

'Answer me, why did I lock you in?' she repeats.

'Because of that,' he says, pointing at her face.

'Because of what? Use words,' she says. She wants him to name it. To say it out loud. Maybe if he hears the words in his own voice, he will feel them. Feel something.

'Because I hit you in the face with a shoe,' he says, matter-of-factly, meeting her gaze directly. She looks back at him. Shame, regret, remorse, none are there. There is something else instead. Something that reminds her of herself and makes her furious. And afraid.

'How do you think that made me feel, Gideon?' she persists, trying to stay level, trying to remember which therapist told her that this was the way to help him exercise empathy.

'I don't know.' He shrugs. 'How do you feel, Emma?'

She kneels now, to be at his eye level, and gets close to him.

'Touch my face, feel what you did to me,' she says, her voice deep, a rumble of fear and fury beneath its surface. Gideon, sensing he perhaps went too far this time, unsure what she will do, stays still.

'Feel. What. You. Did,' she says, emphasising each word in a quiet voice, just above a whisper, picking up his hand, putting it to the bloody gash over her eyebrow. She guides his fingers across the wound and down the path of dry blood on her face.

She closes her eyes and winces. He recoils.

'Feel it,' she says quietly, gripping his wrist. 'Feel it!' she screams.

When she opens her eyes she sees her son, head turned to the side, eyes turned to the wall, pulling away from her grasp.

'Stop,' he says, his voice cracking.

She drops his hand. 'You made a bad choice,' she says, standing up abruptly. 'Put these on,' she says, handing him dry pyjama bottoms and turning to leave the room.

And then, 'I'm sorry.' He apologises to her back.

FIVE

She stops.

'I'm sorry, Emma – Mama – that you're hurt,' he says.

She turns to face him, a tiny shaft of relief cracking through the wall of her chest. Her shoulders drop. She strokes his smooth cheek with the back of her hand, almost gently.

'That's good, Gideon,' she says.

She helps him change clothes, she changes his bedding. She gets the paper plate of raisins and tangerine segments. She sits on the bedroom floor with him. They pretend the dinosaur is eating the raisins.

When the plate is empty Emma says, 'It's still the middle of the night, we should go back to sleep now, all right?'

'OK,' he says.

She tucks him in, turns off his lights, and at the bedroom door she remembers to meet him with love. *Children like him must be loved, and loved, and loved.* That's what the therapist, the last one or the one before, said. But they did not tell her how to love him. They assumed she knew. She doesn't.

But she tries 'I love you, Gideon' and closes the door.

'Why?' he asks the ceiling, then closes his eyes.

▌▌▌▌▌

She taps into the search box, *What prevents scarring.*

Then, *Does vitamin E help scars.*

Then, *My child stabbed me in the eye with a stiletto,* just to see what comes up. Some articles on knife crime, a few angry girlfriends temporarily blinding their cheating boyfriends, a drunken mother assaulting another mother with her shoe over a lost kebab on a night out in Brighton. But no stories with six-year-old boys. No knock-knock jokes.

'C'mon,' Anne says, walking into the kitchen where Emma is sitting. 'Let's fix you up and have a cup of tea.'

'Where's Gideon?' Emma asks.

'He's with Ollie giving the dog a bath. Are you sure you won't go to hospital?'

'But the dog—'

'It's fine, Emma, he's safe.'

I'm never safe, Emma says, inside herself, where her sister can't hear.

She thinks of Anne's baby girl, napping upstairs.

'The baby, did you lock the door?'

'This is madness, you really should go to hospital—'

'Too many questions, you know that, Anne, after last time. They're going to get involved. Did you lock the baby's door?'

'Maybe they *should*,' Anne says abruptly, slamming her medical kit on the table. 'Your sister's doing your stitches for you in the kitchen, you need help, Emmy, listen to yourself—'

'I am!' Emma cries, stunning Anne into silence. 'I *am* listening,' she says, quietly.

After a beat, Emma asks again, 'Did you lock the baby's door?'

'Yes,' Anne sighs. She pulls on one rubber glove, then the other.

'Sit by the window, that's the best light,' Anne says, opening an antiseptic pad. She removes Emma's makeshift bandage, a cocktail napkin held on by several superhero plasters.

FIVE

Anne cleans the wound and finally says, 'It's not too bad, I don't think you need proper stitches, I can just glue it. But, Em, this is your face, you should really have someone in plastics look at it, to make sure the edges of the wound—'

'It doesn't matter.'

'Em—'

'No more doctors, Anne. Too many questions. It's just a little longer, Annie, they said they'll even take him at seven and a half, I don't have to wait until he's eight, at that school, the one in Surrey,' Emma says desperately, words spilling out of her like running water.

'Boarding school? He's so young, Emma, God, he's not a handbag you put on eBay, he's not a car, you can't just trade him in.'

'It's not like that, it's a special school, for kids like him . . .' Emma stutters at her sister's proximity to the truth.

Anne works in silence on Emma's wound. She is surprised by the depth of it, by the force Gideon must have used. But kids are stronger than people think. It isn't the worst injury she's seen a child give a parent. If it were not Emma in front of her, she would recall that those other injuries she's seen in hospital were different. They were accidents. Balls thrown too hard, elbows to eye sockets while roughhousing on the living room rug, scooters spun into ankles.

Even though Anne has forgiven her sister for how she conceived Gideon when she saw them both nearly dead in the hospital the night of his birth, even though Emma confessed what she had done to her because she thought she was dying, even though motherhood has turned Emma inside out, Anne still does not trust her, not even a little, although she pretends to. If Emma were Phoebe, Anne might have been alarmed at what she was seeing, she might have wondered about her nephew, taken it more seriously, she might have believed something was wrong with Gideon. But Emma is Emma. She always has been.

Anne peels off her gloves. 'Kids are hard, Em,' she says. 'He's not exceptional, kids are just hard. I know it's not what you thought it would be when you got pregnant—'

'How many times can I say it?' Emma interrupts. 'Sorry, Anne, that I was such a bitch to you at the worst time in your life. Thank you for helping me with Gideon because I don't know how to do anything. I'm sorry, and thank you, I'm sorry, and thank you, I'm sorry, and thank—'

'Auntie Annie, Auntie Annie, help me!' Gideon suddenly screeches as he runs through the kitchen, chased by Ollie on all fours, pretending to be a monster. Emma watches her son clamber onto Anne's lap, throw his arms around her neck, and scream into her hair as Ollie, the monster, approaches and then launches a tickle attack.

Emma watches the three of them laugh and giggle and carry on. It is a happy, idyllic scene in the farmhouse kitchen with the copper pans hanging from the iron ceiling rack and the butcher block table; it could have been a photo shoot for a parenting magazine or an interior design brochure. There is no place for her in the photo, of course.

She touches her mended eyebrow, looking for something

FIVE

to do with her hands until this performance of ease with her child is over, this show of instinctual lightness that she should have with him but doesn't. She considers pelting her sister's yoga terrorist husband with avocados, but instead she says, 'All right, Gideon, that's enough,' calmly, reaching for his arm, taking back control, doing what a mother is supposed to do. Or what she thinks a mother is supposed to do. She has never known what a mother is supposed to do.

'Oh, don't spoil our fun, Mummy,' Anne says gaily, picking Gideon up, his body curled around her, spinning him round and round. They laugh, and then Ollie grabs one of the surgical gloves from Anne's kit and blows it up. 'Hello, young man,' he says in a silly voice, 'I'm Charlie Chicken, cock-a-doodle-doo!'

'Goddamn it, that's the sound a rooster makes, not a fucking chicken, and I said, enough!' Emma exclaims as she stands and everything stops. The dog pants, a bird sings outside. The kitchen is silent.

Anne puts Gideon down and says, 'Why don't you lie down, Emmy, let me sort the guest room,' and leaves.

Ollie says, 'I'll get out of your way,' and leads the dog outside.

They are alone now in the kitchen, mother and son.

Gideon says, 'Emma?'

She falls into a hard wooden kitchen chair, stares straight ahead and doesn't answer. Gideon says, 'Mama?'

She still doesn't answer. Taking a step closer to his mother, Gideon strokes the side of her face, strokes the new bandage over her eyebrow, and says, 'Feel. What. You. Did.'

∎ ∎ ∎ ∎ ∎

The doorbell rings. Emma's throat catches, her heart stops. Through the door viewer she sees the delivery man. She hopes it's the gown she ordered last week. She's been waiting for it.

'Thank you,' she says, grasping the package like a life raft. She shuts the door. This is exactly what she needs. She has spent the past few hours taking every frame, every piece of art off the walls, after Gideon proved he could tear them down in last night's rage before bed. She removed the nails. She dismantled the line of shoes he had constructed and tossed them in a laundry basket to deal with later. She washed his sheets. She tried to quiet her unease about what he might be doing at Anne's right now.

Anne was so confident when she sent Emma home and offered to keep Gideon for a few hours.

'But the baby?' Emma protested, afraid to leave.

'Don't be ridiculous. Gideon loves Louise, I'll be with them the entire time,' Anne assured her.

'You should have been his mother,' Emma said.

'I know,' Anne said to herself, as she watched Emma drive away.

Alone at home with her new clothes, Emma fills a champagne glass with sparkling water. She rarely drinks alcohol. She usually can't afford not to be alert at all times. She takes her pretend champagne and strips down in front of the full-length mirror. She tears into the package and shimmies into a shimmering black evening gown. The silk satin skims her delicate

FIVE

curves, drapes around her like a living thing, caressing her, holding her. She checks that the cut of it covers all the places she meant to cover, and it does, but she needs one more thing.

'Where are they?' she says, as she opens the drawer of her bureau. 'Perfect,' she says, pulling on the antique full-length black evening gloves, her grandmother's. She looks at herself. She is a vision. She breathes deeply for the first time in days. She smooths the fabric of her dress with her gloved hands.

'OK, well, just this one, if you insist,' she says to an imaginary man at an imaginary party, a slow mischievous smile creeping across her lips.

She runs into the hallway to the linen cupboard and finds the red wine, a gift from a client long, long ago, on the highest shelf in the back. 'What? Really?' she giggles at the man who isn't there. 'I mean, you can, but I'm pretty sure your wife won't like it.' For a moment she can feel an arm around her waist. A brush of lips against hers.

She fills her champagne flute with red wine. She takes a sip and winces. She has not tasted alcohol for many months. And then she downs one, then another, then holds onto the third glass.

Emma swans around the house from room to room, pretending her suitor is chasing her, but she moves carefully because even in her inebriated state she remembers that silk satin will crease immediately and this dress has to go back. And it will, but not before she gets up on the table, not before she plays *Now That's What I Call the 90s,* and not before she belts a song at the top of her voice and the people of the world spice up her life and she slips inside the eye of your mind, and not before, definitely not before, she must confess that her loneliness is killing her but that she still believes – still believes!

And above Britney, above her own voice, she can hear the doorbell. Already? The things she ordered last night?

She climbs off the table, hurries down the hallway, trips over the bloody scatter cushion she screamed into yesterday, somehow she missed it when she was cleaning up, it gets caught up in her silk satin train, it comes with her to the door.

It is not the delivery man, it is not the Net-A-Porter man with her silver dress and her white disco boots. It is a different man altogether.

Hit me baby, one more time.

'Didn't we say two o'clock today,' Liam says in the doorway, not hiding his surprise at what he sees. 'Is this a bad time,' he says. They are statements, not questions.

She cannot catch her breath. She cannot swallow. She nearly asks, 'What day is it?' but stops herself. The query will only make this worse than it already is. At least she knows not to admit aloud that she is lost in time.

She looks down, appalled to see the bloody scatter cushion at her feet, and kicks it away. She knows the red wave has begun under her skin, creeping up her neckline, crawling up to her clavicle. She never flushed like this before she had Gideon. She sees herself as he must see her, unhinged, unmoored.

He is a stark contrast to her: calm, self-possessed, in a crisp blue suit with a waistcoat, no tie, the tailored hems of his cuffs and trousers as sharp as razor edges. His shaven head,

FIVE

smooth as a stone – she imagines for a second resting her cheek on his forehead, how cool he would feel against her blazing flesh. His cologne – he's wearing too much of it, which is the perfect amount – is so strong, it becomes the air of her personal atmosphere. She starts to raise her hand to his face then stops herself.

Shit. She tightens her grip on the doorknob, thinking as fast as she can.

'Are we going in or doing this out here?' he says, looking up at her bandaged brow, noticing the laundry basket full of shoes in the corridor behind her.

'Oh, look at the time, I'm so sorry, do come in,' she says cheerily, holding onto the door to steady the tremble in her hands. *Shit*.

He steps past her into the hall and looks at the dark rectangular shadows on the walls, each marked with a hole where a nail used to be.

She closes the door and lingers as she pushes it shut to buy some time. She wills herself to sober up. Fatboy Slim is praising you like he should over and over again in the kitchen. It's so loud she can't think. She looks at her hands and sees that she is still wearing the long black gloves. She wonders if she has red wine teeth. *Shit*.

'I've interrupted something,' he says. 'I thought you were expecting me.' He folds his arms, noticing the blood-stained cushion that landed at the foot of the stairs on his right.

'No, I mean, you're not interrupting anything at all and, of course, yes, I was expecting you, two on the dot,' she says, faster than she can think of the words. She wants to say no, she was not expecting him, no, she had never expected any of this. That what she expects and what she gets are usually very different.

She stands in front of him, smiles, and pulls at the fingers of her gloves one at a time as she peels them off and says, 'I must look *absolutely* mad,' and she half-laughs with false confidence.

She uses her teeth to pull at the last finger, the limp gloves in her hand like dark dead roses. And he says, 'Absolutely.' He smiles, using the slight gap between his teeth to its full effect.

Time	Destination	Expected
1st 7:06	London Victoria	3 min
South London Service formed of 8 coaches.		
2nd 7:13	Bedford	10 min

07:03

The train is one station away, and the driver is about to release the brake at 7:03 and nine seconds, but he stops. The doors in the seventh carriage are not closed. There is a middle-aged man, a partner at an accounting firm, in head-to-toe yellow Rapha cycling gear blocking the doors with his carbon-fibre Pinarello. He's having trouble getting on board. It is only his third time taking the bike onto the train with the intention of then cycling from Victoria station to his office, as many of his suburban brethren do. He hates cycling, but he found this out only after he spent £500 on his cycling clothes and helmet and £3,000 on the bike. He made the purchases after a recent dinner party because cycling was all the other dads of his son's friends would talk about, so he thought he would give it a try. He thought he might get invited on their Saturday morning cycle rides. And, of course, if he was invited, he couldn't just turn up in a T-shirt with his old mountain bike. So he got all the gear, but the invitation still hasn't come. He thinks it might be because they don't think he can keep up with them yet. Or because of what his son did to that other kid. Or what they all know he did to his son when he found out about it.

Realising that his reflective, waterproof backpack is obstructing the door, he shuffles in, moves his bike further into the carriage, rolls it over a stranger's foot accidentally, and mutters, 'Sorry, sorry, so sorry.' The doors close, then open again and then close, and the train driver releases the brake, and as the train gets under way and picks up speed, the accountant examines his Lycra reflection in the train door windows and wonders why rich people can't just do cocaine at dinner parties like they used to, instead of shaming each other into elitist exercise trends.

The other passengers shift in their seats. Three people internally curse the delay caused by the accountant, one looks at him and says, 'Tory piece of shit,' under her breath, others ignore their nagging bladders, two turn up the volume of their audiobooks to drown out the woman at the other end of the carriage who is shouting into her phone, and another tries not to get caught looking at the saucy text chain being read by the passenger next to them. Some catch up on work emails. Some drink their morning tea from travel mugs. All is proceeding the way it does every weekday morning on this train on this track.

However, the travellers on Platform 1 are currently living the moments that later they will come to think of as *before* – before they recognised the fragility of life, before they comprehended the impermanence of the body, before they hoped that repentance of the soul was real. Before they witnessed the death. Some of them will do something to defy their destiny.

FIVE

Some of them will stay out of the way. Some of them were born knowing there is nothing they can do. Some were born believing they can do anything. Regardless of their individual outlooks, the result will be the same.

Review everyone's positions. Consider what they might do next. Consider what you know that they do not, and will not, until it happens, until the train that is headed towards them is unable to stop in time.

Emma and Liam are on the tracks. Liam is holding Emma's phone in the air to lure her back onto the platform.

Gideon is attached to Liam's back, yelling, 'That's Mama's!', trying to get Emma's phone off Liam by biting into his neck.

Mrs Worth is on the ground with Sonny supporting her on one side and Medical Student on the other.

'I beg your pardon,' she wheezes out with hostility to Medical Student when he loosens the buttons on her coat and unties the bow of her high-necked blouse.

'That's absolutely none of your business,' she says to Sonny, when he asks if there's someone he can call for her.

Despite her cantankerous words, she finds the two young men comforting. She won't give straightforward answers to their questions, but they both notice that she is tightening her grasp on their hands. She is saying nasty old lady things because it is her default position while her chest tightens and her mouth dries and she is filled with panic. Medical Student is familiar with the portents of death in the eyes of the aged, and her aggression suggests to him that she has a lot of life still left in her. Or that she will die very soon. And if that should be the case, he thinks it would be nicer for everyone if she left this world with a better attitude than she is currently displaying. Or perhaps she could just speed it up.

Meanwhile, To Do List is click-clacking in her heels up the station stairs as fast as she can, determined to find a member of station staff to take charge of the situation. She's wearing the wrong shoes for running upstairs, and her high-waisted, tummy control undergarments are making breathing difficult, but she reaches the top of the stairs at 7:03 and thirteen seconds.

'Hello?' To Do List calls out in an authoritative voice. 'We need help!' she shout-speaks to the empty ticket office, receiving no response.

Due to privatisation of the railway, labour unions, the prioritisation of profit, advances in technology, and most people's preference for having fewer interactions with other people because other people are awful, many train tickets are bought online. Consequently, the ticket office at this small, suburban station has limited hours: weekdays, 6:30 to 13:00. This station is also a Category E, Small Staffed, because of its size and location, which means that even at the best of times, it only ever has one staff member for only part of the day. Even with this limited schedule, the office often has its roller blinds drawn with a sign in the window. To Do List reads such a sign now. DUE TO A MEMBER OF STAFF BEING TAKEN ILL, THE TICKET OFFICE WILL NOT BE STAFFED UNTIL 08:30. WE APOLOGISE FOR THE INCONVENIENCE. Unfortunately for the passengers on

FIVE

Platform 1, everything is going to happen long before then, actually, in just a few minutes from now, so To Do List has to make a decision.

As To Do List thinks about her next steps, Emma yells, 'Goddamn it!' at Gideon and 'What is wrong with you!' at Liam in the same breath.

'Here, *Jesus Christ*!' Liam exclaims, throwing the phone to Emma, and puts his hands up. 'I've done it, lad. Now get down,' he says with his voice still raised, standing on the tracks against the platform edge so Gideon can slide off his back onto the concrete safely.

Medical Student, seeing the escalation of the scene with the addition of the child, prioritises vulnerabilities and leaves Mrs Worth with Sonny to help guide Gideon to safety.

Gideon releases his grip on Liam and shrugs away Medical Student's unfamiliar hands. 'That was Emma's!' Gideon says boisterously, then giggles and runs to the station stairs.

White people, Medical Student thinks at 7:03 and thirty-six seconds and exhales at what he believes is the result of Western European permissive parenting. His own children would never behave this way. He misses them dearly.

Emma, her hands on the platform lip, tries to push herself up from the tracks, and Medical Student approaches her next. He looks for someone who might assist or care that there are still two people on the rails. He stares meaningfully at Bad Back, wondering how he can just stand there looking at his phone.

He does not know that Bad Back has just received a text

from his wife that says, I'm going to my mother's. Don't call me.

Bad Back suddenly feels Medical Student's glare, looks up, and says, involuntarily, 'Sorry, mate, bad back,' gesturing at his back.

But he does not have a bad back. Those are just the words that come out before he can stop them. He does not know why he said them, but now that he has, he can't rescind them. He starts to bend this way and that so that Medical Student doesn't think he's lying. *Why am I like this,* Bad Back thinks, shaking his head. *This is why she's leaving me.* He would kick himself if his back didn't fake-hurt him so much.

He looks up at the digital information board. The clock flicks from 7:03 to 7:04. And the word DELAYED flashes up. The 7:06 to Victoria is now expected at 7:09. Bad Back checks the train app on his mobile phone and murmurs, *Oh, for fuck's sake* to himself.

Perhaps you are relieved. There is too much going on to possibly complete the death before 7:06, now that three full minutes have passed. Or perhaps you feel cheated. You expected the death as promised, between 7:01 and 7:06, and isn't *that* a convenient little delay, you're thinking, an extra three minutes written in to assist with the plot.

Your scepticism is understandable, but please remember where we are. In Tokyo or Geneva, the train would be on time. The death would happen on schedule. But this is England, home of milky tea and suppressed emotions, superfluous royalty and dry humour, excellent hats and dysfunctional

FIVE

transportation. A recent study of the UK rail system found that only 56 per cent of trains are ever on time. The BBC said so. Go ahead, look it up. We'll wait. We do a lot of waiting here. For staff shortages, signal failures, general malaise, acts of God, leaves on the tracks, and existential crises in the tunnels. This morning, all trains on this line are required to travel at a reduced speed on a stretch of track that is broken and has been temporarily clamped, extending all arrival times by three to five minutes. In a story such as this set in Britain, there is really nothing more realistic than passengers on a platform all muttering, quietly and with restraint, because their train is delayed.

And you will recall that this is a story about a death, taking place here, in front of you, very soon. And it is likely to be gruesome, and terrifying, and it will change everyone on this platform forever. It is not to be taken lightly. So perhaps you will be gracious enough to allow for three more death-free minutes for those who are about to witness this tragedy. Perhaps you can grant some time for the train to slow down and avoid a derailment and even greater tragedy. Perhaps you can find it in yourself to extend just three more minutes to the person who is about to die. Or perhaps you can't. Perhaps you come from a place where everyone dies on time.

Medical Student shakes his head at Bad Back and kneels at the platform edge, reaching for Emma.

'I've got her,' Liam says, next to her, against the lip of the platform, trying to push her up to Medical Student.

Emma swings a leg up onto the platform with the help of

the men, and when she leans her weight on Liam and his face is close enough to hers, he says something that only she can hear.

'You'll have to kill me first,' she replies to him.

'I'm trying to help you,' Liam says, nearly shouts, roughly letting go of her as Medical Student pulls her up. Liam barely restrains other words that come to mind for women who don't do as he says.

'Madam,' Medical Student says to Emma as he helps her to standing, glancing at Liam, thinking of the only word he knows to address a woman of an undiscernible age in Britain, 'are you all right?' while asking her with his eyes if Liam is a threat to her.

'I'm fine, thank you,' she says as she brushes herself off. 'You're very kind.'

Then she rushes towards Mrs Worth's side, calling, 'I'm so sorry.' She slips her newly cracked phone into her pocket and pulls out a bottle of water from her bag and opens it, placing it next to the old woman.

'I'm sorry, my son, he's, uh—'

'A psychopath,' Mrs Worth says through clenched teeth, clutching her arm.

Emma glares at her, although she's not surprised. She leans down and says, 'I hope you signed a DNR,' taking her water back as she hurries away to grab Gideon, who is running in circles around the bottom of the stairs.

At this same moment, on the platform edge, Medical Student says to Liam, who is still on the tracks, 'Need a hand?' and reaches towards him.

FIVE

'Nah, you're all right,' Liam says, brusquely, waving him away. Liam never accepts anyone's help. Medical Student nods and jogs back to Mrs Worth. Under his breath, Liam says, 'Fucking nuts,' referring to Emma, and hoists one leg easily onto the platform.

And then it hits them, all of them, all at once, at 7:04 and thirty seconds.

The high screech of a siren, loud and insistent. Everyone looks up, automatically, following the human instinct to look skyward when a sound invades the atmosphere.

Liam looks up too at first, then looks down as he pushes with both arms to get onto the platform. His housekeys fall from his coat pocket onto the gravel of the track bed.

'Bollocks!' he yells, and lowers himself back down to get them as the noise pierces his thoughts. No one hears him shout or sees him descend, distracted as they are by the alarm, and who pulled it, and what it means. No one hears him grunt when he hits the back of his head accidentally against the bottom of the concrete platform lip with his full force after grabbing his keys and not ducking low enough when he tried to come out. No one can hear the scatter sound of the gravel in the crawl space under the platform when all of his mighty, muscular, unconscious heft hits the ground.

On the platform, Gideon screeches an imitation of the alarm. Emma chastises him. Bad Back moves his hand to the small of his back in case anyone is watching, and paces. He knew things were rocky in his marriage, but he didn't think she'd actually leave.

To Do List, full of regret, standing next to the unmanned ticket booth, wonders why she panicked and pushed the button for the fire alarm instead of just calling the police on her mobile like a sensible person. In her defence, the alarm does say, PUSH IN CASE OF EMERGENCY. In her haste and desire to be a good citizen, compelled by an overwhelming need to contribute to a resolution of the dangerous drama on the tracks that has nothing to do with her, she did what the button said and has consequently altered the destiny of her fellow travellers. Or perhaps she's just helped to move it along.

She automatically reverted to the actions that people her age associate with emergencies and would have been taught as children, before the advent of mobile phones. It was involuntary. She wonders if it's menopause. She wonders if everyone will hate her if she goes back down to the platform, if they will know it was her. She wonders if she should just leave the station now and pretend she was never there.

Medical Student, so in control just a moment ago, starts sweating, despite the cold. He cannot catch his breath, his hands go numb and tingle as the alarm's high-pitched warning thrusts him back into the war with its sirens and bombs.

A mouse scurries along the track. It stops when the alarm starts and sniffs the air, but then goes on its way, foraging in the rubbish in the gravel and weeds. It can tolerate higher sound frequencies than humans and is unperturbed by the alarm. It climbs over Liam's keys, limply clutched in his right hand. It continues with its rodent business, climbing up Liam's arm and over his face, and crosses the rivulet of blood cutting

FIVE

a burgundy path across the shiny virility of his scalp, on its way to investigate an empty Doritos bag pinned just under his shoulder.

'It'll be all right,' Sonny says to Mrs Worth, putting his big Bohemian scarf over her to keep her warm as she stiffens at the sound.

'My arm,' she forces out as Sonny bends to hear her.

Sonny looks up at the board. He sees the word DELAYED. He thinks, *Mum, is that you?*

It is 7:05. The train is hurtling down the track, on its way to meet our five. A passenger on board spills their tea, the cyclist pretends not to be in the way, a young woman standing by the carriage door feels a pain in her side that she keeps ignoring but shouldn't.

'Don't worry, we'll get you some help,' Sonny says to Mrs Worth.

A passenger planning to exit at the next stop texts a friend waiting at a café near the station, Be there in ten mins.

Unfortunately, that's not true. Because someone is about to die, and we really don't have that kind of time.

Mrs Worth

'Pleasure to finally meet you, I've heard so much about you,' Livvie says, putting out her hand to Mrs Worth. She really puts out only half her hand, only the long slender fingers. The young woman's hand is soft, her nails manicured to a high shine in powder pink. They are not working hands. Mrs Worth notes her carriage, her precise eyebrows, the slightest hint of creases starting at the edge of her eyes from tanning, and estimates Livvie's age to be about twenty-five, a year younger than Nicholas, Mrs Worth's son.

Mrs Worth doesn't take Livvie's hand, only looks at it and says, 'Oh, hello,' as she stands awkwardly in the entrance hall. She is unsettled by the French bulldog circling her ankles, but she tries to ignore it and says nothing.

'Horatio, come here, you si-wwy, leave our gwest aw-one, you si-wwy pup,' Livvie says in a saccharine-sweet baby voice turning all her *l*s to *w*s. Then, with the dog in her arms, she turns to Mrs Worth and says, 'I hope you're all right with dogs. He's the sweetest little thing, he won't bother you, I promise. Can I take your coat, Matilda?'

FIVE

'No, I'll keep it, thank you,' says Mrs Worth, bristling at the sound of her given name coming out of Livvie's mouth. Before Livvie can respond, Nicholas enters the hallway.

'Hello, son. I've met the dog,' Mrs Worth says.

'Hello, Mum,' Nicholas replies, knowing that she is not referring to Horatio. Livvie must have called her Matilda. It will be a long evening.

Livvie doesn't catch the comment because she is watching Nicholas wave at his mother, a single wave in one direction, like he is clearing a foggy windscreen. He does not step forward to kiss her or embrace her the way she would her own mother. The way everyone else she knows would with their own mothers.

Mrs Worth sees her son trying to catch Livvie's eye, to warn her against doing something like calling his mother by her first name on their first meeting, but Livvie is making determined eye contact with Mrs Worth because she read in *Cosmopolitan* that's important for establishing trust with your significant other's mother. Even if she's weird. And creepy. And obviously hates your dog.

'So what happens now?' Mrs Worth asks.

Nicholas gently pulls his mother's coat off her shoulders and says, 'Give me your coat, Mum, and just go straight ahead, have a seat on the sofa, we'll be right there.'

Mrs Worth reluctantly sheds her coat but keeps tight hold of her handbag and leaves as directed.

Nicholas turns to Livvie and says quietly, 'Don't worry, she takes some getting used to.'

'Would you stop?' Livvie says, clutching Horatio. 'Mothers love me, you'll see.'

But Nicholas knows that Livvie, his gorgeous, lovely Livvie, has never met a mother like his, and he knows that as soon as Livvie put out her beautiful hand and introduced her adorable dog, and his mother saw the pretty fingernails and noticed the glossy lip and heard the honeyed voice, she immediately found Livvie and Horatio ridiculous and vacuous and frivolous. Nicholas does too, but that's exactly why he loves Livvie. Life with her is so light, like cotton candy or a peck on the cheek from your high school crush.

But *love* is not a word he uses for his mother. He cares for her deeply, he is indebted to her for her dedication to him, he is awed by the pioneering career she built as one of the first women in her field, forensic pathology, on her own as a single working mother at a time when such women were rare. He cannot believe she works just as hard now, at sixty-five, as she did when he was a boy. But *love* is not a word he has ever used to describe how he feels about her. Nor is it one he has ever heard her say to him.

His childhood with her was not unhappy, but it was not exactly the opposite. 'Neutral' was probably the best way to describe it. Placid and neutral until she would accidentally leave horrific crime scene photos out on the kitchen table when she was working on a case, thinking he was at a friend's house, mixing up the days of his after-school club and his playdates as she often would, her mind full of other, more pressing details about the unresolved deaths of strangers.

FIVE

These moments of his childhood – the ones where autopsy photos of severed limbs and bloody, murdered torsos haunted him in his sleep for months – he would describe as traumatic.

But to her credit, though it was not natural to her, she did sit at the end of his bed when he cried from a nightmare. She did allow him to sit on her lap and put his arms around her neck and cry into her bony shoulder.

She did not cluck and coo at him or return his embrace with the strength he would have liked, but she did say, 'Nicholas, it's sad that those people in the pictures died, it's good to be sad for them. They're people with families, and I help them get the answers so they can catch the bad guys. It's not easy, but it's important. It's the most important job I could ever do.' And Nicholas understood that it was, but he wished that the job of being his mother was more important.

When Nicholas was old enough to ask about his father, he decided not to. He was curious, but he did not want to hurt his mother, he did not want to disturb the fragile balance of their life together. He knew the man must have been tall and must have had dark curly hair, and tawny skin, and deep brown eyes like he did, because he looked nothing like his petite, pale, prematurely white-haired mother. He didn't feel he could ask her because sometimes if he said too much or asked too many questions, she withdrew and went somewhere that he could not follow. A curtain would fall down over her eyes and he could not see her past it.

But luckily for Nicholas, Mrs Worth was a scientist at her core. And when he was fourteen his curiosity about his paternity was satisfied quite fully when she gave him an old notebook to read.

'I found this up in the loft when I was getting the Christmas ornaments. I suspect it will answer your questions – if you have any,' she said, handing him the diary labelled LOG OF RECREATIONAL ACTIVITIES, 1986–87. He knew his mother was forty years old in 1987, the year of his birth. Intrigued, he flipped through the pages. He turned to a date about nine months before his birthday and read the entry:

25.01.1987

Participant: Andrew Sanderson

Description: Approx. 6' 1", medium build, muscular biceps. Age, 27. Slight subcutaneous adipose layer covering the lower abdomen, which although noticeable and could be improved is not repulsive. Hair, black. Eyes, dark brown. Skin tone, medium to dark, cultural appearance is Caucasian, perhaps Mediterranean, though physical features and characteristics suggest possible variable genetic influences.

Occupation: Forensic pathology trainee.

Location of activity: My flat. Primary position, front room sofa. Secondary position, bed.

Duration: Approx 42 minutes preparatory activity, Approx 7 minutes maximum exertion.

Number of thrusts in maximum exertion phase: 212 (Approx)

Heart rate: 112 bpm (Approx)

FIVE

Temperature: 36.8°C

Notes: A pleasurable experience, although participant talked too much, probably due to his age. As a result, I was unable to keep accurate count of my heart rate or the number of thrusts. If the opportunity presents itself, I will repeat the activity; however, I will expect to see improvement in performance after providing critical feedback.

The subsequent entries for the next few months all referred to Andrew. It appeared his performance did improve with feedback and they saw quite a lot of each other. The last entry of the notebook had only one line in the middle of the page.

Test result: positive. Gestational age, approx. 13 weeks.

When he returned the notebook he asked, 'So why isn't my surname Sanderson, Mum?'

'I did all the work, why should he get the credit?' she said.

'Then how come everyone calls you *Mrs* Worth?' Nicholas asked.

'Women who live without men make people nervous, Nicholas. So I added Mrs to my surname. People asked too many questions otherwise, especially when you were born. If they ever ask about "Mr Worth" I just say he's dead, and that shuts them up,' she said.

Nicholas asked her a few other carefully worded questions, like did Andrew know about him (no), did she like Andrew (yes), what happened to Andrew (he married the girlfriend he was cheating on with Mrs Worth). And when he was about to ask if he could find Andrew, his mother put her hand on his shoulder in that awkward way that she had of showing affection about three times a year and said, 'I chose you then and I would do it again. I have no regrets.'

Nicholas handed back the notebook to his mother and replied only, 'OK, Mum.' He didn't have the heart to ask her anything else, knowing how much those words meant and how hard they were for her to say. They never spoke about it again.

Most of their life together was like that, living in comfortable silence, words never having been Mrs Worth's strength. And then, in what felt like the blink of an eye, Nicholas was a young man, going off to university, going off to travel, going off to live, she was relieved to see, a happy life, full of friends, and parties, and laughter and experiences and loves – full of normalcy and fun and people. Her life was full of people too, of course, although most of them were dead.

Mrs Worth was most comfortable in the morgue, in the lower levels of the hospital, among the deceased, who did not judge her peculiar personality, who did not expect banter or smiling or conversation or ask prying questions. They needed her skills and her knowledge more than the living did, she knew it from her first incision into a cadaver in her first year of medical school. It was where she was most at home.

As a forensic pathologist she performed thousands of autopsies and unlocked the secrets of the dead and eased the pain of not knowing for their families. Her work brought criminals to justice and exonerated the innocent and protected

FIVE

humanity from disease. And when she began her career, she was one of the only women who did this work, and it was a huge achievement.

But in her heart her greatest success was that Nicholas was free and happy. The biggest accolade she could receive was hearing him laugh easily. The greatest relief was that people liked him. And that he was nothing like her.

Nicholas has never known what made his mother the way she is. She says very little about most things and nothing at all about her past. But he does know it is not easy for her to be around new people. That sometimes she speaks before she should and says things she shouldn't. That little dogs have always made her nervous. He also knows that she loves him, has always loved him, even though she's shown it in ways most people would not recognise as love.

So when Mrs Worth says, standing in her son's home with his fiancée, 'Hello, son. I've met the dog,' he ignores her nervous insult, and he puts a hand on her shoulder before he helps her take off her coat. He says softly, 'Give me your coat, Mum. Just go straight ahead to the sofa. We'll be right there.'

And when Livvie declares, 'Mothers love me, you'll see,' Nicholas says, 'Of course they do, darling. Just do me a favour and call her Mrs Worth. Just for now.'

▮ ▮ ▮ ▮ ▮

'Matilda, we've got work to do. Prepare the table,' Gerald says. Young Matilda, reading in her room, hears the thud of the sack against the wood of the floorboards in the kitchen where Gerald has dropped it, having just come home from his route. She must try to convince him to have supper first. She always finds it too difficult to eat after they do the work.

Gerald was Mrs Worth's father. He gave her the name Matilda. He gave her other things too that were not as easy to name.

Gerald was a postman, but before that he was a surgeon. And because Gerald died long ago, his violence will have to be explained on his behalf, as Gerald was never able to explain it himself, or to himself, or to Matilda, or to anyone else. If he had, things could have been different for his daughter. Of course, things could have also been the same.

Gerald, a talented medical student, trained to be a surgeon before the war and worked as a medic in a field hospital during it. Two years into his service, shrapnel from an explosion left him with partial vision in his left eye, an occasional tremor in his left hand that the army doctors said was all in his head, and an intense desire to never touch another sick, dying or wounded person ever again. Once he had recovered sufficiently and received a medical discharge, Gerald came home to the burning wreckage of London, with her hollow-eyed widows and old men, her streets empty of children who had been sent away to the countryside, the life he remembered crushed under the rubble of her burnt-out buildings. He found it only slightly easier to live in London than on the battlefields he had left behind.

Gerald, like many of the men who served and survived, was welcomed home as a hero. And like the other heroes, he

FIVE

did not speak of his horror or his fear or his grief. The heroes did not know what words to use or who to tell them to, or see what good would come of describing the terror that awaited them in their dreams each night, or speaking of the panic that seized them inexplicably at the breakfast table, or revealing the shameful need to weep alone because the war still raged within them.

And because the heroes like Gerald did not speak of it, the horror and fear and grief reverberated instead in their harsh words to their children, or their wordless evenings with their wives in their homes where the floors were made of eggshells. They knew their families lived in fear of them and their rage that would come and go without warning, sometimes at the end of a fist, sometimes in yelling at the top of their lungs, sometimes at the bottom of a bottle. The tyranny of their pain made the heroes into tyrants, forcing some of them, like Gerald, to seek control over anyone or anything they could because they could not control their own suffering and they did not know why.

Gerald married Jo, Matilda's mother, when she was only seventeen years old, in 1947. She was fatherless and brotherless due to the war, and being fourteen years his junior, she knew too little of life to put up much resistance to his ways. She was easy for him to control as she was too afraid to disagree with him, and this was reason enough for him to love her. But she had been a mere child during the war that made him the man he became, so she did not remember its brutality, and this was reason enough for him to resent her.

Jo was dutiful and quiet, having no other choice for her own survival than to keep the house and tend to baby Matilda in strict accordance with Gerald's directives, staying out of his way, doing as she was told. When he complained that the tea was cold, she warmed it, and then accepted the slap when the next cup she gave him was too hot. When he threw his breakfast across the room because she was a *silly, stupid girl* who could not even boil an egg, she simply picked up the plate from the floor, cleaned the wall, and boiled another. When he did not come home until after midnight, smelling of beer and cigarettes and other women, Jo pretended to be asleep. She never asked him where he'd been. She wished he would have stayed there longer, wherever it was.

Jo was meek and obedient. There was nowhere else for her to go, and when Matilda was born she became even meeker, even more obedient. The only thing Jo ever did without asking Gerald for permission was to die suddenly in the middle of the night. Jo did not know she had been born with a weak heart, weakened further by Gerald's rage and abuse, and further still by pregnancy. Left alone now with their baby girl and her little face, so much like her mother's, was reason enough for Gerald to regret the kind of man he had been to his young wife. Though it wasn't enough to make him a better one.

With his one good eye and the tremor that was all in his head, he continued to deliver the post. With Jo gone, the sad target of his cruelty buried, he did not, thankfully, turn his ire on Matilda. *She's only a baby*, he'd remind himself; *she's just a little girl*, he would think as she grew, when he could feel

FIVE

rage rising; *she doesn't have a mother*, he'd mourn to himself on behalf of his daughter.

Then he would remember Jo, lying cold and placid beside him that morning he found her dead. He would remember touching her grey cheek and understanding that she was gone. The guilt gnawed at him that he had made the short time she had on earth a misery. Gerald's anger would then become sadness, which was safer for Matilda because it made him silent. And his silence, though it was thick and heavy and impenetrable, at least protected her from his wrath.

But it did not protect everyone. Because Gerald sometimes purposely delivered the wrong letters to the wrong people. He sometimes sat and smoked a pipe in the front room while he put strangers' letters on the fire one by one and watched them burn.

Gerald did his best to suppress, to dampen, to extinguish his pain. But then he found a new way to smother his anguish. He sometimes brought home a sack stamped Royal Mail that did not contain any letters at all, but something else entirely.

He brings home such a sack tonight. 'Matilda,' he says, 'we've got work to do. Prepare the table.' So dutiful and quiet Matilda, fifteen by now, sterilises the kitchen in strict accordance with her father's directives as she has many times in the past five years since he began this strange work, following Gerald's orders and ignoring her own instincts, avoiding looking at the sack until it is time. She covers the table with old newspapers kept for their evening's work. She stands on a stool to get her father's surgical tools from the high shelf.

'Shall we have supper first, Father, before the work?' she asks, hopefully, her stomach grumbling at her.

'Have you found the scalpel?' Gerald says, ignoring her question, placing the sack on the table. Matilda notices that tonight's sack is heavier than usual and that her father is more determined. There is an edge to his voice that it did not used to have when he started all of this. Her heart sinks and her nerves go on alert, but still she stays quiet, and she does as she is told.

▮ ▮ ▮ ▮ ▮

If what they did together was not love, then Matilda did not know another name for it. She knew it was all the love that Gerald knew how to give.

Matilda had been held as a baby by the kind neighbourhood women who helped Gerald in the early years when she was left motherless. By her aunt, Gerald's sister, before she got married and moved to Yorkshire. By mothers in shops who saw Gerald struggling when Matilda fussed, by mothers in doctors' waiting rooms when they saw he didn't know what to do about her crying, by women along his postal route the one day when the neighbour was sick and he couldn't find anyone to mind her so he'd just made a sling and carried her inside his uniform coat while he worked. At the depot when clocking in and out, he put her inside his mailbag for a few minutes so she wouldn't be detected. She didn't cry. She seemed to understand what a bind he was in.

FIVE

But the loving, motherly hands of strangers that come and go are not a substitute for the hands of one's own mother, always there, open and waiting. Matilda had the hands of her father for practical support: transport, feeding, changing. He did not hold her longer than was necessary. He did not hold her just because she was his own. He let her cry through the night until she learned there would be no point to it.

She started walking before she was a year old, not from precociousness, but from a sense even in her infancy that she needed to make herself more convenient for her father to live with. She cried little, and all her minders called her a 'good baby', but if she could have spoken, she would have pointed out that she was just being pragmatic, because she had to be. Because life for her father was already hard enough.

As she grew, he bought her things to play with, he even smiled sometimes when he saw her joy, but he did not play with her, although she wished he would. He didn't know how.

When books replaced toys as her prized possessions, he bought her those too, realising a few years too late that perhaps he should have read to her in the evenings, perhaps she would have liked that, and feeling sad that she was now too old for it. Except that she wasn't, and had he asked, she would have said, 'Yes, Papa,' she would have loved for him to read to her, she would have gladly curled up under his arm and listened to *Anne of Green Gables* or *The Famous Five*. But she knew that he wasn't capable of that. Although he could not hold her or hug her or kiss her on the forehead in the way of fathers, when he stood in a bookshop and thought of her and bought her a book and left it on her desk without a word, she knew that what he left there was his love.

Gerald spoke little to Matilda, and he looked at her even less as she grew and Jo's eyes started looking back at him. He did not ask her questions about school or friendships or her dreams and aspirations. It did not occur to him to ask, as a mother would, and even if it had, he would not have been able to endure her answers, delivered with the same rasp in her tone that Jo had. Matilda would have volunteered small anecdotes from her small life, but she was never sure whether it was safe to disrupt her father's quiet moods, whether if she spoke to him he would nod, or grunt, or simply withdraw further to the place she knew he went sometimes where she could not follow him.

So they ate their meals in silence and sat next to each other after dinner reading, Gerald the newspaper, and she one of her books, while listening to the radio. And every now and then, perhaps three times a year, when she brought home a good school report or won the class prize, he would put a hand on her shoulder and say, 'Well done,' and his large hand on her small frame was heavy, almost painful, but she did not complain, she did not shrug him off, she waited and bore the weight of him, because she understood that it was his love.

When she had just turned ten, Gerald said to her one evening, 'Come here, Matilda girl, I have something to show you,' with something cheerful and bright she had never before heard in his voice, and she ran to Gerald. She saw a light in his eyes. He'd brought her something, and he was happy, and she could not wait to know what it was that made him that way.

FIVE

Whatever it was could not be better than her father calling to her with that sound in his voice and the sparkle in his gaze.

'What is it, Papa?' she asked, a joyful, nervous feeling in her stomach. Sweets? A book? Hair ribbons?

'Go sit down,' he said, 'and close your eyes,' and little Matilda ran to the kitchen table, put her hands over her face and her head down. She was petite for her age, and her legs, still not quite long enough to touch the floor, were swinging back and forth under her chair in excitement. She could hear some rustling, shuffling, and then, 'All right, you can look!' Gerald exclaimed.

Matilda uncovered her face and looked down at what he had put in front of her. Her legs stopped swinging. She held her breath. She stayed very, very still. Whatever this was, whatever the reason he had for bringing it to her, it made him happy. So she would be happy. She must pretend to be happy.

Matilda looked at the tiny body, its striped, matted fur, its minute O-shaped mouth, its sealed eyes that had never opened in its time on earth.

'What is it, Papa?' she managed to say, lifting her voice at the end of the question deliberately, so he would not hear her heart breaking.

'What do you mean? It's a kitten, silly girl,' Gerald said, still in high spirits. 'Born a few days ago, maybe a week. I mean, it's dead now, but you're going to learn so much from this, Matilda. I have so much to teach you.'

A house fly landed on the minuscule corpse, rubbing its hands together as it stood on a dried open wound. The kitten looked as though a rat had got to it before Gerald did. The dark red matting its fur was blood, she realised. She wanted to retch but didn't.

'But where did you get it, Papa?' she said, feeling sick, swallowing the lump in her throat, trying desperately to sound excited.

'What's the matter, don't you like it?' Gerald said, something like an incipient hurt in his tone, something that could easily turn to anger or sadness, that could take him away from her. So she had to like it, she had to love it, because if she didn't he would go silent, he would stop looking at her. He would be so hurt if she didn't love it.

'No, Papa, it's wonderful, I'm just asking how, how did you . . .' She did not look at the kitten while she said this, but then, when she glanced down again, she could not finish the thought.

'Well, there's a stray cat over in the alley by the butcher's on my route. I heard the whining under a pile of rubbish. She had a whole litter trying to feed, but this one was off to the side, dead. The runt. Never had a chance, the poor little soul. So I just slipped it in my pocket. It's an excellent first specimen for you to learn from, although we will have to be quite delicate with it,' he said, waving away the fly and coming behind her chair, leaning over, putting his big man's hand on her shoulder. It weighed a tonne.

'What's a specimen, Papa?' she said, with a squeak in her voice that she hoped he did not detect.

'All in good time, Matilda. You'll see,' he said. 'Now go find

FIVE

the old cutting board and put some water on to boil. We're going to have to learn to sterilise my instruments first. The first rule of surgery, girl – scrupulous hygiene. And we'll need your mother's sewing kit for the pins.'

When her father mentioned the sewing kit of the mother she did not remember, Matilda thought, for just a sliver of a moment, that perhaps this was not so bad, perhaps they would be making a little dress for the kitten. In an old valise that was also once her mother's, she had a tiny dress that her aunt had told her was once hers when she was a baby, that Jo had made for her. She could not imagine what else her father could need the pins for. When she saw, a few minutes later, how he would use them, she understood that something had happened to her life that she would not be able to change.

And then another thought came to Matilda that she had never thought before, now that she had her first encounter with a dead body: that her mother had had a body once too, which also must have gone stiff and sad and quiet like the kitten. Matilda hoped that there had not been any flies on her when she died. And she wished that her mother were here with her now, a real person in a live body that she could touch, with a hand that she could reach for to hold.

■ ■ ■ ■ ■

Matilda survived the dissection of the kitten that first time on the kitchen table, the pinning of its splayed limbs to the old cutting board, and the abdominal incision. She did not vomit until Gerald removed the viscera and presented her with the tiny heart.

'Do you see the beauty of it, child?' he said to her. 'Do you see the perfection?' And he held it gingerly to the light with delicate dissecting forceps.

It was then that she said, 'I'm sorry, Papa,' and excused herself to be sick. She was both fascinated and horrified, nauseated and stupefied. Part of her wanted to scream and cry, and part of her wanted to hold the tiny heart in her own hand to hear the echo of its dead beating.

A few weeks after the kitten, Gerald brought home a dead mouse he'd found when delivering the post to the newsagent. Its distended abdomen, he and Matilda discovered, was due to a large, fatty tumour sitting on its liver. After that, there was the rat, already slightly decomposing and still in the trap that had caused its demise, which Gerald had found round the back of the posh cheesemonger. A squirrel, a crow, a pigeon, a seagull followed.

'It's so sad, Papa, so many dead animals along your route,' innocent Matilda said, believing wholeheartedly that all the animals had simply been found by her very observant father.

'Yes, very sad,' Gerald said.

With each body they followed the same procedure: don aprons and rubber gloves, sterilise the instruments, cover the table in newspaper, get the old cutting board, remove the pins from Jo's sewing kit. Afterwards, they would clean and scrub all of the surfaces and floor diligently, with the smell of disinfectant soon becoming the most prominent in the house.

FIVE

Their evenings changed markedly. Instead of listening to the radio and reading, Gerald taught Matilda how to run the scalpel down the midline of the abdomen without nicking the organs underneath. He had Matilda practise sutures on squirrels and pigeons, teaching her first the continuous over and over sutures, then progressing to the subcuticular and horizontal mattress sutures.

Gerald showed her how to carefully cut away and then harvest organs of the various creatures that came to their kitchen table. They put the healthiest specimens in jars of formaldehyde, labelled them, and stored them in a cupboard in the kitchen that had become their makeshift operating theatre. They did this with the most deformed organs as well – enlarged bird spleens, ruptured squirrel livers, diseased pigeon lungs.

Once the necropsies were finished, the skins and furs and carcasses and feathers and viscera and bones that they were not preserving for Matilda's education were buried by Gerald at night, in the dark, under the tree in the back garden.

And so this was the nature of their love. Matilda understood that worse than the war, worse than his bad vision and the tremor, worse for her father than losing Jo, worse for him was losing this, his calling, his talent, and his purpose – surgery. Manipulation and control of bodies. Science. He did not speak of healing, curing, saving. He had lost too many men on his operating table to believe in them any more.

But when he found a way to get surgery back, the meticulous practice of cutting the skin, peeling back the flesh, delving into the organs under the dome of the ribcage, holding these components of life in his hands – not the mundane life of some mediocre, meaningless, individual but Life itself, Creation – the first thing he did was give it to his daughter.

Matilda understood this from the very start, so she didn't complain. She knew her father was a fragile man, and he would never recover if she rejected this macabre embrace. She accepted his strange affection with every bone they sawed through and every organ they sliced. Gerald had no other way to love her, and she had no one else in the world to love.

She stopped needing to retch. After a year or so of practice, Matilda thrilled, in secret, when she opened biology books in the local library and could name each organ, each nerve, each muscle of the two-dimensional diagrams of frog anatomy, drawn so neatly and intricately on the pages. The drawings were pretty, perfect, unsullied by tumours or traumas, bruises or ruptures. But Matilda knew what really lay beneath the skin, attached to the bones. She had seen the undigested contents of a stomach, fluid in the lungs, how the hammer of a rat trap causes fracture of the vertebrae. The part of her that was still her old self, the girl she was before Gerald began his unorthodox training, was ashamed, suspected that something was wrong, and that part of her thought about asking. Or maybe even telling. But she was too afraid of asking or telling, of what would happen if anyone knew.

The her that she became the more she learned from her father was also the most shameful part of her, because that part truly loved what they were doing. She knew there must be something wicked about how Gerald acquired the bodies, and

FIVE

odd about their kitchen cupboards full of organs and skeletons. But she also found them utterly compelling, and wonderful and miraculous because Gerald showed her the genius of respiration and circulation; digestion, reproduction and excretion; the brilliance of the nervous system, the endocrine system; of blood vessels and skin and egg and bone and feather, and she knew these could only be what some people called God. And she had seen him, at work through her father's shaking hand, under the light of the single bare bulb that hung above their kitchen table.

■ ■ ■ ■ ■

'Papa?' Matilda is afraid. She knows from the shape of the sack that her father has not brought home a stray kitten or rat or crow this evening. When he pulls the body from the sack, she knows that this time he's done something he shouldn't have.

'What's the matter?' Gerald says when he sees her stricken face. 'It wasn't easy, you know,' he adds, irate and tired.

'How did you get him?' Matilda asks, worried, not asking why, or how could you, or what will happen to us next.

'Look at the body. You tell me. Silly, stupid girl. Don't you see evidence of the cause of death?' Gerald says, washing his hands in the kitchen sink and speaking to her over his shoulder.

She looks at the unnatural angle of the creature's neck. 'Don't look so appalled, child. Good old Rusty had it coming to him. Mrs Endlesham wouldn't put a stop to him urinating on my rose, so I did it for her. It's half dead by now, the plant, I mean, not the dog. He's very dead, but it only happened today, still fresh, so a good one for you to work with. It seemed a good opportunity.'

Matilda shudders. 'What's the matter?' Gerald demands. She senses a new fatigue, and his voice is stretched, covering something.

'Has something happened, Papa? Are you well?' she asks as gently as she can.

'Stop your dithering and get to work,' he says, bluntly, coldly. He is shutting down, turning away from her. She approaches the table and notices that the body is not in a Royal Mail sack. It is in a burlap bag for potatoes. She looks at the clock and notices that he is home quite early from work.

But Gerald is not in the mood for questions. Matilda proceeds with a heavy heart, and echoes of the old nausea she used to feel are rising as she pulls on her gloves and prepares to make the first incision.

The day after Rusty's necropsy, as Matilda walks home from school, she sees Mrs Endlesham walking with her children, looking for their small Jack Russell. 'Rusty! Here, boy!' Mrs Endlesham's little boy, about nine years old, cries out. He is visibly distressed. The family catch Matilda looking at them from across the street. She looks away quickly, her heart racing as she hurries home.

'Papa, you must never do that again. I know Rusty was a nuisance, but he was a pet, and the little boy was so upset. Please, Papa,' she pleads with Gerald at supper that evening. They are eating on their laps in the front room because Rusty's corpse is occupying the kitchen table. It is a warm day, and

FIVE

he is decaying rapidly, the flypaper hanging from the kitchen ceiling is coated with bugs, but Gerald has insisted that they cannot dispose of him yet. They have not finished the work.

'Disapproving, are we now, Matilda? Concerned suddenly about all God's creatures great and small?' he says, as he chews a vicious forkful of lamb stew, a slight trail of its juices clinging to his chin. 'That's rich coming from you, Papa's little surgeon. How many have you logged in your notebook there? One hundred? One hundred and fifty?'

Matilda puts her fork in her bowl, her dinner untouched. He never used to get angry with her. Silent, morose, annoyed, but never angry. She does not know how to respond, but she does know that he must never do this again.

'One hundred and forty-two. But that's not what I'm saying, Papa, I just – I'm worried—'

'Worried? You should be. If they catch *you*, silly, stupid girl, if they see what *you've* been up to, you have no idea what they'll do to you. If you know what's good for you, you'll let me worry about the details. You just keep at the work and do as you're told.'

Matilda does not know what he means, who *they* are, who will catch her, but she is too afraid to ask.

To her great relief, Gerald brings nothing home in the sack for the next three days. The work on Rusty has been extensive and she is still cataloguing and recording his organs and their findings. But she has to repeat her plea when Gerald brings home a French bulldog who nipped at his ankles once on his route, and then a miniature poodle who used to bark at him every day when he delivered the post to her elderly owner, and then a ginger cat who hissed at him on one occasion when his shaking left hand caused him to lose his grip on a parcel and drop it, breaking the glass inside. He tells Matilda these things as though they have just happened, but he no longer comes home in his uniform. She knows he no longer has a route.

'Papa,' she says, putting her hand on his arm, after they dispose of the last of the cat. 'I think it's time to stop now, I think that's as far as we can go. I've learned so much from you, Papa, but we can't go on like this.'

He wrenches his arm away. 'Like *what*, you horrid little ingrate?' he says, quietly, almost snarling, with anger in his eyes. 'I'll do as I please. And if you don't want to help, then you just stay out of my way.'

That is when a curtain comes down in Gerald's eyes and Matilda cannot see him past it. He withdraws further and further. He leaves less and less money every week for her to do the shopping with, and more and more jars fill the cupboards. He no longer asks her to prepare the table or sterilise the instruments. He does this himself now, or, more often than not, does neither. She finds the kitchen table wet and fluid-stained in the morning, her father's scalpels and forceps strewn about the surfaces, dried with blood. When she looks closely at the new jars, she notices that his handwriting on the labels has grown jagged and illegible and that the specimens are nicked and tattered, their severed blood vessels frayed at the ends.

Matilda goes only to school and back and stays in her room when her father is in the house. She eats little. She waits to hear

FIVE

the key turn in the lock, his uneven step on the floorboards, the thud of a sack. She waits to hear him call for her, but he never says her name. In the rare moments when they pass each other in the house, he seems surprised to see her, as though he has forgotten that she lives there. She knows it will be better for them both if he does. The months wear on. When Matilda leaves for school in the mornings Gerald is still in bed, and she finds him bent over his work in the kitchen when she returns home. He leaves in the night without saying where he is going. She hears him returning in the early hours. His steps grow heavier. So do the sacks. The house no longer smells of disinfectant the way it once did when they were scrupulous about their cleaning methods. It reeks of rotten flesh and formaldehyde.

One night when she has heard him leave, Matilda finds her mother's old valise and packs her few items of clothing, including the tiny pink dress once made for her with love. She runs her hand along the spines of her beloved books to say goodbye. She thinks about taking *Gray's Anatomy*, which her father gave her last Christmas. She knows from the stamp inside that he did not buy it but that he stole it from the library. She has pored through its pages, but now she wonders with a shudder why he gave it to her. She does not dare to think what else he had in mind for her to learn. She comes down the stairs and takes a last look at the kitchen of her childhood home, covering her mouth and nose so that she does not have to breathe the stagnant, foetid air. 'I'm sorry,' she says to no one, but hopes that somewhere Gerald can hear her. He returns home very late and does not notice until morning that she's gone.

Two years after their first meeting, Mrs Worth watches Horatio walk with Livvie down the aisle to meet Nicholas at the altar. She has declined to attend any of the pre-wedding events, like the rehearsal dinner and the 'Bridal Glam Mimosas and Make-up!' preening session on the morning of the ceremony, though Livvie was deliberately courteous about inviting her. Mrs Worth did not want to be there almost as much as Livvie did not want her to be there, and at least there they agreed.

After the ceremony, Nicholas has a quiet moment with his mother.

'What do you think, Mum? I'm a married man now. Listen, it would mean a lot if you would finally let Livvie call you Matilda. It would go a long way to making things easier, between you, I mean, but for me too.'

Mrs Worth has watched Nicholas and Livvie smile and kiss and hold each other throughout the day. She is, in her own way, happy for them, or rather, she can recognise their happiness and she is grateful that her son knows such a feeling. Mrs Worth's own understanding of love has been so muted and warped and stunted that she doesn't realise that what disturbs her most about Livvie is not her frivolity and lack of depth. It is her ease with love, and the ease with which she gives that love to Nicholas, an ease Mrs Worth has never had even with her own child and that she has even less now that he has grown up and found love for himself.

FIVE

So Mrs Worth instead answers her son with, 'No, I don't think that will be possible.'

'Mum, please, we're family now, you've got to give her a chance, for me.'

'The dog is wearing a tuxedo, Nicholas.'

'Mum, it's just a bit of fun.'

She has never told Nicholas how she knows Livvie, that she met her before he did. If she had told him right after their first meeting that day maybe things would not have got this far, maybe she would not have lost her son to this ridiculous girl. But the moment for truth is long past, and he has chosen her, and Mrs Worth will simply have to accept it.

Several years before Nicholas met Livvie, Mrs Worth stopped in a Boots pharmacy on the high street. She'd been on her feet for twelve hours, her hands aching from clutching her surgical tools all day, her neck stiff from leaning over the body of the poor young woman they'd found in the Thames the week before. But it is her knees, getting arthritic, that are really troubling her. Mrs Worth is sad for the dead girl and she is tired. She catches her reflection in a mirror at the cosmetic counter. She looks haggard and old, like the walking dead herself.

She is walking down the pain relief aisle when a thin blonde woman with a severe ponytail, wearing a tight black sheath, stilettos and sunglasses, despite the late hour of the day, brushes past her, stops a short, sweaty male employee, says, too loudly, 'Where's the lube? You know, lubricant?' and follows him as he scurries down the aisle.

Good Lord, Mrs Worth thinks, *poor man,* retrieving her

reading glasses so she can find the Voltarol for her knees. She takes it along with some ibuprofen, a ChapStick, and a Kit Kat to the queue and watches all of her items fall to the floor when she is cut off by a young man in a hurry who is determined to get in line ahead of her.

'In quite a rush, aren't we,' she says, irritated, struggling to pick up her items without bending her aching knees.

'What?' the young man says, rudely, over his shoulder, barely casting her a glance. 'Sorry.' But he does not bend down to help her and stares straight ahead. No one in the queue helps her.

She finally picks up her things when a young shop assistant opens another register at the cosmetics counter behind her, just opposite the tills where they keep the perfumes in locked cabinets, so Mrs Worth heads there and puts her items down, satisfied to be served before that rude young man after all.

'You can't buy those here, this is cosmetics only,' the young girl says. Her long and perfect powder-pink nails tap once on the counter.

'But surely it doesn't make a difference? It all goes to the same place?' Mrs Worth says, indignant.

'You have to buy cosmetics if you want to check out here,' the shopgirl says, bored, annoyed, dismissive.

'I have a ChapStick, arguably that is a cosmetic,' Mrs Worth says, refusing to move.

The girl sighs loudly, pouts her lips and says curtly, 'Look, you can't check out here unless you're buying perfume or cosmetics, all right? If you're not, then you need to go to the other till, please.'

FIVE

'I would like to speak to your manager,' Mrs Worth says, digging in.

'What? Why?'

'Because you are rude, and this policy, if it is, in fact, a policy, which seems dubious, is nonsensical, and I would like to purchase these items and be on my way,' Mrs Worth says, looking around for someone with half a brain to help her.

'Oh my God, fine,' the girl says, as she starts to scan Mrs Worth's things.

There is thick, angry silence between them for the few moments while the young woman completes the transaction.

'Thank you,' Mrs Worth says, in a clipped tone. As she walks away, relieved the confrontation is over, she distinctly hears the words 'stupid old cow' muttered behind her.

She approaches the door, and just as she is about to open it, the rude young man crosses in front of her, takes the door handle, and shouts out, 'All right, Livs?' in greeting to the awful young woman, who calls back, 'All right, babes, see ya later,' and waves at him and smiles. He pulls open the door as though Mrs Worth were invisible, as though he could put his hand straight through her. The heavy door shuts abruptly in her face. She looks over her shoulder at the shopgirl telling the lubricant woman that her nail shade is *pussy pink,* and they laugh as she scans her items, none of which, Mrs Worth notes, are cosmetics.

Livs. That is who Nicholas has chosen. Mrs Worth recognised her as soon as she saw the perfect pink nails on the hand extended to her at their first meeting. Livvie was just a girl when they'd had their encounter, perhaps she has changed. But Mrs Worth knows that people don't change all that much, not really, except for the fact that sons leave their mothers. She does not know how to tell him that he is the only person in the world that she has ever loved. That to be his mother was the privilege of her life. That he will regret tying himself to this empty-headed, shallow woman and her ugly, spoiled dog. So she says, 'I've had enough for today, Nicholas. Have a lovely time.'

Though abruptly leaving the wedding before the cake is even cut without saying goodbye to the bride might be a reason that many people feel would justify not speaking to one's mother for five years, this was not the moment that did it for Nicholas. He knew his mother was strange and he knew he couldn't change her, and he loved his wife for her bubblegum view of the world, and he had so much else to think about and look forward to. He told Livvie that his mother loved the wedding, she just wasn't feeling well. She thought Livvie was beautiful. And he put all her other words to the side. For now.

A year later, Livvie is pregnant with their first child and announces it at a family Christmas that Mrs Worth reluctantly attends at the newlyweds' home with Livvie's parents. The announcement is made as they all drink 'Mimosas!' by the tree, and Livvie opens a gift addressed to Horatio.

'Oh my gwood-ness, Ho-wa-tio! What's in he-were, gwood boy?' Livvie exclaims in the exaggerated baby talk she uses for her dog. She opens the box to reveal a doggie bandanna.

'What does this say, love bug?' Livvie says, a giggle in her voice, handing it to Nicholas.

FIVE

'It says, "My parents are getting me a human!"' he reads out, cheerfully, as Livvie squeals and her parents rise and gesticulate and almost spill their mimosas in happiness. Mrs Worth stays in her seat.

'Isn't it wonderful, Um, Uh . . .' Livvie's mother says, warmly taking Mrs Worth's hand after hugging her daughter. She always refers to Mrs Worth as 'Um, Uh', unsure what name to use for her that is both polite and also loyal to Livvie.

'Yes, it's about time they thought about giving that dog away, very sensible, although I'm not sure what all the fuss is about,' Mrs Worth says, pulling her hand away quickly from Livvie's mother.

'What did you say?' Livvie cries, hysteria rising in her voice. '*Give* him away? We're not giving him *away*!'

Nicholas catches his wife before she goes any further. 'No, Mum – we're having a baby. We're not giving Horatio a new owner, we're giving him a baby. Isn't it great?' he says, trying to put a chuckle in the sentence.

'Why would you give a baby to a dog?' Mrs Worth says, and then, after a beat, 'Oh, I see.'

An awful silence descends on the room until Nicholas breaks it with faux lightness and says, 'I think all the old folks are in shock, Livs!' trying to smooth it over. He sees his mother bristle, sees Livvie's eyes quickly filling with tears.

'She ruined it!' Livvie cries, flying from the room with her dog under her arm and her mother in tow.

For many, this might be the moment that would justify not speaking to one's mother for five years – her inability to be excited for the birth of one's first child expressed through her unveiled hatred for one's beloved pet, and on Christmas Day, no less. Yet this still is not what will sever Nicholas from his mother for half a decade.

Nicholas sighs deeply, rubs his forehead, and thinks about the two women in his life. He tells his gorgeous Livvie, 'Look, her mum died when she was a baby. Her dad was weird, all messed up from the war. She never had a family except for me, she's been on her own since she was sixteen. And you know, she has this crazy job that most people can't even think about. You're so loving, your heart is so big, darling, just make some space for her, OK?'

'Why does she hate Horatio?' Livvie asks, her impossibly blue, round eyes blinking at him.

'She doesn't, she just never had a pet. And she told me she was bitten as a kid, so she's scared of dogs, that's all it is. She loves you, and she'll love the baby, I know she will – how could anyone not love you?' he says, lifting Livvie's chin, planting a kiss on her forehead.

'How did *she* manage to raise someone as lovely as *you*?' Livvie says, wrapping her arms around her husband.

Nicholas remains patient with his mother through this encounter, and the next, and the one after that. When his son, Rafi, is born, he ignores his mother's comments about the choice of name. He intercepts the set of surgical tools that she brings as a gift for Rafi's second birthday. He even manages to broker a peace when Livvie, pregnant with their second child, is told she needs a C-section, and Mrs Worth describes the procedure in such graphic detail that Livvie vomits.

FIVE

But there finally does come a moment that Nicholas cannot save, forgive or explain away. The time does come when he has to choose his mother or the mother of his children. And sadly for mothers, that choice is never hard for their sons to make.

■ ■ ■ ■ ■

'Thank you so much, Mrs Worth,' Livvie says, evenly, trying very hard to disguise her red-hot rage and resentment. It is a Friday in the summer holidays. Rafi, now age six, has stayed home from day camp because of the twenty-four-hour rule on diarrhoea. His younger brother Robi (pronounced 'Robbie' but spelled, of course, Robi), now four, should have been at a playdate at the house of a preschool friend, but the mum had to cancel because everyone in the house had lice. Livvie's usual sitters aren't available in the mornings, and if she doesn't get to her interview on time, this job will slip through her fingers, just like all the others. Her mother is on a cruise, her sister is working, and Nicholas is in Paris for a meeting.

'You'll have to call my mum,' he says. 'Sorry, Livs, just this once, you know if I was home I'd drop everything.'

'God, why is the whole world against me!' Livvie wails. As she complains to her husband, she notices in the bathroom mirror that her roots are coming in. They're quite bad under the blonde, showing not only her old mousy brunette but grey as well.

'Ugh!' she moans loudly. Horatio sits at her ankles as she plucks stray eyebrow hairs and shouts at Nicholas on speaker while she tries to make herself presentable.

It's just a little part-time job, just something to get her out of the house and away from the children and back to some sort of life. But it's public facing, doing free make-up and selling expensive cosmetics in an upscale boutique for rich middle-aged ladies. She really should look more put together than this, should have her hair done, should have lost ten pounds, should have topped up her gels, should have had a facial, and not only does she have to go in looking like a rag, hoping her extensive cosmetic skills speak for themselves, but now she has to call her *fucking* mother-in-law to ask for a *fucking* favour.

They've been married seven years now, and Livvie doesn't even care any more that she still can't call Mrs Worth by her first name. She just doesn't use a name directly with her at all, and otherwise just uses what the kids call her, Dr Gran. They mostly stay away from each other and each hide behind Nicholas for their communications. It's easier that way for everyone.

And when Livvie looks at it objectively, compared to her friends, she's pretty lucky.

It's not like Mrs Worth is a super involved grandparent. She still works in the hospital morgue part-time, which makes Livvie want to gag when she thinks about it, but at least that means she doesn't have the time to come over and meddle and be in the way and tell her she's doing everything wrong.

Nicholas calls his mother faithfully once a week, but she never asks to speak with Livvie. So this arrangement really isn't so bad. Mrs Worth isn't nice, and Livvie knows she doesn't like her, but she's not nosy or pushy. She doesn't insist on seeing the kids. She isn't overbearing or passive-aggressive like so many

FIVE

of the older women Livvie knows, like her own mother. She's just passive. And while usually that's not a problem because they ignore each other, today it makes Livvie nervous. Her mother-in-law has been alone with the kids only about four times since they were born. The most recent two occasions were disastrous, both boys in tears when Livvie returned, both screaming in the middle of the night after having bad dreams. Rafi refused to sleep in his bed for a week after the last time because Dr Gran told him, in detail, about the procedure for killing chickens in factories to make the chicken nuggets he had had for dinner that night. He still won't touch them, even now.

But today, Livvie needs her help. There really is no other option and it's either call her or cancel the interview. It's only a couple of hours, and it's in the daytime, so how much could really go wrong? She might say weird stuff to them, but she would never hurt them. She's a doctor, after all, Livvie reasons internally. *Yeah, a doctor for dead people,* the voice in her head reminds her.

'Life is really hard for mothers, Horatio,' she says to her companion, and makes the call.

■ ■ ■ ■ ■

'Do you really cut up dead people?' Rafi asks his grandmother.

'Yes,' Mrs Worth says, looking at her grandson over her newspaper at the kitchen table. She goes back to reading.

'Why?' Rafi asks, flatly.

'To find out why they died,' Mrs Worth says.

'Do the ghosts come to tell you?' Rafi asks.

'Ghosts?' Mrs Worth says, alarmed, putting her paper down. 'There are no ghosts. Ghosts are pretend. I work in a hospital, with doctors and police. It's a serious place.'

'Do you cut open dead kids?' Rafi asks.

'Sometimes. But it's very sad,' she says.

'Why?' Rafi says.

'Because no one wants children to die,' Mrs Worth says.

'How do you do it? Do you chop them up or do you use a pizza slicer? Mum just bought one of those, it's very cool, want to see?' Rafi says, running to the kitchen drawer to find it.

'Now wait just a moment. No pizza slicer. That is absolutely the incorrect implement for an autopsy. It's not nearly sharp enough. You clearly have no understanding of human physiology whatsoever,' she says.

'Pizza?' says Robi, shirtless and trouserless but wearing socks, underwear and a baseball cap, popping out from under the kitchen table.

'What are you doing under there? And where are your clothes?' Mrs Worth says.

'Clothes are boring,' Robi says.

Mrs Worth sighs. 'Now look, you two can't just wander around here in your underpants doing nothing and saying all kinds of nonsense. Now go and play, or whatever you do.'

'OK, Robi,' Rafi says, ignoring his grandmother and leaning over his brother, wielding the pizza cutter in the air. 'I'm sorry, but it's really bad, and we're going to have to *cut* you in half.'

'Good God!' Mrs Worth shouts, grabbing the slicer from

FIVE

his hand and laying it on the kitchen island. 'That is not a toy! And you would never get through a whole body with that, anyway. Now look, we need to be more productive than this. Go and get me one of your felt-tip pens.'

They decide that Robi, as he is partially clothed, will be the patient. Mrs Worth finds two shower caps in the bathroom, one for her and one for Rafi, and they put them on. She explains the necessity of not contaminating the body with skin or hair cells. She shows the boys how to scrub up. Then she gets the disposable gloves and masks she always carries in her purse and puts a set on Rafi.

'I want one,' Robi complains, feeling left out, so she puts a set on him as well.

Then, feeling very solemn about his job as the patient, he lies down on the kitchen table.

'Pretend you're dead,' Rafi says to him. 'Be really still and don't breathe and close your eyes. Dr Gran is going to *cut you open* and *take out* your heart and stomach, and then we're going to go into your brain and push it out your ear.'

'No!' Robi screeches with gleeful horror.

'I will do no such thing!' says Mrs Worth. 'Now pay attention and you'll learn something. Where is the heart?' she asks Rafi.

'There?' he says, pointing at Robi's left shoulder.

'Close, but not quite. It's lower, here, slightly to the left, closer to the centre,' she says. 'Robi, make a fist.' She has him put it on his chest in the correct position and draws a circle around it. 'That's the heart, you see? Every person's heart is about the size of their fist.'

Robi looks down without moving his head, trying to stay still, as Dr Gran continues. 'So to get to the heart, first we have to deal with all of this skin and muscle and bone that's above it. What are these?' she asks the boys, drawing a light line along one of Robi's ribs. She teaches them about the ribcage, how it protects the organs underneath.

'So if that's the heart, where's the patient's stomach, doctor?' she asks Rafi. He points to his brother's belly.

'Well, yes and no, that's too low, it's under there, but it's also more to the left. It's in what we call the left upper quadrant. You see, we divide the abdominopelvic region into four parts, which helps you know how to find things,' Dr Gran says, and she draws two long, dotted lines on Robi, dividing his torso into quarters.

After explaining which organs can be found where, Mrs Worth, with Rafi, turns Robi on his side. She draws lines to show where to find his lungs and to explain that the ribs wrap around all the way to the back. Then Mrs Worth's phone rings in the other room.

'Don't go anywhere, boys, I have to answer if it's the hospital,' she says.

If she had spent more time with her grandsons or ever exchanged more than polite pleasantries with Livvie or ever babysat more than four times in six years or had any real maternal instincts, Mrs Worth would have known not to leave the boys alone. Earlier, she would have reflexively put the pizza slicer back in the drawer immediately, thinking many steps ahead of the children the way practised mothers and

FIVE

grandmothers are conditioned to do, rather than just resting it on the kitchen island within their reach.

'I know, I know!' Rafi shouts with glee, having thought of a brilliant idea.

He opens the fridge and takes out the family-size bottle of ketchup.

'Here, now I'm gonna to put this on you, and it'll be like *blood* and we're going to do an operation!' he says to Robi.

'OK,' Robi says, obediently lying back down on the operating table.

'And I'm gonna need this too, to make it like it's real,' Rafi says, taking the pizza cutter from where Mrs Worth laid it.

'Ready? I'm not going to hurt you, it's just pretend,' Rafi says, resuming his position standing on a kitchen chair, leaning over Robi's supine body.

'Doctor, it looks really bad,' Rafi says in a deep, serious voice as he squeezes ketchup on Robi's abdomen.

'What are you doing! What are you *doing*!' Livvie screeches, and Horatio starts to yelp as she opens the back door of the house leading into the kitchen. 'Stop it! Stop it right now!' she screams.

Whether Robi sustained the cut prior to Livvie's entrance or whether Rafi's hand slips and cuts his brother after his mother startles him with her yelling is hard to say. And really, it's beside the point.

Either way, 'Ow, ow, ow!' is the sound that comes out of him, followed by terrified tears, because his vivid imagination is confused by what is ketchup and what is blood all over his torso.

'I'm sorry! I'm sorry! I'm sorry!' is what the stricken Rafi says, dropping the pizza slicer, believing for an awful moment that he has actually murdered his brother, because the ketchup smeared all over him is very convincing to his child's brain.

'I only left for a minute,' is what a ghostly pale Mrs Worth says when she runs into the kitchen and, stunned, surveys the scene.

'Why is Robi naked, why is he on the table like that? What did you do to him?' Livvie shrilly cries again, as her outfit gets smeared with ketchup when she lifts Robi from the table.

'He was playing dead, Mama. She says she cuts open dead kids,' Rafi hiccups through horrified sobs, holding his ketchup-covered hands out in front of him.

'He's not naked. They had questions about physiology,' is all Mrs Worth can think to say.

'You're sick, you know that? Sick!' Livvie screams at Mrs Worth. 'You're not normal! No normal person cuts open dead people. Dead kids? What are you telling them? Physiology? He's four years old!' Livvie shouts, pulling both her sons away from Mrs Worth, who stands frozen and foolish in her shower cap and gloves.

'I thought . . .' she starts to say but then decides against it. She takes off the mask and gloves and lays them on the table. She quickly scans Robi in Livvie's arms. 'He's not badly hurt, it's just a surface wound,' she says.

'Oh, so that makes it OK? He shouldn't be hurt at all. And do you know how hard it is to get ketchup out of clothes!' she yells at Mrs Worth's back as she gathers her things and leaves.

FIVE

'Dr Gran, wait!' Rafi says, running after her, feeling guilty and confused about getting his grandmother in trouble, not quite sure why what they did is so wrong.

'You stay with your mum now,' she says, opening the front door. She doesn't look back.

Livvie quickly sits Robi by the sink, and within seconds of rinsing him off, it's clear that he just has a tiny nick from the pizza slicer.

Relieved but furious, Livvie sternly tells the boys, 'You are *so* lucky, *never* play with that again, do you hear me? This could be so much worse.'

Unfortunately for Livvie, it is about to be.

Mrs Worth gets into her car, puts on her seat belt, turns the key in the ignition. She checks her mirrors. Although she will never be able to trust her memory on this point, she does check them. However, after she backs up, after the bounce and muted thump of the wheel against the body, after the yelp, after Livvie shouting, 'Who let Horatio out? Who let him out!' after both little boys stand on the front steps, crying, and after she sees their mother leaning over the small body in the rear-view mirror, it is not surprising that she will always question herself about whether she saw the dog. About whether she drove over him on purpose. About whether she drove away without stopping because she was in shock, or ashamed, or afraid, or all three.

She will remember clearly Livvie's high-pitched exclamation of 'You're sick!' She will remember knowing that it's true. She'll remember that she didn't offer to look after her grandsons over the years because she was afraid she wouldn't know what to do or would say the wrong thing. She knew nothing about children and dogs and the fun and loving and laughter of grandmothering. She'd never had a grandmother. She'd never had a mother. She was afraid of hurting them all somehow because she didn't know enough about people, about family. And, of course, hurt them is exactly what she did. She's so much more comfortable with the dead, whom she can't hurt at all.

She'll remember thinking that Livvie is brave, defending her children like that, saying what she thinks is right in the face of something wrong, and she will wish that she could have been brave, long ago, when Gerald hurt little creatures and made her cut them open and made her feel strange and all wrong. But she did what she was told. She said nothing at all. And so let what they did follow her for the rest of her life.

■ ■ ■ ■ ■

When Nicholas gets home and learns what happened, he calls his mother.

'Are your sons all right?' she says.

'Not really, I mean, they'll be fine, but—'

'That's all that matters. I have to go now,' she says, hanging up, burning with shame. And that is what she says every time he calls after that for several months. He cannot text her because she shuts off her personal mobile, keeping only the one she uses for the hospital. She will not open his emails. When he calls her house, she says only the same few words, because she can't bear to ask about the dog, or Livvie. She can't bear

FIVE

to know she has, in the end, become the monster she tried to suppress for so long.

Mrs Worth thought she had left those awful days of her childhood behind and done something positive with her life to overcome the ruin of Gerald's madness. But it has never gone away. She managed to have a beautiful child of her own, who became a loving husband and father, and yet, though she has run from it for years, decades, she can never escape that kitchen, with its flypaper and jars and bare bulb, the cutting board, the pins, the bones and the bodies.

She never had the courage to challenge Gerald, only to leave him, silently, just as she had always followed his orders and adhered to his rules – in silence. She's in her seventies now, a doctor, a grandmother, and while it's too late for her to change, too late for her to be anything other than odd and strange and not like other people, she can do one thing that she knows normal people do. She can say the one thing Gerald never said.

'Thank you for seeing me,' Mrs Worth says, standing in Livvie's living room.

'That's all right,' Livvie says coolly, sitting upright, hands folded, legs crossed, on her sofa. 'Please sit down,' she says, politely.

'I won't, I'm not staying,' Mrs Worth begins. 'It's been some months now, I know, and I should have come earlier. I have something to say to you. Livvie, I am sorry. I know you loved your dog like one of your children. I don't really understand why or how but that's not my business. I'm very sorry.'

'Wow, how heartfelt,' Livvie deadpans.

'I won't say that I didn't mean to kill your dog, because I can't be sure about that. But in any case, that's what I came to say,' Mrs Worth says. She hears the sound of something metal turning behind Livvie, *squeak, squeak, squeak*.

'You can't be sure?' Livvie repeats. 'You can't be *sure* you didn't intentionally try to kill him?' In the momentary silence between them, Mrs Worth hears it again, *squeak, squeak, squeak*.

She looks down, near Livvie's feet, to see small metal wheels, attached to a small harness, attached to a small French bulldog.

'Well, surprise!' Livvie mocks, patting her companion on the head. 'These are Horatio's Walkin' Wheels. French bulldogs have weak hips, you know, hip dysplasia? I'm sure you know about that since you know so much about *physiology*. The knock from your car certainly didn't help, so he has to use these sooner than he would need to, but hey, at least he survived your assassination attempt.'

'He's alive?' Mrs Worth asks, unable to find her breath.

'Yep, even though you tried *really* hard to kill him. He made it,' Livvie says, contemptuously, rising from her seat, standing protectively in front of Horatio. Horatio gives a little growl.

'I thought . . . Why didn't you tell me?' Mrs Worth says, desperately.

'Tell you what? That you didn't kill my dog even though you wanted to? That my kids still have nightmares about watching their grandmother's attempted murder of their pet?' Livvie says, her voice rising righteously.

FIVE

'No, no, that's not – I didn't want . . .' Mrs Worth says, stuttering, words escaping her.

'It's what you *wanted* to happen, of course it is, you just said so,' Livvie raises her voice, laughing incredulously, walking towards the old woman.

'No! That's not right, that's not what I said, you just listen, you *silly, stupid girl*!' Mrs Worth yells, clenching both fists, eyes shut tight, face raised upward, Gerald's voice echoing in her throat.

There is an audible sharp intake of breath from both women, their eyes wide, as they each take in the words. Mrs Worth hears her father. Livvie hears only Mrs Worth.

'I see,' Livvie says, taking a step back, calmly, coolly comfortable with her upper hand. 'You practise autopsies on my children, you run over my dog, and by way of apology you come into my home and call me stupid.'

'No, wait, I didn't mean that, you're not listening—'

'No, I'm not, I'm not listening, MA-TIL-DA,' Livvie says, stretching out the syllables of Mrs Worth's name, getting louder with each syllable. 'And I'm not going to listen anymore, because you've said more than enough. Get out of my house.'

Horatio wheels out from behind Livvie's legs and gives another low growl of support and barks. Mrs Worth clutches her handbag, turns on her heel, and leaves.

That evening, when Livvie updates him on the argument, Nicholas once again calls his mother.

'Mum?' he says.

'She will never forgive me,' Mrs Worth says.

'Not anytime soon,' he says. 'But Mum, I tried so many times to tell you about Horatio, we could have cleared this up months ago if you had just talked with me, it didn't have to come to this.'

'Take care of your family now, Nicholas. I don't know what to do with a family.'

'What? Mum—?' Nicholas says, feeling impending devastation.

'I'm better with the dead. Take care of yourself. Your boys are lovely. Goodbye,' she says.

And so, when it finally happens, the moment that breaks them apart, Mrs Worth makes the choice for Nicholas between his mother and his wife, a final act of motherly love.

The first few months are strange, and Nicholas feels his mother's absence and the sting of her rejection. He keeps trying to call her but then he stops. She went too far this time. He can't fix it, and honestly, he doesn't want to. He doesn't have the energy to chase her. He has too much else to do now, it's his turn to live his life, with a career and a young family who relies on him. And after a few more months, then a year, life expands to fill the place she used to take up with growing children and a rolling dog and a promotion at work and moving house and changing schools and the children's sporting events and food allergies and music recitals and Rafi's dyslexia and Robi's eczema and regular haircuts and dental appointments and parent-teacher meetings and a global pandemic and homeschooling and Christmas and birthdays and then Livvie starting a new online business and becoming a social media

FIVE

influencer with her own line of specially formulated organic cosmetics.

There is a launch party with champagne, even a sponsored endorsement campaign, and Nicholas is so proud of her and she is a model for other work-from-home mothers and gives inspirational speeches at women's empowerment events and is offered her own self-esteem podcast and is even on a list of 'Mothers Who Mean Business' in a national magazine. And then there is a cough she has that won't go away. And then blood tests, hospital visits, surgery, treatment, hushed conversations late into the night about how to tell the boys. It happens incredibly fast, too fast, she is too young, everyone says so. And then one morning she is barely conscious in the hospital bed they moved into the living room, and her sons hug her before they go to school. She is gone before they come home.

Nicholas's own grief is so huge he can't even feel it because his worry for his kids is so much bigger. They don't have a mother any more – where does he even begin to deal with that. But then he remembers that *he* still does.

She's awkward and difficult to hug and she's cold, but if there's one thing she knows more about than anyone else it's this – death. He sends her a letter with details of the funeral. He knows she'd seize up if he called her. She doesn't reply to the letter, but he's not surprised. She was never very good with words.

Time	Destination	Expected
1st 7:06	London Victoria	07:09

This service has been delayed. We apologise for the disruption to your journey.

2nd 7:13	Bedford	Delayed

07:05

On an empty bench at the end of the platform, beneath a poster for a local orthodontic clinic, lies a discarded newspaper. It is folded in half. The corner of the top sheet lifts slightly and ripples because of a sudden, slight draught. The page is suspended, trembling in the air for just a second before it drops.

The train is coming.

The subtle movement of the newspaper indicates a shift in the atmosphere, the velocity and weight of the train as it hurtles down the track, influencing the air currents, signalling imminent arrival, or, in the case of our five travellers, imminent death. The train is not quite visible yet, but it will be, very soon.

Because of the distraction of the emergency alarm, which is not loud enough to encourage evacuation but just loud enough to force everyone to shout, Bad Back, Medical Student, Emma, Gideon, Mrs Worth and Sonny have not noticed the slight flutter of the first page of the newspaper on the bench. Liam, unconscious under the platform, also does not notice it. If he were awake, he might feel the rumble under his spine indicating that the train is getting closer. But they all miss the warnings.

They do not get the message. They are too busy with what is unfolding in front of them and within them.

 To Do List stands paralysed until 7:05 and eleven seconds, when she realises that if anyone sees her standing next to the alarm they will assume she triggered it. She run-walks to the elevated covered walkway that bridges Platforms 1 and 2 over the tracks to survey the situation. She notes there was no point in sounding the alarm because no one has evacuated and no help has arrived. To Do List does not know that the alarm does not summon the fire brigade automatically, although that is a common public misconception. Station protocol at such a small station is for staff to first investigate the situation, inform emergency services if necessary, and then evacuate the passengers once they have accurate information. This is due to the prevalence of false alarms pulled for non-emergency reasons, such as personal belongings dropped on the tracks, children playing a prank, or the uncontrollable rage felt by some commuters at the circumstances of their lives that have trapped them in a cycle of early morning train journeys, working, maintaining a terrible diet, drinking too much, and going on budget holidays, only to return to the same station to wait for the same train to take them back to work again two weeks later. But today there are no railway staff emerging to help. It is all for nothing, another useless, meddling thing To Do List did in a fruitless attempt to be—

 'Hey!' she calls out. 'Hey!' She begins waving her arms. She cannot get anyone's attention. 'Down there!' she squawks and points, but no one can hear her.

FIVE

'Oh God, oh God!' she pants frantically as she run-walks over to the stairs, another seven seconds closer to someone's death, intending to descend them, but in her haste twisting her ankle and tripping down half the flight before she catches herself with the banister.

'Fuck a duck!' she cries, clinging to the banister, her torso horizontal, trying to regain her footing. At the bottom of the stairs, Bad Back turns his head. He got tired of pacing, so although no one was watching him, at 7:05 and five seconds, while To Do List was dithering, he made a big show of taking a seat on the stairs by grabbing the banister stiffly and swinging himself around to sit. But at the sound of her exclamations above the alarm, he turns and catches an unfortunate glimpse of To Do List's undercarriage, encased in its nylon tormentor as she barrels toward him, dangerously close to revealing the secrets of her middle-aged femininity beneath her work skirt.

But undeterred by the exposure of her distressed gusset to the public, or at least to this nondescript commuter lump, she orders, 'That man is on the tracks! Go!' like a fallen general giving his final command.

Bad Back, however, does not move. *Oh no,* he thinks. *How will he pull this off.*

As To Do List and Bad Back waffle ineffectually, Sonny calls, 'Eh, man . . . hey!' to Medical Student, touching his arm across Mrs Worth, trying to get his attention over the blare of the alarm. 'Are you OK?'

Medical Student nods. Mrs Worth, no longer able to hide

it, suddenly cries above the siren, 'My arm!' and clutches her left arm, letting out a guttural groan of pain.

'Shit, what do we do?' Sonny loudly asks Medical Student. 'Do we call an ambulance? Does this alarm trigger the cops?' He looks up at the clock on the display board. 7:06. DELAYED. That word. *Why,* Sonny thinks.

Medical Student nods, frozen in a different kind of pain, squeezes his eyes shut, squeezes Mrs Worth's hand at the same time, and wills himself out of the war, away from the living memory of air raid sirens, into the present.

'My arm!' Mrs Worth cries out again and starts to pant. Medical Student's eyes open wide. Over the old woman's shoulder, he sees his friend Pascal, clutching his bloody arm before he falls to the ground and disappears. He could not help then. He must help now. 'Yes, madam,' he says. 'We are here, I know it hurts.'

'Go!' To Do List shouts over the siren at Bad Back, as she begins to indelicately bum-shuffle down the steps.

I can do this, Bad Back thinks. He gets up gingerly, leaning heavily on the banister, puts his hand to the small of his back, and awkwardly jogs to the edge of the platform but adds a limp, hoping to retain authenticity.

He looks over the edge of the platform and sees Liam, unconscious. All the blood rushes to his face. *God,* Bad Back thinks, *I'm such a plonker.*

'Man on the tracks!' he calls out over his shoulder and begins waving his arms to get the attention of Medical Student and Sonny. 'Man on the tracks!' he yells again.

FIVE

'Man on the tracks!' To Do List echoes him from the bottom of the steps.

Sonny looks at Medical Student. 'Go,' Medical Student says, coming back into himself. 'I am calling the paramedics. I've got her.' He holds Mrs Worth as Sonny runs to the platform edge at 7:06 and thirty-six seconds.

'Oh shit!' he exclaims, when he looks over the edge and sees Liam lying in the crawl space under the concrete lip.

Without a moment's hesitation, Sonny jumps down onto the tracks and jogs toward him.

This is it, Sonny thinks. *Not long now.* 'Man on the tracks!' he repeats.

He is not sure if he is imagining a rumble under his feet. But the headlights of the train in the distance look real. They're faint and far away but not too far. And not far enough.

'Man on the tracks!' Sonny shouts again to anyone and everyone and no one as he jogs towards Liam. He's not sure what to do, or what he wants to do, or how to do it, or if he should.

He thinks many things all at once:
This man could die.
I could save this man.
I could die.
I could save us both.
We could both die.
Together.

'Hey, wake up!' calls Sonny. Liam doesn't understand the loud voice though he can hear it. He feels the slightest scratch of a tiny paw on his ear. In twelve seconds, when he opens his eyes, he will see the train.

'C'mon, mate, wake up!' Sonny shouts again. He will see it too.

Sonny

'Good morning, little baby-man,' she says to gurgling baby Sonny at 4 a.m. He is busy in his crib, not crying but swinging his arms and legs up and down and round and round. He tilts to one side repeatedly, the start of rolling. He is too young for all of this motion, she thinks, but he is probably going to be an Olympic athlete. Her son is advanced. Special, obviously.

'Put him in the swaddle,' her tired husband slurs from his side of the bed. 'Maybe he'll go back to sleep.'

'Hello, my baby,' she says quietly, as he squirms and kicks. She gets the designer swaddle with the pocket for his legs and the Velcro fasteners to keep his arms in place. They've read that swaddling is meant to calm young babies, to help them sleep better by mimicking the cocooned feeling of the womb.

He is so sweet, wrapped up this way, arms pinned to his sides under the cloth, still for a few moments, just his little head visible at the top, with his big eyes looking at her in wonder, a shaft of early morning light creeping through the side of the blind.

'Back to sleep now, baby,' she says. And just as she turns

her back to return to her bed next to his crib, she sees her son raise one tiny fist, very slowly, in the air.

She leans over the side of the crib. He has escaped the swaddle again. She doesn't know how he does it. He looks like a very small but determined leader of a socialist revolution.

'He's doing it again, I told you, just like Che,' she says over her shoulder to her half-asleep husband. He opens one eye and sees the little fist waving above the edge of the crib.

'Good boy,' her husband says in his thick Scottish brogue. 'Stickin' it to the man.'

She kisses her extraordinary baby on the forehead. '*Viva la revolución*,' she says.

When he is four months old, the swaddle is abandoned. Sonny rolls, back to front, front to back, sooner than any other baby in the baby group that his mother takes him to every week. The other babies are content lying on their backs, chewing on their hands. Some of them cannot bear even a moment's separation from their mothers. But she keeps her hand near him, always near him, letting him roll, or wrestle with a set of plastic teether rings, while the other babies greedily feed, or plaintively cry, or lazily sleep on their mothers. And their mothers, looking at her active infant, say to her, 'My goodness, he must keep you busy.'

She says to her husband that evening, 'So she says that to me, very condescending, and I said, "He does, it's so exciting to have a child who's so advanced." Meanwhile, all their babies are lying there like fat little lumps, crying.' And she and her

FIVE

husband look at their baby Sonny in his bouncer, which he is bouncing with considerable force.

'Ah, those fat little lazy bastard babies, not like my little muscle man. Aren't you my little muscle man?' her husband says to their baby as Sonny kicks his feet in agreement.

He picks up his son. 'He's perfect, he's ours,' her husband says, and she loves that when he says, 'ours' it's like the growl of a bear, the sound of protection.

When Sonny is six months old, he wakes from a nap and pulls himself up to standing using the bars of his crib, then flips over the side and falls out.

His mother hears the thump and runs to his room. She finds him on the floor and rushes to him, hundreds of thoughts flooding her new mother's brain. But he is not hurt, he is not crying, he is not shocked. He is smiling at her, and if she is not mistaken, he is proud.

'Can you believe this kid?' she says to her husband that night, holding their son. 'Maybe he'll be a gymnast. A stunt man. A pilot.'

'What a strong lad,' he says, and kisses the top of his baby's head, and when he says 'strong' she hears how much stronger that word is than when other people say it.

At nine months, Sonny is walking. At ten months, he is running. At twelve months, the grandparents and cousins come to the house to celebrate his first birthday. A window is left open in the living room. Adults are distracted, eating, chatting with the other grandchildren and watching them do cartwheels and backbends.

Sonny climbs up the back of the sofa to the sill of the open window. He stares at the world outside and reaches for it. He feels a breeze on his little palm, sees the leaves of the tree in the front of their house rustle, and reaches and reaches. Then he dives.

His mother grabs him by the seat of his trousers just before he jumps, one hand gripping the back of his baby corduroys, the other holding a glass of wine. She hadn't had time to put it down before she leapt to save him.

As soon as she brings him away from the window he runs off after his cousins. Her dress is soaked in cabernet. The adults are horrified, but when she looks at her husband they both burst out laughing.

'That's our boy!' her husband says to the room of terrified eyes.

When Sonny is eighteen months old, his mother turns her back to lock the front door, and he runs into the street. A commuter on a bicycle swerves to miss him and swears at her. She swears right back, unconcerned about what her child hears her say.

When he is two, she bends down to tie her shoelace and he runs into the street. A car stops short. The driver swears at her. Sonny swears back.

'That's right, defend your mother's honour,' she says, picking him up and flipping the driver off as the car pulls away. But she only wears slip-on shoes when she is out with Sonny after that.

When he is three she is pulled aside at Little Footies soccer class to be told that Sonny is disruptive and does not take

FIVE

turns. She knows he doesn't take turns. He's bored. In the time it takes the other children to find the ball before it inevitably rolls past them, he is able to kick it across the whole gym and into the toddler goal. Twice.

'So I said, "Actually, I was meaning to speak to you. I think this class is too slow for him. He's just much more talented than these kids and they're holding him back," and I marched us right out of there.'

'That's my girl,' he says, and kisses his wife. 'They can shove their little footies up their little arsies!' And he swings Sonny round and round in the kitchen.

Sonny starts nursery school. Words are used in reference to their son from the lexicon for bad children, like *oppositional, noncompliant, loud*. But his parents hear *energetic, curious, lively*. They are not worried. They don't care if he doesn't nap. They love that all he does is run, that he is not interested in rules. To them, these are signs of high intelligence, exceptional creativity. Their little rebel, Sonny, is pure joy, and they will not dampen his spirit to make him colour inside the lines.

Their happy little family does happy family things: they go for pizza, to the movies, to the swings, and on their walk home Sonny sits on his dad's shoulders and tries to reach the sky. At bedtime, his giant of a father and his fierce little mother hold him tight, and he falls asleep dreaming about running in the sunshine.

One spring morning her husband has to be in the office early. He slips out of bed. It is a bright morning, unusual for London. He decides to cycle. He needs the exercise. He sneaks into Sonny's room and kisses him lightly on the head. He kisses his wife and says, 'Bonnie lass.' She is sitting bleary eyed at the kitchen table, already on her second cup of coffee.

He puts on his helmet. He pushes away from the kerb. The streets are mostly empty still. It is the last five minutes of his life, although, of course, he doesn't know it. He thinks about the day ahead, his first meeting, his presentation after lunch. A call at 10 a.m. He notices a beautiful magnolia in bloom in someone's front garden. He hears the van but does not see it. Just before the impact, he thinks that he should bring some flowers home tonight for his wife. She is such a good mother to their lad, their Sonny.

■ ■ ■ ■ ■

If it were not for her son, she would get into her bed and not leave it for three to four years.

She would pull down the blinds and stop the clocks so that she could forget the difference between day and night and she could just sleep and sleep, and when she woke she would watch terrible reality television until she fell asleep again. No, not reality television. They watched reality television together, *The Bachelor, Britain's Got Talent,* reruns of *Come Dine with Me, American Idol.* Maybe she would just watch her DVDs of *The Golden Girls,* the complete set her husband bought her one Christmas.

If it were not for Sonny, she would start drinking at 10 a.m. and not stop until she blacked out on the floor, in the hope

FIVE

that she might choke on her vomit while unconscious or die of alcohol poisoning and then she could be done with it, all of it. She could die, tragically, from grief, and everyone would be sad, and then in a few years, her sister and her parents and her friends – the ones who attended their wedding and the ones they went to everyone else's weddings with for that decade when they were young and carefree – they would all think of her and her husband and smile and tear up and say, 'Remember when' and raise a glass. They would be missed, but people would say they were together in heaven, and sigh, and then everyone would go to work the next day. Now and then they might think of them randomly, maybe while in the supermarket, maybe while on the train going to work, but everyone would survive those thoughts and continue living.

She remembers that time, that decade before everyone had babies, when they were youthful and full of expectation and had a wedding to go to every weekend. They were grown up enough to know where they were headed but still young enough to hold the promise of their future in the pocket of his suit jacket where he was carrying her lipstick for her because it wouldn't fit in the tiny clutch that matched her bridesmaid's dress. And they'd steal away for a moment during the cocktail hour, and they'd look at that future and they'd know that it was just for them and that it would be wonderful.

This, what is happening to her now, was not part of that. And she cannot survive the thoughts and does not know how to continue living. She does not want to wait five years until it will sting her just a tiny bit less, just a fractional tiny bit less, but everyone else will already be at the 'remember when' stage, so that when they toast him they'll think they'll be doing something nice for her, remembering him, but actually they will be boiling her alive, they will be blindfolding her in front of a firing squad and pulling all of the triggers.

But still, there is Sonny.

Children are the strongest antidote to grief, not because of their unconditional love or their joy or because they take pain away, nothing like that, nothing like an inspirational quote embroidered on a pillow for your sofa. Children are the antidote because of their unrelenting needs, their continuous, voracious, narcissistic, selfish insistence on living, their unceasing demands that those needs, no matter how trivial, be met immediately and urgently.

For example, on the morning of his father's funeral, Sonny wets the bed. It's the morning of his father's funeral, but he still needs breakfast. And clean socks. He tries very bravely to put on his shoes himself because he understands from the change in his mother's face when she strips his sheets and puts on new ones that he needs to be good, he needs to be grown up. Except he does not know how to do the laces.

When his Auntie Gabriela speaks to him gently and bends down and tries to help him, he will not let her.

'Can I help you, Sonny?' she says, starting to tie his left shoe.

'No!' he shouts and pulls his foot away.

'Mummy! Mummy!' he calls, in the standard, ear-piercing way he always calls for her.

'Sonny, your mum is trying to get dressed, just let me—'

FIVE

'No!' he shouts at Gabriela, and runs around the house, frantically, from room to room, searching for his mum.

He finds her in his parents' bedroom, sitting on the edge of the bed, still in her pyjamas, staring into space.

'Mummy, my shoes,' he says, going right up to her, his face so close she can feel his breath on her cheek.

'Mummy, my shoes,' he repeats, trying to break her stare by holding her face and looking straight into her eyes.

He is too young to understand that the smooth untouched pillows on his father's side of the bed are killing her. That before he came into the room, she saw them and had to turn her back because the sight of them – plumped, fresh, ready to be slept on – is like a needle in her eye, is like her fingernails being pulled out one by one while she listens to fingernails being dragged across a chalkboard at the same time.

'My shoes, Mummy,' he says again when she doesn't respond.

Gabriela, who has run after Sonny, stumbles, panting, into the bedroom, saying, 'Sorry, sis, I tried to—' but stops when Luna raises her hand. Gabriela feels redundant and ineffectual, she feels bad that she couldn't do this one little thing at least for her grieving sister, help her nephew get dressed.

But Luna just stands silently from the bed, hoists Sonny onto it so his feet dangle above the floor and kneels in front of her son. She ties his left shoe, then his right.

Gabriela, who is thirty-two and does not want children, and is in a polyamorous relationship, and thinks traditional heterosexual marriage perpetuates sexism and inequality, does not like this image. She does not want her grieving sister to be kneeling at her nephew's feet, like some Jesus and Mary live-action recreation. Gabriela goes to her and tries to lift her to standing so that Sonny doesn't get some weird patriarchal images mixed up with the grief and what is bound to be post-traumatic stress disorder, but Luna stops her.

Luna says, hugging Sonny's legs, 'There you go, baby, you look very handsome, Daddy is very proud of you. Go play now, OK? I'll come get you when it's time to go.'

'OK, Mama,' Sonny says, as he hops off the bed, straight down into Luna's lap, hugging her with every part of his small being. 'Tackle,' he says in his deepest voice with a Scottish accent, as he tackles Luna to the ground. He has always been good at mimicking his dad.

'All right, OK, boy, off you go,' she says, her limbs tangled with his, as he pushes off her shoulder with all his weight to get himself up and steps on her hand with his newly laced-up shoe.

Luna stays on the floor for a minute and says to Gabriela, who she knows is disapproving of some or all of what she has witnessed, 'Don't be so appalled, I'm forty-one, it's easier to be closer to the floor.'

'What?' Gabriela asks.

'So I'm ready when he tackles me twelve times a day. It's just easier if I'm already close to the floor.'

Luna then pulls herself up on the side of the bed. Her husband's smooth pillows that he will never sleep on again are in her field of vision, and they devastate her again and make her say, 'Why,' but it is not a question.

FIVE

'I don't know,' Gabriela says, holding her sister's hand. 'Would it help if I put them away?' she says, understanding intuitively that it is the sight of the pillows hurting Luna in this moment.

'No, it's OK, just do my hair, will you?' she says, and before she reaches the mirror, Sonny is back in the room, shooting them with pretend lasers, commando-crawling under the bed, getting dust all over his clothes, jumping on top of the rumpled duvet in his shoes, and finally collapsing, dislodging his father's pillows and sending them to the floor.

That is where they remain for a few months after the funeral, although every time Luna crosses the room she sees them, until she stops sleeping in the room so that she does not have to cross it and does not have to see them.

One rainy day, Sonny finds the pillows in the path of the tornado that is the only way to describe his movement around the house and strips the cases off to make a cape and something he calls a Bone Catcher. He uses the pillows to build a fort. Then he gets hold of the scissors and rips the pillows open and throws the hypoallergenic, antimicrobial synthetic white stuffing that was meant to ease her husband's allergies into the air to make snow all over the room.

'Look, Mama!' he shouts, with a joy she cannot imagine but is grateful that he still possesses. 'A blizzard!'

He does all of this while Luna watches, with white polyester clumps sticking to her hair, and she wonders how much of her husband's DNA is still in the fibres of the pillows, and she does not scold Sonny for turning it into snow.

She also does not stay on top of the bills, and takes leave from work, and does not wash her hair because it hurts, and does not buy milk when it runs out, and does not make Sonny eat vegetables or limit his TV watching, and tries to remember what she's supposed to do next and has absolutely no idea.

But at least the pillows are gone.

■ ■ ■ ■ ■

Two years pass. Luna is grateful for the mundane mandatory tasks that distract her from the monumentally horrific, unimaginably terrifying, gaping chasm of her grief. She stands on the edge of it every morning, amazed that once again she has awoken, surprised to find that she is still alive, and she wonders what she must have done in a previous life to have caused the karmic disaster that is her current reality.

But, always, there is Sonny.

She has to wash his clothes and buy him pyjamas and read to him and take him to other children's birthday parties. She has to give him antibiotics for ear infections and has to cut his hair, which is the same copper brown as his dead father's. She has to take him to school, she has to work.

If she knew that her husband's last thoughts were of her and their son, of bringing her flowers on the evening that he did not survive to see, it might make it easier, it might help. But there is no way of her knowing that truth and so she cannot take comfort in it.

So she finds relief in the repetition of laundry and vacuuming,

FIVE

in looking after Sonny, in keeping going, in trudging through to the end of each grey day until it becomes black night.

Sonny is sad too, of course, but he is so young, time and reality are still so flexible and malleable for him, that she knows his memories of his father have become a story, a favourite fairy tale imprinted on his mind that he will always remember fondly. That he remembers his father's voice, not from the memory of hearing it spoken, but from how it sounds on the family videos they watch on repeat.

Although the videos start to replace his actual memories, they do not replace the feeling that is having a big, loud Scottish father with a scratchy beard and broad shoulders from where Sonny could see the whole world. Just before he falls asleep, Sonny can still feel that feeling sometimes, of sitting on his father's shoulders and reaching for the sky, but he has never told his mother about it because he has learned not to say things that will make her too sad.

Every morning Sonny greets her with just one word. 'Hugs,' he says, rubbing his eyes, and she moves her coffee cup before he jumps on her or throws himself at her or finds another way of attaching his whole body to her torso and squeezing her so that she is smothered in his love and faint, underlying anxiety.

She knows that part of the reason for his morning ritual is the consistency and repetition of it, and part of it is the need for his parasympathetic nervous system to find calm through physical pressure. And part of it is sadness, missing the man who was strong enough to swing him around by the arms and tackle him and fireman-lift him and pretend to box with him, always getting knocked out in first round, always there to absorb his fierce, constant physicality. She is sorry that she cannot do these things because she lacks the physical strength to do them; roughhousing and wrestling do not occur to her as demonstrations of love, they are not natural to her, they are the language of love between fathers and sons that she does not know. But hugs she can do.

Dinner, however, she can't. And she doesn't.

All the other domestic chores she manages – the dishes, bleaching the shower, taking out the rubbish, sorting the recycling – but not dinner. She cannot bear dinner.

If she were alone, she just wouldn't eat it. The thinking, buying, preparing, cooking, paying attention to time, not burning, adding vegetables, caring, giving a shit about what it tastes like or looks like are just more than she is capable of.

Her husband cooked. He made fresh pasta from scratch and knew how to roast a chicken and understood things about steak. She has not eaten any of those things since he died. The thought of him, of a dishcloth on his shoulder, his head bowed, his face in profile focused on slicing garlic or squeezing a lemon, stops her breathing. She literally cannot breathe if she picks up pasta, chicken, steak, lemon or garlic in the supermarket, if she tries to nonchalantly put them in her shopping trolley like they are just food and not granite rubble filling her pockets to weigh her down while she drowns in the river of her grief.

But there is Sonny. Always.

Growing Sonny, hungry Sonny, who must be fed. So she

FIVE

buys ready-made pancakes and puts them in the toaster and tells Sonny that it is 'Breakfast for Dinner Week'. And they eat pancakes and cereal every night. For 'Sandwich Week' they have ham and cheese on toast for seven days, maybe eight.

During 'Chicken Nugget Week' he says, 'Mummy, I think in other people's houses sometimes they have different dinners.'

'Who told you that?' she asks, curiously, wondering if any adults at school have asked him about things at home and got onto the topic of food and now know about her struggle with dinner.

'The TV,' he says.

'All right,' she says, overcome with guilt now that she realises the depth of her dinner negligence. 'Let's go then,' and she takes him to Pizza Express.

They have not eaten in a restaurant for a long time, maybe a year. She is nervous. She orders a large pinot grigio to help with the noise, the people, the strangeness of strangers' laughter in public. She marvels at how people continue to live and eat and sing happy birthday. She wonders how it is that they don't know that her husband has died, and how it can be that his death has not affected them.

'Look at the ice, Mama, look how fast!' Sonny shouts.

He is delighted with his blue drinking glass. It contains water and a few cubes of ice. Sonny loves spinning things, and when he discovers that by spinning the glass just a little bit he can make a whirlpool in his drink, he is beside himself with glee.

'Sonny, my baby, that's very interesting, but we don't want it to spill and make a mess,' she says, calmly.

'But Mama, look!' he shouts again. She is conscious that a woman two tables away has glanced over her shoulder at his exclamation. A man near them has not looked up but has turned his head slightly and shifted in his seat. Luna moves to stop Sonny, but he has already sloshed water out of the glass onto the table.

'Sonny,' she says, in a calm but warning tone. He is over-stimulated by the restaurant, the noise, the people, the sound, she sees it. She should have come at a quieter time. She knows her child, so despite the over-the-shoulder glances of strangers, she knows the answer is not to grab the glass from him but to talk him down.

'Baby, it's wonderful, I know, the whirlpool, but in my bag I have—'

She reaches into her bag to look for the spinning toys he's obsessed with, the top and an old Nine Inch Nails CD with a spiral on it that Sonny finds absorbing when he spins it on a flat surface. But the pinot grigio has blunted her reflexes. She is too late.

'Mama, look!' he shouts again, and picks up the glass, hoists it in the air, and water spills on his head and seat and ice cubes clatter to the floor, and before she can stop him he hurls the glass across the room.

He does not know until he's done it that it's the wrong thing to do. He did not mean to hurt anyone. He just really liked the deep-blue colour of the glass, and how spinning the ice cubes

FIVE

made a whirlpool, and he likes to throw things that he likes, and he forgets that you're not supposed throw things inside, even magic glasses with whirlpools inside of them.

The glass hits the chair legs of a middle-aged white woman several tables away and shatters at her feet. She complains loudly and waves down a waiter dramatically, unnecessarily using all of her limbs.

She says, in full voice, standing up gingerly from her seat in distress, 'That's quite a shock that's given me, quite a shock,' and she pointedly looks at Luna.

Luna knows the people around her don't understand why she is not reprimanding her son. She knows they expect her to raise her voice, to grab him by the arm and pull him out of the room and scold him or make some other outward display of disappointment and horror on *their* behalf to demonstrate to *their* satisfaction that she will mete out the justice *they* surely would have expected and received when *they* were children. But Luna has never been one to do what other people want her to. And they don't need to understand. Her husband is dead. How dare they look at her son, at her, like that.

She looks around at the other tables, for a moment, at other children with other mothers. Children focusing greedily on the food in front of them, children colouring the children's menu quietly, children sitting on laps and eating pasta contentedly, older children reading books at the table while the adults talk. Dull, obedient children. She wonders where the other children are, the ones like hers. The other mothers, the ones like her. If there is a restaurant somewhere just for them, with holes in the walls and climbing equipment and mini-trampolines at each table where energetic, advanced, extraordinary children are applauded and are not stared at for throwing things from the sheer joy of being alive.

'Honestly, people should learn to control their children, that could have hit me in the head,' the older woman complains loudly to the waiter who arrives with the dustpan and brush for the glass.

Luna remains calm. She offers to pay for the broken glassware, she asks for their food to be packed up, and she pays for a gin and tonic to be sent to the woman's table, not knowing that right at this moment she is trying to get her entire meal for free from the restaurant manager.

Luna apologises to the many staff members involved in the clean-up. She apologises to the diners at the next table. 'I'm so sorry,' she says.

But Sonny feels the disapproving stares. He sees the unfriendly strangers looking at his mother. He wishes he hadn't done it so these people would stop looking at her. 'I'm sorry, Mama,' Sonny says, as tears flood his eyes.

'I know,' she says, 'I know,' because they both know he doesn't mean to do these things, but that he also can't help it. She squeezes his hand, but she is distracted, trying to get their things to get them out of here.

'I'm sorry, Mama,' Sonny says, pulling on her sleeve.

'Thank you,' she says to the waiter with the mop, as she bends to the floor with a napkin to try and assist. 'Let me help.'

FIVE

'I'm sorry, Mama,' Sonny yells, clinging to her arm as she tries to help.

'I know, baby, I know,' she says, abandoning the napkin, hearing the crescendo in his voice that means they have to leave, now. She looks for the quickest way for them to exit, leaving the bags of food on the table, trying to take her beautiful boy away from all of the eyes looking at him, and from the eyes that are trying not to look.

The only way to leave is by walking past the woman's table, and as they do she says, 'Best of luck, you'll need it, love, with *that* one. I'm afraid we all know where he's headed,' and she clinks her fresh gin and tonic with her saggy dinner companion's glass.

Luna ignores her, keeps walking, until she hears, 'Doesn't even *bloody* apologise,' and then she stops.

He's perfect, he's ours, she remembers.

And before she can stop herself, Luna says, 'Why don't you choke on a dough ball, bitch,' and as silence descends on the busy dinnertime rush, Luna feels good. She feels great, actually.

Flush with victory, she turns to usher Sonny out of the restaurant, her head held high, and she thinks how she can't wait to go home and tell her husband all about it.

But when she reaches the door of the restaurant, she remembers that he's gone. How wonderful it was to forget that she has lost him for just a moment. How joyful, how mundane, how blissfully ordinary to feel the feeling of him, living, waiting at home for them, ready to hear her story.

Whenever she needs him after that, she calls on him and he speaks to her, especially when she needs his help with Sonny.

She has rarely said his name since he died, afraid of how the word echoes in the air without his big, hulking body in the world to absorb the sound, afraid of how his name – Graham – now refers to an absence. Instead, she calls him *Babe*, quietly to herself. It's what they called each other, and that is easier to say somehow, because it was her name too.

Babe, she says, *what am I going to do with him? That school doesn't get him. He's always in trouble.*

I trust you, Babe, he says to her, in her heart. *Our little rebel.*

At parent-teacher evening she is told that Sonny likes to climb a particular tree in the corner of the playground and that he refuses to come down when break is over and the bell rings. That he won't stop spinning the water cups at break time even when he is asked to repeatedly. That he enjoys show-and-tell but that he tells stories about aliens and narwhals that he met over the weekend instead of talking about real objects and events because he likes to make his classmates laugh. That this behaviour is disruptive. That she should encourage Sonny to prepare show-and-tells that are grounded in reality.

'Well, *in reality*, his father is dead,' Luna says. 'Would you like him to talk the kids through childhood grief next week?'

Good one, Babe, Graham says, sitting next to her. *Really lean into the death.*

'Of course not, no, I'm so sorry, perhaps you've

FIVE

misunderstood what I meant,' the teacher stammers and shifts in her seat.

'No, I understand you perfectly,' Luna says, 'and I think you understand me too.'

A month later, she receives an email. They have completed reading assessments and Sonny is reading below age-related expectations. She must come in for a meeting.

The teacher shows her the phonics reader, an anaemic story from the Biff, Chip and Kipper series. She turns to the first page and reads its single sentence. 'Look at me, Mum,' it says, with a picture of a boy on a bicycle. Graham taught Sonny to ride a bicycle without training wheels before he was four, far younger than any other children they knew. Of course, Sonny was bored by Biff on a bike. And what the hell kind of name is Biff anyway.

'He barely got through the first two pages and just wouldn't – *or couldn't* – move on,' the teacher explains, with a raised eyebrow of concern underscoring every word. 'I think he may have been shutting down to mask his confusion about phonics. He said it was boring and just got up and went to the block corner,' she says, expecting Luna to be appalled, and confused that she is not.

'Interesting,' Luna says, waiting to feel her husband beside her. 'Age-related expectations.' She ponders the term, and then she hears him, *Let's do this, Babe.*

And before the teacher can respond, Luna says, 'Have you tried giving him something more challenging if he's bored, to keep his attention? Let's see what he can do, shall we?'

Steady on, woman, he says, beside her.

Luna brings Sonny in from the corridor where he was sent to wait. She takes a copy of *Charlotte's Web* from another child's desk. The pink spangled pencil case on the desk reads, AMELIA. She knows the child, and her insufferable parents who cannot contain their pride at how 'advanced' their daughter is. 'She's already read *Charlotte's Web* independently, so we're moving on to *Harry Potter,* even though she's only just turned *seven,*' she heard her mother say faux-discreetly to her friend at pick-up, as though Amelia had just discovered the cure for cancer and they were waiting for the call from the Nobel committee.

'Read this sentence, would you, Sonny?' Luna says, opening the book to the first page.

Sonny sits on her lap and makes her hold the book so he can spin a rubber band on his finger while he reads, slowly, stumbling here and there, but accurately. '"*Well,*" *said her mother, "one of the pigs is a runt. It's very small and weak, and it will never amount to anything. So your father has decided to do away with it."*'

'That's bad, Mum,' Sonny says. 'They're going to kill him because he's small.'

'Yes, but don't worry,' Luna says, looking at the teacher, 'they've underestimated Wilbur. He'll be OK in the end.'

When Sonny is playing out of earshot in a corner of the room, Luna says, 'I know he's loud and he asks too many questions and he doesn't listen and he moves a lot so you assume the problem is him, and not this boring nonsense you gave him to read. It's easier for you to say that he's not engaged than it is for you to

FIVE

do your job and engage him. Instead, you want to raise your eyebrows at me and expect me to defer to you and apologise. You're going to have to adjust those expectations too.'

Targeting the eyebrows, that's stone-cold, lass, Graham says.

But Luna is not as confident as these exchanges with the teachers suggest. As time goes on, she knows that Sonny is struggling to focus and falling behind. She sees that children like to be around him because he's fun and quirky but that once he goes off on a tangent they're not sure what to do or say. When they can't keep up with his banter and his imagination, they tell on him. They have learned from the teachers that if they don't understand him it must be because he's done the wrong thing rather than just the different thing.

Teachers label him *hyper, overactive, unfocused.* They discount his ability and intelligence. He is the first suspect in every classroom disruption, the first name blurted out when other children look for someone to blame. When he responds to an unjust accusation from a teacher, it is called *answering back.* When he defends himself against an unfair judgement, it is called *being disrespectful.*

Words like *diagnosis, medication, disorder* end every meeting she attends about Sonny. And while she researches these words and considers what to do for her *creative, imaginative, talented* boy, she also asks, at every meeting, 'Yes, but what does he do well? And how does he excel?'

And when they can't tell her she decides that their other words are therefore meaningless. Her husband is dead. Her son is a miracle. She decides that anyone who doesn't get that can fuck right off.

And Babe, then he doesn't belong there. So I'm going with this one. Small class sizes, lots of structure, lots of outdoor space, lots of sport. I'm not thrilled about the demographics, but maybe it'll be better for him?

I trust you, Babe, he says to her, in her heart.

Luna sells their house in London and downsizes to a spacious garden flat in an affluent suburb near a private school and a commuter train station. She decides to use money from the sale of the house and Graham's life insurance to pay for Sonny's private school education.

She knows he is bright and also that he is not like other children and also that she would never want him to be. Her son is the exuberance, the humour, the volume, the kaleidoscope thinking that was Graham. And she will not let anyone put out his flame.

The prestigious private primary school is a feeder school for a prestigious private secondary school for the sons and daughters of wealthy politicians who publicly support higher budgets for failing state schools, the future heirs of minor members of the royal family, and the progeny of Russian oligarchs, Nigerian oil barons, and Malaysian industry magnates who are much more academic, worldly and accomplished than the minor royal children, to the discreet but clear annoyance of the minor royal parents.

Luna tries her best with the other parents. She is conspicuously single among their traditional couples, conspicuously

FIVE

not *really* British, she knows, in their eyes, with her Spanish name and Caribbean heritage, although she has lived in the UK from the age of five, and conspicuously not a product of private education herself, which carries greater weight in their world than her PhD in postcolonial Latin American literature from Oxford and her career as a professor.

But for her boy, she tries to soften the edges that have hardened to protect her since Graham's death. And she has to admit it's not so bad. Everyone is kind and polite to her, even though she can't contribute to conversations about second homes or sailing or skiing in Switzerland. She quickly realises her mistake in thinking it would not matter that she and Sonny live in a garden flat when she attends the first mums' evening in the palatial home of the second wife of one of the owners of a famous company, built by twin brothers, a rags-to-riches kind of story she remembers vaguely from her mother's women's magazines from years ago.

Luna excuses herself from a conversation about the best stables in the area and sips her drink, surveying the room.

Babe, Luna says while taking a sip of champagne, which is not prosecco but the real stuff. *I wish you were here, I'm so bad at small talk.*

You're not so good at big talk either, babe, he says, *to be honest.*

And this makes her laugh, because he always made her laugh, and she takes a deep breath.

They're just people, he says, *they just want to be liked, just like you.*

I don't need to be liked, she says, defensively.

I know, you're a real hard arse, he says, with air quotes she can almost see from the corner of her eye, *but just pretend, would you? It's for the lad,* he says.

So she puts on a smile, and finds the hostess and compliments the marble floors, listens to her story about her housekeeper, and remembers that this is for Sonny. Always Sonny.

■ ■ ■ ■ ■

Click, click, click.
Spin. £119.74
Click. Spin.
£576.95
Click, click, spin.
£0
Shit.
Click.

Sonny tells people he is a recent graduate because he recently pretended to graduate. And he reasons that it's not like people ask to see your degree, it's not something you carry around in your wallet, like your driver's licence, right?

A driver's licence is also something he has failed to obtain, because he didn't finish the block of lessons Aunt Gabriela bought for him for his birthday, or sit the theory test, but he will. He'll definitely get back to that too. Someday.

He decides that, since no one ever thought he'd make it to

FIVE

university anyway, finishing a majority of his degree is a huge achievement, actually. He almost finished the whole graphic design course, and that's so much more than anyone ever thought he would do.

When he was a child, none of his teachers ever believed, like his mother did, that he would make it this far. Of course, her attitude towards them didn't endear either of them to the staff. Her strongly worded emails, her constant defence of him, even when he was in the wrong and she knew he was, did not have the impact she thought they did.

Instead, her outrage caused the opposite response. She fought for him every time he was in trouble, and every time the teachers and the headmaster thought she was just a little crazier than the last time.

'Was she frothing at the mouth today?' he overheard the deputy head say to the school secretary, and they both laughed when the secretary delivered Luna's latest message. They didn't notice that he happened to be passing by the office on his way to a class. It wasn't hard for him to guess they were talking about his mother.

He felt awful that he had turned her into this. He just never knew he was doing *it* until he was old enough to recognise at least some of *it* when *it* was happening, but even then he wasn't so good at controlling *it*. Even with the meds, even with the therapy, even with a mother like her.

What made it harder wasn't just that he had something in his brain he couldn't shut off, it was that his mother refused to accept that she couldn't change it. She would not believe that no number of irate phone calls and radical defences of his most irrational and ridiculous behaviours was going to change the pace of his thoughts, his need to move, the things he forgot, the things he lost, the things he never finished, the sleep he couldn't sleep, the meals he didn't eat, the speed of his brain, the exhaustion of living inside his attention-deficit head, inside his hyperactive-disordered body.

He had sports. Ever since he could remember, the only time his brain and body felt like they were part of him simultaneously was when he was doing some kind of sport. He could focus when he was running (he won all the county medals for cross-country) or kicking a ball (he had been top scorer every season since he was twelve) or on a rugby pitch, where he was rarely tackled because he was just too fast for everyone that went after him. He understood tacitly that the only thing keeping him at his fancy school was the sports, as in, he hadn't been kicked out yet because they needed him on all the teams so they could keep up their national rankings and advertise their sporting excellence to prospective parents.

Also, there was his face, right there on the cover of the glossy admissions brochure, with his copper Afro-Latino spiral curls and light brown skin, right next to Afan, a Malaysian kid, who had just won some robotics thing, who was sitting next to a Nigerian kid, Chickezie, who went by Charlie, who had also just won some young entrepreneur thing, sitting on a wall together, laughing, with William, George and Harry, who were representing the traditional whites.

When Sonny was called to the office and he saw William,

FIVE

George and Harry, who had recently won Model UN or the Maths Olympics or whatever, Sonny could not imagine why he would ever be mentioned on the same list as them for anything. Until he saw Afan and Charlie. And the photographer. And then he understood. He could pretend he was asked to be there because he was one of the best athletes at the school, but he had a feeling it was because he had the most interesting hair – big, colourful and curly, his hair was a perfect symbol of the school's commitment to diversity. So Sonny figured that the school wouldn't kick him out until the administration was ready to pay for new brochures.

'And did Sonny tell you, Mrs Bell, that he was throwing the other child's shoe around the gym when the incident occurred?'

'No, he did not, and I fail to see the relevance, Mrs Murdoch, unless you are suggesting that Sonny deserved to be pummelled in the head with a basketball repeatedly because the punishment for moving another student's shoe at this school is enforced concussion?'

Sonny couldn't take it, he had to interject. 'Mum! Just listen, it *is* relevant. I took it, I took his shoe, I threw it to another kid, I grabbed it to hit him with it. He was being a shit – sorry, Mrs Murdoch, for saying "shit" – and we were in a fight. He deserved it. We were fighting, Mum. That's why he chucked the ball at me, it was a fight. I was fighting.'

Luna looked at him, focused on his green eye, and said, 'No, you were not. And even if you were, you wouldn't do that unless you were provoked, and you struggle with impulse control—'

When he did the wrong thing it was never his fault in her

eyes, even when it was. And besides the occasional fights and disrupting class, there was the academic stuff too. He was really good at geography, history, philosophy. He thought they were interesting and he was great at class discussions, at asking questions and making comments that no one else had thought of. He could see patterns and poke holes in places that the other kids, so entrenched in rote learning and performing for their robotic conformist parents, just didn't think to look.

And some of his teachers saw this innate curiosity in him, this unique way of seeing the world. But he couldn't get it onto paper. His ideas moved too fast for him to catch them and write them down. It was too hard to sit, in silence, confined in a room for an exam, so his results never showed what he actually knew. It was the same refrain, over and over again. He didn't apply himself, he didn't focus, he needed to slow down, he wasn't organised, he didn't hand his homework in on time, he didn't wear the right shoes with his uniform. In so, so many ways he was smart, but the message from school was that in so many more ways he was inadequate.

'You're perfect,' she would say to him, every time she was called in for another meeting to 'support' him and he had to sit there, and endure it, and watch her face fall when his teachers disagreed.

She'd rail against them. 'Yes, but what did he do well?' 'Yes, and did you have the same discussion with the other child involved, with his parents, whichever William, George or Harry it was?' She refused to believe the truth, which was that he just couldn't do it.

FIVE

'You're ours,' she would say after, and Sonny didn't know what to do with that because the person included in the plural pronoun had long been dead, had long been only a big, burly memory of a bear-like man carrying Sonny on his shoulders so he could try to touch the sky.

But he resolved to finish his degree for his mum. Someday. She had worked too hard to get him there. So he would do it, he would, just not right now. Because she was dying.

He felt paralysed when she told him about the cancer, about how far gone she was, about how she would fight but the chances were slim that she would win. She would really only be buying time. He could not absorb the words she said, *aggressive*, *metastasis*, *tumours*. He'd always thought she would be old one day. That he had time. That by the time she was an old lady he'd have his shit finally together enough to give her the best old lady life ever, to buy her a house and give her grandchildren and fly her first class to Jamaica whenever she wanted to go.

But none of that would happen now. He'd run out of time. He stopped going to lectures, doing his work, taking his meds, he just stopped. What was it for? He stared at the walls instead.

He did not tell his mother that he was failing. He didn't want her to think she had to sweep in and save him on her deathbed from yet another Sonny-made disaster. He wanted her to believe he was on the path she'd paved for him.

After a few weeks of wallowing, he saw a counsellor at school. And newly inspired, he got up one morning, got dressed, took his medication, and got ready to go back to class and to talk to his professors and to fix this, the way she taught him to. But when he checked his phone while he ate his cereal, he clicked on an ad for a free bet on a casino site. He's not sure why he did it. He just did. An impulse.

After the first six hours, he'd won £3,000. And the elation, the hit of dopamine, the surge of electricity to his brain, the flutter of excitement in his stomach, the endless possibility there in the phone screen, were the answer to his problems. It was so easy: click, click, click. He didn't think about Luna, he didn't think about the mess he'd made, he just thought about the click, the spin, the relief.

The losing didn't matter, the losing meant he just had to keep going so he could get to the high of winning. Because playing, even when he was losing, was better than meds, than running, better than his art and design, because his pure focus on the game made his brain stop buzzing and put the treadmill of his mind on pause. Everything stopped. And he was still. And it was bliss because stillness had always been so elusive.

He lost track of the days after that. He ignored emails from his teachers, messages from friends, letters from the university administration about his ineligibility for graduation. He missed the meetings he was asked to attend, missed the parties his friends invited him to. He kept going to work at the gastropub where he was a waiter, and now that he had abandoned his classes he took on more hours so he could earn more, so he could play more.

As soon as he was paid, he'd type in his debit card numbers and keep playing. He applied for different credit cards, he got

FIVE

offers in the post for them all the time, and then he typed those numbers into the casino sites too and kept playing.

He did not use the card he held jointly with his mother, the one she paid the bills for, the one they used to review together every month to help him learn money management because his mother said people like him often had trouble with money.

He used that card for his living expenses while he was at uni, that was their agreement, but he was tempted, many times, to type those numbers onto the screen, to just play ten or twenty pounds here and there. But he wouldn't be able to explain away the charges, and he would just picture her face and stop himself.

As she got sicker and sicker and less able to keep track, when those monthly reviews were dropped, overtaken by her illness, he saw his chance. *You are such a piece of shit, you are such a piece of shit,* he said over and over as he typed in the numbers of that card too and burned with private shame.

The games were all he thought about. Every minute. And when he wasn't working he was playing. And even when he was working he was playing. It happened enough times, playing on his phone when he should have been waiting tables, that he lost the job. No matter. Soon the new term would start, and his student loan money would come into his account.

He spoke to his mother every day and lied to her and felt awful for it. And when the end of his last year of uni came, he told her not to worry, not to feel bad about not attending his graduation. It was just a lot of speeches and robes after all, it was just a day, it didn't really mean anything, not with her being ill, and besides he had his friends there. Technically, Sonny told himself, this was not a lie to his dying mother because graduation really did not mean anything to Sonny because he was not, in fact, graduating.

That was three months ago now. He moved back into the spacious garden flat in this boring suburb where he'd grown up. His room was just as he had left it. When he came home, Luna asked to see photos of his last days at uni and he showed her pictures of his friends in their caps and gowns that he had saved from screen shots of their posts. He had even texted her a selfie on the day wearing his roommate's cap and gown, pretending it was his own. She did not press him for details. She was so ill by the time he got home and on so much medication that she did not have the strength for probing questions. Only acceptance.

He was relieved not to have to devise more lies, but he was also sad that she was not seeing through him. She was not detecting, with that inner sense that only she possessed, that something was wrong. And that was the real sign that she was dying.

Click, click, spin.
£756.72
Click, spin, spin.
£1356.29
Click. Spin.
Shit.

FIVE

He's been told that they are now in the last weeks of Luna's life.

He owes £3,000 on one credit card, £5,000 on another, £10,000 on another. He owes Gabriela £2,500, a loan he asked for because 'it was a tough time and he didn't want to worry Mum'. There is, of course, his student loan debt, which will have to be paid back too, eventually. There are five to ten friends he is avoiding contact with now because he owes them all money. He doesn't know how much.

But when he plays, he doesn't think about all of this, he doesn't worry about it, his brain is flooded with spinning wheels and bright colours, and numbers that go up and bring him incredible elation, and numbers that go down, which he is now numb to, which he ignores, waiting for them to go back up again.

One morning, after he stays up playing until sunrise on his favourite site, he goes to the kitchen, unable to remember the last time he ate. Luna is sitting at the table, her hands curled around a coffee mug. He was not expecting to see her there, it's been weeks since she's ventured out of her bedroom.

'You've been avoiding me,' she says, a sliver of the former strength of her voice still glinting like steel in the first light of day coming through the kitchen window.

'What? No, I haven't,' he says, guiltily.

'I haven't seen you for three days,' she says. 'I know because I don't have too many of those left. I'm careful with them.'

He suddenly feels like he did when he was little, in the mornings, when he needed to feel the pressure of her arms, when he needed her embrace to ground him, to keep his body from feeling like it was floating away, when he needed her to root him, when he needed to tether himself to her, to be bound by the gravitational pull of her love.

'That's OK,' she says, 'because it gave me and Gabriela time to sift through and organise all the letters that have been arriving here for you.'

'Mum, I—' He feels his face flush, a burning feeling rush up his neck. He feels caught, trapped.

Luna goes on, 'I know you've been gambling. I know – now – that you've been doing it a long time. It's not your fault, Sonny. People with ADHD are really susceptible to it. Look, addiction is an illness, just like . . .'

And even though she is so frail, and hollow-eyed, and exhausted, he snaps at her.

'No, Mum. I do dumb shit. I make stupid decisions. Just accept it. They're not special choices, or disordered choices, or illness-related choices, they're not less bad, they're just regular, fucked-up mistakes, that stupid fucking fucked-up people make. I am just a fuck-up,' he says, turning away from her, starting to pace, wishing he could run and run and run.

Luna looks at him. She puts a hand to her chest, closes her eyes, takes an effortful breath. He looks over his shoulder at her, he notices that she lifts her cup with both hands.

She takes a sip. Having gathered a little strength, she says, finally, 'No, Sonny, I don't think so. Because if you're a fuck-up, then that means I'm a fuck-up, that I didn't do a good job, and *I* – Sonny – *I* am not a fuck-up. Because if the stupid shit you did over all these years is just you being a fuck-up, and not

FIVE

because you're a genius with a messed-up brain, or a beautiful soul who is an addict, or a victim of your genetics or the loss of your father, if none of that is true, then *I*, as your mother, *I am the fuck-up*, not you. *And I. Am not. A fuck-up.*'

Sonny looks at his mother. She is out of breath from speaking and he is startled by it. His mother, once so fierce and strong, now half the size she used to be, her black eyes huge in her hollow face. He thinks he can see her heartbeat through the papery skin stretched across her breastbone, the only part of her not entirely swallowed by her towelling robe. He has not looked at her, really looked at her, since he moved back home. He can't bear the sharpness of her cheekbones, how the necklace she never takes off, with his and his dad's initials on tiny medallions, is absent from her neck because the metal irritates her chemo-fragile skin.

'I'm sorry, Mama, I'm sorry,' Sonny heaves, and he starts to sob, and he kneels beside his mother's chair and puts his head in her lap, carefully. He presses his arms gently around her. She is so small now and he is so tall, like Graham. Luna is almost child-sized in his embrace. And even though he is touching her so lightly, she can feel her little boy as he once was, squeezing his whole torso against her, pressing his whole being to her, like his life depended on her. Because it does.

'I'm sorry, Mama,' and he says it with the same urgency and pain as when he was small, when he was so sorry, so, so, sorry for all the things he did.

'Not sorry, Sonny,' she says, 'never sorry,' holding her son's head in her lap, stroking his hair that is the same copper brown as his father's. And they stay this way together for some time until she lifts his head, and she looks at his green eye and then his brown eye.

'You can fix this,' she says. 'But it will take a while, and it won't be fixed before I die. But you'll have to do what I say, and if you don't, I'll know, and I'll come back, and I'll haunt you.'

Great, Babe, Graham says. *I'll come too.*

'Good news, your dad says he'll come too,' she adds when she hears him, his voice much louder now than it used to be.

'Mum!' Sonny exclaims, 'Jesus, you're so morbid. That's not funny,' and he laughs through his tears in spite of himself.

Sonny knows he will remember this moment for the rest of his life, of laughing with his mother, his arms around her while she was still living, a glint of mischief still there, in her eyes. He will remember laughing with her, but also this feeling like a firing squad is pulling all of the triggers, of rocks in his pockets weighing him down in the river of his grief, at the thought of her going and leaving him here, without her.

■ ■ ■ ■ ■

'Your mother left very explicit instructions that I am now going to explain to you, so just stop me if you have any questions,' the lawyer says.

'OK,' Sonny says, grateful that Gabriela is beside him, because he knows as soon as the lawyer starts talking that he won't remember anything she says. He has not gambled since the day in the kitchen with Luna. He spent every day after

FIVE

that with her, holding her hand, talking, laughing. He slept on the floor next to her bed. She was gone two weeks later.

Everything that came after her death has been a distraction – the memorial, the people who had to be contacted, and all the things to sign and do, even though Luna had, of course, planned every last detail so Sonny wouldn't have to worry about it. And so somehow, the need for the games has got out of his system. He was surprised, he thought he would need to feel the electricity and then the numbness, but he hasn't wanted that. He has only wanted to be good these last few weeks, to be good for his mother so that at last she wouldn't worry. Because he knew she would worry about him, even when she was dead.

The lawyer continues, 'The flat is yours now. She owned it outright with no mortgage. She wanted you to have it, to keep until you get on your feet without having to worry about rent, and you can live there, or rent it out for extra income, which she thought you might want to do eventually.

'After that, there was about £100,000 she had in savings, some of it still left over from your father's life insurance, which she was clever about investing. Your mother was a very thoughtful woman,' the lawyer says.

Sonny smiles sadly because this seems like the socially appropriate moment to do that. *Thoughtful* was one way to describe his mother. *Strong-willed, a force of nature* and *pathologically insistent on his success* were others. Sonny can't remember this lawyer's name even though she just said it a few minutes ago, and he thinks how strange it is that she knows these intimate details about his life but that he doesn't even know her name.

'However, about £25,000 of that was already accessed to pay your outstanding debts and settle your bills with various credit cards, collection agencies and your university,' the lawyer, whose name might be Helen or might be Emily, continues. 'The remaining money will still go to you, but it will be held in a trust, and in order to access it you'll have to meet certain conditions.'

'Her master plan to control me from the afterlife,' Sonny says, with a sad grin.

'The afterlife won't know what's hit it, Sonny,' Gabriela says, trying not to cry. On second thought, maybe Sonny should not have brought Gabriela. She has been trying not to cry since they got here.

'If you comply with the conditions, you'll receive the remainder in thirds. You'll receive the first £25,000 when you have finished your degree and held a part-time job for three years with no outstanding debts and you're living a financially solvent life. You will also attend Gamblers Anonymous during that time. Gabriela will have full access to all of your bank accounts and credit cards. You'll receive the next £25,000 once you have a full-time job and have remained gainfully employed for two years. After that, if you can prove full-time employment with no outstanding debts, you will receive the final £25,000, liquidating the trust. If you don't meet these conditions and provide the proof required by the trust, the money stays where it is until you do. There are contingencies in place for redundancy,

FIVE

illness or other things that might come up, but that's the general structure. Does that make sense so far?'

'Yes,' Sonny says. 'She thought of everything.'

And she did. Except for how it makes him feel to know that she loved him so much and trusted him so little.

▌▌▌▌▌

He does it. Everything his mother wanted him to do. Finishes his degree at night, works in the day, Gamblers Anonymous meetings, no debts, no gambling for three years. It is hard, really, really hard, he slips up a couple of times, but mostly he stays busy, he has Gabriela checking on him, and when he makes a mistake they deal with it right away and he moves on. Part of him wonders if deep down he is doing it so he can get the cash so he can gamble as soon as he has it. But when the first £25,000 arrives what he feels is nervous. He takes his aunt out to dinner and they tell stories about Luna and laugh until they cry.

'She's so proud of you,' Gabriela says.

'How do you know? Does she talk to you?' he says.

'She never shuts up,' Gabriela says, and they both laugh.

'Hey,' she says, just before leaving. 'Do you want me to hold the money for you? Will you be OK?' And in his aunt's face he sees his mother's younger face, the Luna of his adolescence.

'You know what,' he says, 'I think I will. I've learned a lot, I've got to trust to myself,' he says. 'But thank you,' and then, 'Do you think I can do it? I mean, maybe I should give it to you to hold,' he says, suddenly doubting himself and all of his hard work.

And it is here that Gabriela should have listened to Luna, who was calling to her, who had learned a few lessons in the afterlife, but the champagne has clouded Gabriela's hearing, because instead of saying, 'I know you can do it,' she says, 'You know I'm always here, you've always got a safety net,' which does not mean he can do it. It means, when he fucks up, which is likely, she will help.

But Sonny devises a plan. He puts the money in a savings account at a different bank from his usual one, and refuses to set up internet banking so he can't easily get to it, and throws away the ATM card that comes automatically with the account, and doesn't even look at the PIN number that comes in the post, and receives only paper statements that he doesn't take out of the envelope and that he throws away immediately when they arrive. He puts Gabriela's name on the account so that she also gets the statements as a check, a buffer, to keep him honest. He installs Gamban on his phone and his computer so he can't access any sites. He stays busy, working, running, working, running, and after work one day he is running late for a meeting and he stumbles into the room and trips over a bag that belongs to Valentina.

'Sorry,' he whispers. She smiles. He sits in the row of seats behind her, still feeling the brush of her hand against his skin when he gave her the bag, and stares at the back of her head and her shiny, long raven hair and doesn't hear a word anyone says because by the end of the hour he is madly in love.

FIVE

'It's not a good idea to date people in the programme, you know,' she says, drinking coffee with him in a place around the corner after the meeting.

'I'm full of bad ideas,' he says, smiling.

'So am I,' she says.

And that is their start. Valentina is a piece of his life he did not know was missing until she came into it and filled up all the blank space. Sonny finds out that love is something new that can make the buzzing stop, that calms his mind and brings his brain and body together. Valentina is much further along in recovery than Sonny. She went to rehab for her addiction seven years ago, when she was nineteen, with the support of her family, surrounded by their love until she was strong enough to stand on her own. She considers her addiction to be in her past, but she still drops into meetings now and then, just to check in, as a way to stay vigilant, and now as a way to support Sonny, but always as a reminder to herself of how far she has come. Or how far she thinks she has come.

Valentina moves into the garden flat. They talk about a future that encompasses his dreams and hers. They talk about selling the flat, moving to London, or renting it out, maybe taking time off and travelling. Sonny thinks, to himself, about maybe buying Valentina a ring and getting married, maybe taking her to some remote, beautiful, spiritual place to make their vows. They both ignore the spark that ignites inside when they get the flat valued and find out how much they could sell it for. He does not acknowledge the flicker of the flame that starts to burn, he does not say his is the only name on the deed, that the money will be his, actually.

He does not mention that the next £25,000 is wired straight into the lonely stray account that he doesn't use. He has told her so much, so many things, he has even told her that the meetings were his dead mother's plan for him, he said he goes to honour his mother, but he does not mention the money, the trust, its requirements. They have talked for hours and hours about the secrets gamblers keep, the plots and plans they make to hide the shame, the debt, the broken voice inside that cannot say *stop*. The thing he does with everyone else he does with her too. Especially with her. Because he knows her brain, so much like his own, and he loves her but he doesn't trust her. Not fully. Not yet. Maybe not ever.

And now he is in the last year before the end of his mother's master plan, the last year before she finally lets him go with the last instalment of her painstakingly saved savings. She taught him that he could do it, and he has done it. She was right. He was fixable.

'Do you ever think about it?' he asks Valentina, in bed one morning.

'Every day,' she says, without having to ask what he means.

'I'm afraid to sell the flat. I'm afraid we can't handle the money,' he says.

'We have to forgive ourselves at some point, Sonny, we have to trust ourselves,' she says.

'Do you trust me?' he asks, staring at the ceiling, holding her hand to his chest, where he keeps his secret.

FIVE

'Yes,' she says, because she wants to trust him, she almost does trust him, she loves him so much but she knows him too well to trust him. As well as she knows herself.

Soon it is his twenty-sixth birthday. When he wakes up, he opens then closes his eyes again and listens. He tries to hear his parents, but he's never been able to, not the way his mother always said she could hear his dad.

After work he goes to his favourite restaurant in Soho to find Valentina waiting with a bunch of his friends. A surprise party. 'Make a wish, Babe!' Val shouts to him, and he blows out the candles.

'From all of us,' Greg, his friend from work says, handing him a card, as they drink and eat cake.

And Sonny says, 'Oh, you shouldn't have, mate,' as he opens the birthday card and he hears the sound - *flit, flit, flit* - of twenty-seven lottery scratch cards falling out onto his lap. One for every year of his life, plus one for good luck.

Greg doesn't know, of course, none of their friends know about him or Valentina and their secret struggle. They've told everyone that they were at a bar when he tripped over her bag and fell in love with her. A half-truth, almost whole.

He holds the cards in his lap while his friends banter, wine is poured, beer is sloshed, a waiter drops a tray, glass breaks, everyone laughs. Panic surges through him. He could give everyone at the party a card to scratch all at the same time and propose to split the winnings. He could take the envelope to the bathroom and flush it. He could hand it to the homeless man sitting outside the restaurant. He could sit in a dark room in the middle of the night and scratch each card methodically, carefully, and feel the relief it would bring.

'Wow! So fun!' Valentina says, not looking at him, grabbing the envelope, stuffing the cards inside. 'Let me put that where we won't lose it, you know how Sonny is always losing stuff!'

When he can get her alone, he says, 'What have you done with it?'

'Don't worry, I've got it,' she says. Her voice tells him one thing, her eyes say another.

On the train on the way home, when they are finally alone, finally somewhere quiet, he says, 'God, that was awful, where is it?'

'In my bag, we'll deal with it at home,' she says.

'No, now,' he pleads. 'When the doors open, throw it out at the next stop.'

'Don't make a scene,' she says, and pulls her bag closer to her.

Finally, at home, she runs into the kitchen, coat still on, she pulls the scissors out of the drawer, and - *flit, flit, flit* - she empties all the cards onto the counter. 'C'mon, cut them up, you can do it,' she says, and hands him the scissors.

'Why are you being so dramatic, why didn't you just throw them away?' he asks, confused.

'Do it!' she yells, and then, short of breath, 'Show me, show me you're past this.'

'What?'

'I saw how you looked at those cards when he gave them to you, I saw the sparkle in your eye, Sonny, you're not over it, you're not. Show me it's over, that you want this life, we sell

FIVE

this flat, we travel, we move on, show me you love me more than this thing, show me.'

So he cuts each card into four pieces, one by one. And takes the pile and throws them in the air like confetti, and grabs Valentina, and holds her. In her rush, in her fury, she didn't think to count the cards before he cut them up.

'Of course I love you more,' he says. 'The most.'

Later, when she finds a scratch card in his jeans pocket while doing the laundry, he will tell her that he kept it to prove to himself that he had beat it. 'See,' he will plead, 'it's not scratched off, I didn't do anything. I didn't use it.'

But the card does not hurt as much as the bank statement she opens. One of the ones she's noticed before, that he throws unopened into the bin. One that says he has a balance of £50,000 he never told her about.

'I love you, but I can't stay,' she says, when he gets home from work.

'Wait, what do you mean?' he asks, sitting down across from her, the table between them.

'I have to leave for a while, I'm not sure we're good for each other, Sonny,' she says, holding out her hand across the table, which is holding a scratch card.

'That's not mine, I swear,' he says, pushing back from the table, startled, that same trapped feeling he had when he was small, when he was scapegoated by other kids for something he didn't do.

'No, it's not,' Valentina says, sadly. 'It's mine. I hid one from you too.'

Valentina goes back to her parents' house. She is supported and surrounded with love and understanding. She goes to meetings in a different church hall so she won't run into Sonny. She gets therapy. She gets on track.

Sonny has no parents to go back to. He has something else instead, and he is £32,000 in debt twenty-seven days after his birthday, one day for each year of his life, plus one for good luck. He is in debt after emptying the lonely stray account, after selling his grandfather's watch, after maxing out the only credit card he still had, the one he managed to hide from Gabriela. He knows he will not get the last instalment of his inheritance and he does not want it. It has cost him too much already. It is not like his mother said, it is not fixable, and when he broke her rules she didn't come back to haunt him, in the end, although he waited for her. Luna wasn't as strong as she thought. She can't reach him from the afterlife after all.

■ ■ ■ ■ ■

He chooses the pin-striped burgundy suit. It reminds him of Dorothy on *The Golden Girls*. He watched every single episode with his mother the year after his father died, and even though he was so young, he has distinct memories of Dorothy and Sophia, probably because they made his mother laugh and that reassured him that she was still his mother, because nothing else made her laugh in those days.

He found the suit at his favourite vintage shop. The tag read, 'Long Tall Sally', and he liked that. It felt like a brand

FIVE

Dorothy would have endorsed. The trousers hit him well above the ankles and flared out, and the jacket was small for him, but the shrunken look of it suited him.

He buttons up his black shirt and ties his skinny satin black tie. He goes with the white patent wingtips, no socks, because they are unexpected on this cold winter morning in this season. But they make the stripes in the suit pop and they tie it together. Black shoes are too predictable, too safe, two things he is not.

He ties up his hair in a high topknot. He expertly arranges his long curls so that they spring, just so, over his brown eye. It's cold, but he doesn't want to wear a coat. Too restrictive in case he decides to run, or jump, or he's not sure, but he wants to be able to move freely. While he still can.

So he puts on Valentina's Bohemian claret and orange poncho that she left behind in her haste to leave him. But he wears it as a scarf. It smells of her perfume still.

He texts her: I miss you I love you everything that is mine is yours. He does not expect a reply. He does it so she'll have evidence of his wishes when the time comes.

He could earn enough to pay it off in a year. His salary plus a few freelance gigs, as long as he was sensible about his spending. That is not the problem, that is not the point.

Sonny is not going to stop. Ever. He can pay off the debt, and put blocks on his phone and computer, and he can run, and he can love Valentina and immerse himself in his work. But something will happen and then he will do it again. And then again. He will have secrets, and tell lies, because he cannot stop. He is so tired of himself.

Outfit on point, he is ready to leave for the station. It's important to look like it's a regular day and he's just a guy on his way somewhere, waiting for the train so no one suspects him. Before he goes, Sonny looks around his flat where he once lived with his mother, where she spoke to the ghost of his father, where she died. She had chosen the spare bedroom to stay in once they knew the end was coming. She wanted Sonny to have the main bedroom when the flat was his and she did not want him to have the memory of her dying there. He walks into the spare bedroom now and lies down on the floor where he used to sleep in her final weeks and tries to feel her, hear her, but there is only silence.

His mother tried so hard to fix *it: it* – his addiction – *it* – his brain – *it* – his hyperactivity, his not fitting into a world that was not built for people like him. Her unshakeable belief that he was hampered by *it* and that if only *it* could be medicated, accommodated, recognised, controlled, his life would be different, he would be like everyone else, better than everyone else. But *it* and Sonny are one. There is no Sonny without *it*, and there is no addiction and no attention deficit and no depression without Sonny. He is the common denominator.

He is about to turn off the lights and leave for the station when a thought occurs to him. On the back of an alumni magazine from his old prep school that is on the table with the rest of the post he writes, 'Gabriela, it's not your fault. Please make sure Valentina gets the flat. Thanks.'

Sonny locks the door and starts his walk to the station. He

FIVE

walks through the streets of the suburb he has known for most of his life, a place where his mother did not fit and where he fit even less, but that was, in the end, their home. He reaches the station. He checks his watch. It is 7:01. He descends the stairs. He hesitates for just a moment before he steps down from the last one. His foot hovers over the concrete. He thinks about how he will never walk down a flight of stairs again, about how brilliant humans are that they invented stairs so many thousands of years ago.

Sonny looks at the tracks beyond the yellow line. He reckons the yellow line is about twelve steps away. One or two beyond it is the platform edge. He takes one step, then another. A few more steps and then he will stop and stand. He will try to look natural. Then he will take a few more, and then he will be close enough to the edge when he needs to be.

He takes a step now and thinks of Valentina. He is conscious of the cold morning air, how it is sharpening his vision. He takes another step and thinks of his father, who he knows loved him, even if he does not remember it, and he briefly feels a feeling like flying. Sonny looks at the digital information display. It says that the train will be on time.

With his next step, Sonny adjusts Valentina's scarf, and he hears a mother's voice, not his mother, but someone's mother shouting, with a tone that mothers of difficult children have that is so familiar to him, like a song from his childhood. 'Goddamn it!'

And he cannot take another step because an old white woman with short white hair in a black coat has fallen at his feet. And before he knows what he's doing, like a reflex, he is kneeling at her side.

'Um,' he says, 'are you all right?'

'Of course I am, don't be ridiculous,' the old woman says, insulted.

'OK,' he says, unsure what she means. 'Are you here with someone?'

'Do I know you?' she asks in a tone that makes him feel as though his question was too personal.

Before he answers the old woman, his heart says, *Mum?* And he waits to hear Luna for the second time this morning, but he still doesn't get an answer. Or maybe he doesn't realise he already has one.

'Uh, no, I don't think so. Look, do you think you can get up? Maybe you shouldn't get up, actually. You hit your head, I think,' he says, looking down at her, then up at the digital information display.

It says that the train will be here soon.

Time	Destination	Expected
1st 7:06	London Victoria	7:08

Delayed South London Service formed of 8 coaches.

2nd 7:13	Bedford	7:16

07:06

Perhaps now is a good time to mention that, whenever possible, train drivers and dispatchers do try their hardest to make up lost time when delays happen. Even a minute improvement on a delay is an important contribution to the smooth running of the railway. Especially during the morning rush. Our passengers are quite busy at the moment, but if any of them happened to look up at the digital information board, they would see that it now says that the delayed 7:06 to London Victoria is currently expected at 7:08, a minute sooner than the previously reported 7:09. That's why Sonny can see the train. That's why they can all feel it coming.

Sonny came here this morning with a different death in mind. A death that did not depend on the actions and inactions of others, on the decisions of those present to act with their instincts, or against them, or in spite of them. He had not accounted for the involvement of old women and immigrants and commuters and strangers. He had not expected them to be here, interrupting his death, getting in his way.

Sonny reaches Liam, and at 7:06 and thirty-six seconds he

sees the blood. *I don't have to do this*, he thinks. *This isn't my job.* And yet he says, 'He's hurt, we've got to pick him up!' to the others on the platform, involuntarily, not in control of his own speech.

The closest person to Sonny is Bad Back. Bad Back knows what he should do. Drop the charade, grow a pair, realise that no one cares if he's lying because this isn't actually about him – *how many times has his wife said that* – and go help this tall skinny guy get that big guy off the tracks. But he doesn't move.

He considers running away now, up the stairs, out of the station, to the car park. He could get into his car and drive and drive and drive, away from here, from his life, his wife, his job, and start again somewhere, where no one knows him, and no one looks at him, and no one bullies him into raising money for charity, and no one forces him to lie, and no one gives him social anxiety, and he can stop getting into messes like these, stupid entanglements caused by his own poor reflexes, and bad instincts, and general shitness as a person. He wants to be less of what he is. Not perfect, not amazing, not successful, just a slightly less shit version of himself would be a massive improvement.

Self-involved and indecisive, Bad Back is standing by, mouth agape, marvelling at Sonny's bravery, when To Do List limps over, sweating, panicked to the platform edge.

'Oh my God!' she shrieks, too loudly.

'*Paw Patrol* is on a roll!' Gideon, being carried by Emma, exclaims next to To Do List.

FIVE

He is staring down at his tablet as Emma shifts him with difficulty from one hip to the other. She shoves the tablet in front of him and grabs him and is on her way to the stairs to leave when To Do List warns, 'Man on the tracks! Go!' And Emma's heart drops because she knows without being told who it is.

'We've got to help!' To Do List cries hysterically at Bad Back. She limps down the platform to Sonny, waving her arms and exclaiming, 'I'm a qualified first aider! I'm a qualified first aider!'

'Liam . . . Liam! . . . Liam!!!' Emma calls in a crescendo as her hunch is verified, and she runs lopsided down the platform with Gideon attached to her side.

Sonny doesn't register the shouts of the women because Liam is starting to wake. 'Uh,' he groans, lightly at first. 'Let go, let go,' he slurs at Sonny, one eye open, a ferocious, roaring pain in his head so fierce he can barely breathe.

'You're all right, mate, we've got to move you, you're all right,' Sonny is surprised to hear himself say, the words coming from some deep inner reservoir of strength propelling him through this, making him do all the right things for this man that he cannot do for himself.

'I'm a first aider!' To Do List asserts above the alarm. 'Is he breathing?' she says breathlessly, when she reaches them. She can barely speak, having not done this much exercise for several years. She gets down on all fours and tries to reach ineffectually for one of Liam's arms from the platform.

'Chase is on the case!' Gideon calls out delightedly,

engrossed in his show as Emma puts him down to sit on the bench. He looks up from his tablet at the adults on the track, once. Then again. Then again.

'He's heavy! We need help!' Sonny pleads, looking over his shoulder with difficulty, to see the train getting closer. And closer.

'I know him,' Emma says, which is important and irrelevant.

'Get that guy!' Sonny shouts, out of breath, struggling with Liam, a limp rag that weighs a ton. 'With the old lady!' and Emma runs to Medical Student, brushing past Bad Back, who is still watching from the side, as she quickly checks for Gideon's position over her shoulder.

'They need you!' she calls to Medical Student.

'Talk to them,' he says, handing her his mobile. 'It's a heart attack, it's the paramedics,' and he runs to Sonny and Liam.

'But . . .' Emma starts to protest. She can't sit here with this lady, not with Liam over there, not with Gideon. But Medical Student is gone before she can say anything. She reluctantly takes the phone, and says distractedly to Mrs Worth, 'Don't worry.'

'C'mon, man!' she hears one of the men yell further down the tracks. *Oh God*, she thinks, *oh God*. The alarm continues blaring. It is 7:07.

'On three!' directs Sonny.

Sonny and Medical Student lift Liam to the platform edge, where he sits now, hands to his head, legs dangling over the side.

'Here, move your legs, move them like this,' To Do List

FIVE

says, pulling at one of Liam's legs, trying to get him fully onto the platform.

'Get off me!' Liam says to her gruffly in a haze of concussion.

'You have to move!' she screams, pulling at him, when he swings one giant arm, like a drunk man, and wallops her in the face. She staggers backward, her nose bleeding, her tears flowing. She is crying from pain, and from finally understanding that she is not needed here. She is not wanted. And she cannot help.

'Move!' Medical Student yells at Sonny, as he scrambles to pull himself up onto the platform. He cannot understand why Sonny has moved to the centre of the track. 'C'mon, man!'

'Go help,' Mrs Worth says to Emma, clutching at her arm, breathing laboriously.

'But you're—'

'Alive,' Mrs Worth says, and groans through another tightening of her heart.

'The tall one wants to die,' she pants at Emma. 'Go,' she commands, with all the strength she has. Like Medical Student, Mrs Worth can recognise the portents of death in someone's eyes when she sees them.

'OK,' Emma says, quickly placing the phone next to the old woman.

'Gideon!' Emma cries as she runs towards him. 'Liam!'

'Liam, Biam, Liam, Biam, Liam, Biam,' Gideon says in a sing-song way to himself, still watching his show.

He stands up slowly, still holding his tablet in front of his face so he doesn't miss a moment of Chase, the police pup, riding in a helicopter with Sky, the sky pup, and he starts walking towards the big man holding his head. He balances on the edge of the platform, like a tightrope walker, putting one foot in front of the other.

'Oh shit,' Bad Back says feebly, when he sees the train getting closer and sees that Sonny is still on the tracks, standing still. He thinks of his wife, what he will tell her about today, and the shame he will feel in the telling. *Fuck it*, he thinks, and runs to the platform edge where everyone is standing.

'The paramedics should be there shortly, stay on the line,' the operator says on Medical Student's mobile lying on the ground next to Mrs Worth. She cannot hear the operator, with the alarm and the commotion on the tracks, so she does the only thing she can.

'Man on the tracks,' Mrs Worth says with a great effort, as loudly as she can to the phone, feeling the vibration of the train coming down the track through the concrete underneath her, before her eyes close.

It's time.

There will be no last-ditch rescue, no superhero making an appearance. There is no open-ended scene where you are left guessing if perhaps everyone survives in the end and the story is just a comment on the fragility of the human condition and the diversity of human suffering; a clever mechanism to remind us that everyone has a story, and not everyone is who or what they seem. While the human condition is fragile and while everyone does have a story and while we do not know

FIVE

what goes on behind closed doors while we are judging books by their covers, et cetera, et cetera, you have known since the beginning, since you got to this station this morning, that there are five main characters and one of them will die.

And now it's time.

Liam

'I must look absolutely mad,' Emma says. She pushes the door shut behind him and pulls at the fingers of her gloves with her teeth. She points her chin down and lifts her eyes up at him as she pulls at the last one, a provocative reflex, a muscle memory of sultriness.

He is not lying when he says, 'Absolutely,' but he smiles at her, as if he is joking, to put her at ease, knowing what effect his smile has on women. On this woman.

He steps into the entryway and looks at her. There is still a hint of Kate Moss about her, in the cheekbones. But standing like this, a bloody cushion at her feet, her brow bandaged, her gown hanging on her hollow frame – the seductress is gone, replaced by a ghost.

'Liam,' she starts to say, then stops. He follows her eyes to the corner by the door, where they land on Gideon's Spider-Man wellies. He waits for her to say something about the boy, but she doesn't. He guesses she has stopped herself so she doesn't fuck this up.

'Never mind,' she says, 'nothing,' and half-smiles.

FIVE

He follows her to the kitchen, 'Praise you like I should . . .' echoing against the bare walls, as he steps over the laundry basket of shoes, kicks the bloody cushion to the side, and completes the deranged obstacle course that is the entryway to her home.

'Emma, what's . . .' He starts to ask what is going on here, not sure he wants the answer, but she can't hear him over the music. She interrupts.

'Let me make us a cup of tea, then we can look at the contract,' she says loudly, beckoning him to sit down. She cuts off the music. 'This is business, after all,' she trills into the now-silent air.

He sits on a stool at the centre island and watches her move hurriedly about the room as she puts away the evidence of her party for one. She's lonely, it clings to her like sad perfume.

'I'll just put the kettle on,' she says, turning to fill the kettle in the sink. 'Shit,' she says quietly to herself, frantically dabbing at water drops on the silk satin. He sees the price tag hanging under her arm.

'Worried you can't return it?' he says, mockingly, a bit cruelly, he knows. 'I don't think you should,' he says, to make it up to her. 'Looks lovely on you.'

Bastard, she thinks. 'I have nowhere to wear it to these days,' she says humbly, with a sad smile, as she pulls open the drawer in the kitchen island where she hopes – she prays – she has left the papers for him to sign.

'Let me just grab the contract, it's here somewhere,' she says, with the slightest tremor in her voice. She's a little drunk, though he knows she's pretending not to be. She's frantic, rummaging in one drawer, then another, then another.

'Got my life shoved in a drawer?' he says, meaning to diffuse her panic but making it worse.

'No, I've got it, it's here, somewhere, somewhere,' she mutters to herself. He moves to the stove. She seems not to hear the high, higher, highest whistle of the ket—

'Got it!' she proclaims, loudly, clutching the contract to her chest, turning to face Liam in the sudden silence. He's holding the boiled kettle and turns off the burner. Fire and water, he thinks. Which one is she. Which one was she.

'Emma, I don't think—' Liam says, placing the kettle down, taking a step towards her.

'See, I found it!' she says, yelping though she doesn't mean to, holding the pages up. 'Just have a seat, I'll make your tea.' She almost sings the words, breezily, heightening the poshness of her accent like a shield. Although that doesn't affect Liam the way it does most people, it just makes him double down.

'Have a look at these, I think you'll find that everything is as agreed,' she says, putting the papers in front of him, slightly crumpled, looking a bit worse for wear but still intact, like her. He sees the smallest drop of blood on the top right-hand corner of the cover page. He knows that his signing of this contract is her only way out. She has to get him to sign it or she won't be paid. And if she isn't paid, she can't send the boy off to the 'special school' and out of her life. Liam knows all of this, but he has other plans.

'I'll be back in two ticks, just going to change,' she trills,

FIVE

and she turns to leave, one step, two steps. She stops. She can't move.

He takes a sip of tea, holding the cup with one hand. She turns around and sees the fabric of her silk satin train strangled in his other hand, tethering her to him.

'Sorry, love, but I can't seem to get a word in edgeways with you. I'm not signing this. And Danny doesn't mean to do this, I know he doesn't, and anyway, I have an offer for 'im,' he says, keeping his hold on her satin leash, taking another sip of tea.

'Please, let me go,' she says, calmly, quietly.

'Why's he doing this?' he asks, his voice tightening as he wraps the silk satin tighter around his wrist.

'Please,' she says, trying to still the tremble in her voice, trying to pull away from him without damaging the dress, because she has to return this dress, it cost £2,300, she needs that money.

'I loved 'im my whole life, Em, this can't be how it ends,' Liam says, pulling her to him by the crumpled satin in his hand, spinning her round to face him. 'Can it?' he says, in a whisper, quietly, his breath, her oxygen.

'I, I . . .' she stutters, trailing off, wanting to lean into him, to disappear into him. But she gave in to that once. And once was enough.

'How'd this happen?' he says, breathing the words into her ear, touching the bandage on her eyebrow. She feels the weight of his hand on her wound after he pulls it away, like a handprint in wet sand.

She doesn't answer.

'Your eyes,' he says, unable to name the colour of her irises. He doesn't know the word for the crystal of spider webs holding drops of water after rain.

'Let me go,' she says, heartbeat thumping in her ears. 'Please.'

'If you needed money for the boy, Em, you just had to ask,' he says, his eyes locked on hers, never breaking his gaze. 'Tell me what you need.'

She stands frozen.

'Make Danny change his mind. Tell 'im I have something big happening, global level, he can come in on it with me. Tell 'im to forget all this petty shit about his boyfriend and his hurt feelings. The meeting's tomorrow. It's two young kids, real brains, a once-in-a-generation idea, they've got it, it's going to be massive, worldwide. Make 'im go with me, I'll take care of you, Emma. I'll take care of Gideon.'

He slides his arms along the back of her waist, pulls her in, pulls her hips into his, whispers, into the back of her neck, 'Will you let me take care of you?'

Emma closes her eyes tightly. *Yes.*

He wants to fix this, this madhouse, this madwoman. What she needs is a man around here. It's sad really, that she has to learn it this way, the hard way, the hardest way. He's met the boy a few times, introduced as 'Mummy's friend' during the brief reignition of their affair when he had some trouble with Elizabeth the Second, which was his name for his third wife, Beth, the second Elizabeth he'd married. Of course he went back to Beth. 'No hard feelings?' he said to

FIVE

Emma, Gideon hiding behind her legs. 'Of course not,' she said, and didn't mean it.

He dropped in the Christmas Gideon was four, after he did all the usual stuff with his two youngest. The boys got given a Nintendo Switch, but they cast it aside, more interested in the Xbox they also got that morning, which they also cast aside for the miniature Range Rovers they could drive around the garden. He rewrapped the Nintendo and left it on the doorstep, *For Gideon, From Santa,* with a little winking smiley face to let Emma know it was him. 'Who's Jason and Marcus?' Gideon asked, looking at the crumpled gift tag stuck to the back of the box. Liam didn't know Gideon could read. That's when she asked him to stop, to stick to their agreement. It hurt more than it helped. Hurt her.

But now and then he'd still intercept them on the way to school, pretending to be walking in the opposite direction, his way of keeping tabs, of letting her know he was watching. 'All right, little man?' he'd say, and smile, seeing the gap between Gideon's two front teeth and feeling his heart break. 'I think you dropped this, love,' he'd say, and give Emma a hundred-pound note, or a gift card for games on the Nintendo. She didn't accept the gift card. 'He threw it against the wall. In a rage. Thanks, though. Now leave us alone.'

And he did, for a while. Yet they have ended up here again, like they always do. She pushes him away, he pulls her in, the game they've played for years. He wants to fix this. It's what he's best at. Taking care of people. He's done it all his life.

'Wouldn't it be nice to be taken care of?' he whispers to her. She closes her eyes. *Yes.*

But Emma is so tired of men. The one who hired her to do this deal, the one she chose to be the father of her child, the one her son is on the torturous road to becoming.

And she will take care of herself.

She deftly pulls at the straps of her dress and tears the stitches, unzips the side of the bodice. In a moment, in a motion, her gown falls to the floor, freeing her, pooling in a black puddle around her feet. Liam stands impotently with the satin of her train still in his hand, when she steps out of the dress to face him, barefoot, clad only in a black lace slip, the violent road map of her skin unveiled. It is not an invitation, it is not a flirtation. It is a statement of fact.

He sees the bruise on her left thigh, the size of an apple. A long burn mark on the inside of her slim calf. A thin red line, a scratch, extending down the inside of her arm. She is so pale, her blue veins, her bruises, her scars illuminated on exposure to the air. Her skin looks like a battlefield against the dainty luxury of the expensive lingerie. She is like two different women standing in one flesh. The waif and the mistress. He cannot picture her as someone's mother. As the mother of his son.

'Are you sure you want to take care of us, Liam?' Emma asks, coolly, as his eyes run over her.

'God, Emma,' he gasps, 'did the boy do this?' urgency catching in his voice as he steps towards her. He wants to pull her into him, cover her, shield her, make her part of him. But it is Gideon, part of him, that has done this to her.

FIVE

'You haven't seen what I've done to the boy,' she says steady, unflinching. He's not going to fix her. She won't let him.

'What do you mean? What are you saying?' Liam says, appalled. 'Where is he?'

'I'd think twice before you make offers you'll regret, Liam,' Emma says, ignoring the question, as she turns away from him and he watches the luminescent angles of her delicate shoulder blades reflect the light. He thinks of butterfly wings. And knives.

▌▌▌▌▌

Had Danny and Liam been born today, technology would have detected Danny's heartbeat and shown his compromised position in Doreen's uterus. It would have given medical professionals the evidence to make appropriate suggestions for interventions resulting in the healthy birth of both boys. Doreen would have had a planned caesarean section, and Danny would not have been left in the back of her womb on his own, fighting to begin his life.

But Liam and his brother were born in 1970, and so Danny's heartbeat was missed under the roaring thump of Liam's in the midwife's stethoscope. Only Doreen's body knew of his existence, and so it inflated her lungs and made her scream, and it contracted to push him out, tiny and blue, while everyone was still distracted by the chaos and the miracle that was the birth of the wailing, robust Liam.

In the end, despite the confusion and shock of finding

a second baby where they had not known there would be one, despite Doreen's plunge into paralysing terror when she learned she had two boys and that one of them was almost dead, despite God not giving the infant Danny any grace, they had managed to save him, although not all of him survived.

There were parts of him that could have been but that never would be, and so they would become something else. The parts of Danny that were meant to run and jump and bounce and bound like his brother did not remain after his birth. The parts of him that were meant to fasten buttons and tie shoelaces and write in cursive did not make it. It was the absence of those parts that he understood caused his father to name him 'Cripple', which he used to mutter at Danny before he left for work in the morning. Until one day his father said nothing at all, just closed the door to the flat behind him and never came back.

Little Danny didn't mind their father's leaving, though little Liam did, because Danny understood that their father had named Liam 'My boy' and after he was gone there was no one left to call him that. Doreen just used the names she gave them.

Doreen only used the words that were necessary. She was a good mother and a loving mother. In the times in between her shifts as cashier at Sainsbury's and cleaner at Marks and Spencer, just before she'd leave for work when Liam came home from school to look after Danny, she'd say things like, 'I mended the holes in your socks' or 'There's cottage pie but it's mostly carrots,' which her boys knew meant, 'I love you.'

Sometimes she'd come home, worn and frayed, like the dreary curtains left by the previous tenant in the living room

FIVE

of their tiny flat that she had never had the time to wash, and she'd take sugar packets out of her pockets that she secreted from the employee break room at work. She'd pour a whole packet each into their cups of warm milk, and all she'd say was, 'The drink of kings,' and she'd hold Danny's cup of milk still for him while he drank it with a straw, and she'd ruffle Liam's hair while he downed his in one gulp.

When she said these four words, Liam, a literal thinker, remembered the word 'kings' and held onto to it, and kept it close, and believed it was meant for him. But Danny heard a lesson – nothing is ordinary if you don't want it to be – and this was the real difference between the boys as they grew into men.

■ ■ ■ ■ ■

In the beginning, they weren't sure what Danny knew and what he didn't know, what he could do and what he couldn't. That is the nature of cerebral palsy. In the beginning, Doreen knew she would be able to do little about the physical difference between her baby boys, but the difference in their futures, she knew, she could make level.

Doreen was told by a doctor that Danny might not speak or walk or read. She was told by another to be grateful that he was not her only child, because she would not be able to have any more. She was told by an auntie about hope, by a neighbour about God not giving more than she could handle, and by the priest about how merciful it was that Danny would never be aware of his limitations.

She was told, she was told, she was told, she was always being told something by someone who looked at her and her boys and saw only deficiency, because they never asked Doreen to define abundance.

Always after she was told, Doreen, being a woman of few words, simply tucked the loose strands of her auburn hair behind her ears, lifted her chin, and said, 'Thank you,' with the slight sound of Ireland in her voice and one arched eyebrow that conveyed the exact opposite of gratitude. Then she wrapped her sons up warm and held one on her hip and held the hand of the other and walked out into the world with them.

She was not concerned about what she was told because she knew that the tellers did not know that the hearts of her sons were identical, even if nothing else was, and that each one beat in rhythm with her own. The tellers did not see her beautiful boys at night, little Liam sleeping curled around his brother's stiff limbs. They were not there the day that Liam shouted, 'Mum, look at 'im!' while Danny took his first steps, leaning on his brother, did not hear her say, 'You two are miracles,' holding back tears as she held them close. They did not see how Danny, bright as a spark, helped Liam with his English homework because he wrote everything back to front, did not see her pride when they held each other up, her joy when she heard them laughing at some secret joke only they knew.

After the beginning of their story, and approaching its middle, Doreen and her boys found their way. There was, of course, derision or pity, and often both, everywhere they went. People saw Doreen, with her tired green eyes, as the poor,

FIVE

pretty, long-suffering mother, Danny as the poor 'spastic' boy, Liam as the poor neglected normal child. Doreen never argued or corrected this misinterpretation of her family, and if she was offended she never let anyone know it.

She saved her words instead for reading to Danny every day until he learned to read himself. When it was clear to her that he was far more intelligent than his teachers recognised at the local school, she took on an extra shift and paid for a succession of tutors, many of whom she dismissed almost as soon as they entered the flat and introduced themselves to Danny in a slow, loud voice or with an undertone of condescension, or with pity, like he was a lost kitten. When she found the one that spoke to Danny like he deserved to be spoken to, Doreen said to her only, 'You can come back tomorrow.'

The brothers did everything together. Liam, big and strong for his age, pushed Danny everywhere in his wheelchair. When they played football with the other lads, Danny would be in goal with Liam, as Liam sometimes pushed him round to block a shot, sometimes got him to standing and had him lean on him in goal as they lunged together with varying success. The other children around them grew up knowing the twins as a unit and for the most part never questioned it. The few times anyone imitated Danny's slow speech or laughed at a jerky movement or let slip a 'spaz', they had Liam to answer to, and they never did it again.

But this happened rarely, and not just because of Liam's brawn. Danny was clever, a schemer, a master manipulator of the public's interpretation of his life. And while he could not run or kick or play hide and seek, he soon figured out that he could pretend to have seizures in his wheelchair right in front of the till, which distracted shopkeepers long enough for one of the gang to take a few Mars bars without notice, and everyone would get at least a half. Or Liam would push Danny into the cinema and suddenly catch an uneven bit of carpet, tipping Danny onto the floor, creating just the right diversion for the other boys to sneak past into the theatre undetected. 'Nice one, Danny,' they'd all whisper when he and Liam eventually joined them, passing their free popcorn down the row.

There did inevitably come a time when their group's attention turned from playground games to chatting up girls and they no longer cherished stolen sweets but preferred cans of lager to drink in the park at twilight, when they were still too young to go to the pub.

'He'll be fine in goal, Mum, don't worry' became 'I can't take him out tonight, he'll get too cold' or 'We'll be in the park, mate, it's too hard with the chair or the crutches, you'll fall' and Danny would spend the evening with Doreen while Liam went out to feel what it was like to be by himself in the world, without a wheelchair in front of him, without one eye always on his brother. And Danny felt the ache of being left behind, felt the acute pain of his difference, once disguised by the games of their childhood that everyone had now outgrown.

But always when Liam came home from these forays into manhood, he'd wake his brother and breathe whisky and beer on Danny while he told him who he saw, and what this girl

FIVE

or that girl looked like, and how far he had got with her or, more truthfully, how he had got nowhere at all.

'You should've been there,' he'd say, before turning over in the single bed next to Danny's in the room they still shared, the alcohol drowning out the throbbing guilt in Liam's chest.

On one of Liam's Saturdays out, when he said that the pavements were too icy for Danny's crutches or too slippery for the chair, or the place would be too crowded, or he was taking the Tube and there were no lifts, Doreen looked at her son, so handsome, that gap between his teeth a charming imperfection in his perfect face, and she said, 'Don't do anything stupid,' by which she meant, 'Come back to us, we need you,' as she closed the door to the flat behind him.

Then she turned and looked at her Danny, and she saw the hurt in his eyes. Doreen made tea and pulled out the Trivial Pursuit board she'd found down at the Oxfam shop for two quid. All the little pie pieces were missing, but the question cards were all there, which was the most important part. Rather than take turns with Danny, Doreen just asked him the questions and put a matchstick in a pie slice for each correct answer until every little pie was full. He rarely missed one. Then she'd take out the stack of unsold *Telegraph*s the newsagent down the road had saved for her all week and they'd start on the crosswords, the only words exchanged being the clues Doreen read out and Danny's answers: *peripatetic, banal, impresario*.

Doreen was confident that the agility of Danny's mind would carve a path for him to security in his life. She knew that he would not be destitute or dependent, that his talents would take care of him. Her deepest worry for him instead was his isolation and the growing distance between her boys. Up until this point in their adolescence she'd thought their bond was unbreakable, but now she was not so sure. It was natural for Liam to break away, but she hadn't thought that it would happen so soon or that he would leave Danny behind so easily. But more than that, she felt an urgency. She had the sense of an ending coming nearer, a whisper in her ear that she was running out of time, and she worried that her mother's love would not be enough to fix things. It was her deepest fear, which, of course, she never shared with anyone.

When the crosswords were done and it was time for bed, Liam was still not home. Doreen saw Danny's eyes resting on the clock, his loneliness marked by each tick of the second hand. She held her boy's head in her hands, and she said, 'I know you need him, lad. So, make him need you more.'

Danny put her words away, in the same place he put the memory of the drink of kings, and kept them there.

▌▌▌▌▌

At this point in the story the boys are eighteen. There has been a tacit understanding in the family that Danny will go to university, that a degree is his best chance for employment and independence, and that Liam will go out to work. At first, each brother is excited by their prospects. But only one of them stays that way.

FIVE

Liam has been looking forward to what a job would bring. Money to take girls out. He would help Doreen; she could finally do fewer shifts and she could spend more time helping Danny type up his coursework and get on with his studies. He might even buy an old car and rebuild it.

Work is not easy to find without qualifications and experience, but Liam is young and strong, and so, undeterred, he takes what he can get. He tars roofs, cleans chimneys, digs landscapes, clears rubble, does hard, physical jobs that require his strength. He rises at dawn and comes home in the dark, his fingernails permanently blackened, his muscles hardened, his back aching. He works six days a week, sometimes seven.

He works this way for a year, then two years. He takes a couple of girls to the cinema but he scoffs when they also expect dinner. He doesn't buy a car to fix up. Doreen does only one less shift a week.

When he comes home, bone tired, he finds Doreen and Danny hunched over textbooks, laughing at some inside joke. Liam then gives Doreen half his pay, and the laughter, though it has nothing to do with him, sounds like reality smirking at the little bit that's left in his wallet. He doesn't come home for dinner for several weeks, preferring instead the company of other working men in the pub. He leaves before Doreen and Danny wake, half his pay always left by the kettle.

When he finally does make an appearance one night, Doreen says, 'Working yourself into the ground, lad,' by which he knows she means she doesn't approve, and he should come home after work and spend time with his brother, and he should stop drinking his pay, though she still gives him a plate of sausages with extra mash.

'The life of a king, Mum, don't you remember?' Liam says, an edge to his voice as he gulps a beer.

Doreen busies herself in the kitchen while he eats, slightly shudders at the sound of her son's voice, his tone, his East End accent so much like the father he doesn't remember. Then finally she says, 'There's more out there for you. Danny is—'

Liam cuts her off. 'Oh, you mean the boy wonder? Reaching for the stars, is he, Mum? Well, someone's got to pay for those dreams. Looks like the only one 'ere who can do that is me.' And Liam picks up a sausage with his fingers, eating it almost whole.

'Don't eat like a caveman,' Doreen says, which he knows means that this is Danny's best chance. They all know that. He knows she means she expects him to put his brother first, always, because that is what it is to be a man.

'And don't forget who was buying the sausages before you ever brought home a tuppence,' she says, with irritation, clearing the plates from the table, chastening her son.

But Liam won't let her do it this time, won't let her say two sentences and think she's solved the whole problem and had the last word. He thinks of the chimneys and the gutters and the dirt and the rubble in the heat and the rain while they were sat here, reading books. He pushes away his plate, pushes away from the table, forgets his strength and his size in the tiny kitchen, the chair tips over, the table shakes.

'How long, Mum? How long is my penance? How many roofs will I have to tar, and shit bosses will I have to listen to,

FIVE

and holes will I have to dig before I've repaid God for how I was born? I know things aren't easy for 'im, but they're not easy for me either, you think they are but they're not, and I'm paying for it every day,' Liam says.

Doreen says nothing.

'Do you hear me, Mum?' Liam says.

Doreen surveys her son from her position at the kitchen sink, cloth in one hand, rubber gloves in the other. She notices his height, his width, his strength, the spitting image of her own father, thank God, thank God he has not grown to be the man who fathered him instead, and then she says, 'Yes, I hear you, lad. Now, put the mouse back in the house, Liam, and clear the table,' which means, 'Your fly is undone, you big oaf, and stop feeling sorry for yourself.'

They look at each other for a moment. He laughs and so does she, and he zips up his jeans and brings the dishes to the sink.

'Mum, I . . .' he says, and doesn't finish, and she knows he means 'I'm sorry'.

She pats his cheek. 'It will be all right, lad,' she says, and even though she believes this, he does not.

But Danny, who hears everything from the living room sofa where they thought he was taking a nap, does not laugh. He cries. And he makes up his mind.

▌ ▌ ▌ ▌ ▌

'Let – me – help,' Danny says to Liam one Sunday morning, leaning on his crutch. Liam looks at him. Danny sees resentment dulling the shine of his brother's eyes. It is a look Danny remembers, an ancient memory of a father they once had.

'How?' Liam says, his sentences growing shorter, like their mother's. Danny knows what's contained in the 'how': How could you help, how could you earn some money so I don't have to do it alone, how can this be all there is?

Danny has the answer. It is on the sign he saw outside the local pub on his way to the library. QUIZ NIGHT, CASH JACKPOT.

Liam is sceptical and uncomfortable. 'You know I have trouble with those sorts of things, Danny.' But Danny says, 'Try – once.' And once is all it takes.

'What British city was formerly known as Duroliponte?' the quizmaster calls out as heads bow to sip their pints and confer around the tables of the Rose and Crown. The punters this evening don't know yet that they have no chance at winning with the twins in the room.

Liam leans over to Danny, who covers his mouth with one hand and says as quietly as he can, 'Cam – bridge,' in his halting way.

'What is the symbol for tin on the periodic table?' comes the next question.

'S – n,' says Danny, with a long pause between the letters.

'Who was the only prime minister to ever be assassinated?'

'Spen – cer – Per – ce – val,' says Danny, focusing hard on getting out all the syllables and getting his breath so he could be understood above the din of the pub, because he knows

FIVE

that Liam's never heard of Spencer Perceval and it's a hard one for Danny to articulate.

Danny knows all the answers but can't write them down fast enough, and Liam can write them down but recognises few and can't spell any. But no matter, together they sweep the jackpots at all the pub quizzes in East London.

They win £25 at the first quiz, £35 at the next, and they keep going and keep winning. They return home victorious, and Liam puts their winnings in a jar that he keeps on the high shelf of the wardrobe in the room he and Danny still share. Then puts on a dash more Brut, brushes his teeth, smooths his hair, and says, 'Are you sure you don't want to come, mate?'

'Tired – now – see – you – la – ter,' Danny drawls as he watches Liam leave to meet the lads for one more pint before the pubs close.

'Ah, you're a legend, I'll be back soon,' Liam says as he leaves, clapping his brother's bony shoulder with his strong hand.

Part of Danny wants to go with Liam, will always want to go, but after an evening of questions and disbelieving stares and curious glances and unkind murmurs from the drinkers and quiz goers that they beat out, he's had enough of being on show.

Tonight, after Liam leaves, Danny enters the kitchen on his crutches and sees Doreen at the table, staring at the bottle of Dubonnet the boys bought for her after their victory, not daring to open it. They won a lot, £72, the most they'd ever won. It was a rolling jackpot that kept growing because no team could crack the questions until Liam and Danny arrived and took it all. Liam also got talking to an electrician at the bar who needed an apprentice, got the number and a sliver of hope that there was more waiting for him, like his mother said there would be.

When Doreen dies not long after this evening, there will be £1,004 in the jar. By then Liam will have learned that all this time everyone thought he was thick, he really just had a mechanical brain, and he learns from the electrician to read machines and wires and circuits the way he never could read words.

The twins will combine their winnings with the tiny sum Doreen leaves them to start their first electrical business. Danny will handle the administrative end while Liam does the design and the practical work. They will grow it into the largest assistive technology firm in the United Kingdom, D-Tech, the 'D', of course, for Doreen. They will be known internationally. They will become wealthy and important men – kings after all.

But this evening, still some time away from all of this, under the dull kitchen light, Danny says, 'Go – on – Mum.'

'I should save it for best, for company,' Doreen says, running her thumb over the Dubonnet label and looking at her son.

Danny puts out one of his hands for her to hold. 'He – needs – me – now,' he tells her.

'Good lad,' Doreen says, and pushes the hair out of her Danny's eyes. 'Suppose one sip won't hurt,' she says, and carefully opens the bottle.

Doreen dies when she is sitting in her favourite chair in the front room of the same flat she brought her boys home to

FIVE

twenty-two years ago, newly born. On her right, Danny sits in his wheelchair, and on his right, Liam sits on the settee, only the arm of the sofa between him and his brother. It is Saturday evening. They are watching *Stars in Their Eyes*, which is Doreen's favourite show and which her boys watch with her because they love her.

Doreen says, 'Three, lad,' to Liam as he spoons the third sugar into her tea and passes it to her. They're having tea after supper and some biscuits from a tattered box she brought home from Sainsbury's that she got for half off plus her employee discount.

She sips her sweet, sweet tea and thinks to herself for the thousandth time in twenty years that she really should launder those curtains, and regrets that now she won't have the chance, as a thunderclap no one else can hear explodes inside her head. The pain is immense, but she sees her Liam, so big and muscular and broad and handsome pointing at the screen and making his brother laugh. As the feeling drains from her left side, Doreen regrets that she never had the money to fix the gap between his teeth that she knows secretly bothers him, but that she has always loved. The last thing she sees before her vision is lost and another blood vessel explodes in her brain is her Danny, smiling with the box of biscuits in his lap. As her breath stops, Doreen can still hear his hoarse, gasping laugh as Liam says something rude about the lady on stage impersonating Barbra Streisand. *Lads*, she thinks, her lads, and the word feels like a smile. And as the mug of tea drops from her hand and her soul leaves the room, she regrets nothing at all.

Liam was about to tell her and Danny about Kate. That they want to move in together. That they're going to find a flat nearby. But before he has a chance to mention it, Doreen drops her tea and dies.

The twins grieve their mother, as they will the rest of their lives, in the way that sons grieve mothers and daughters don't, until the daughters become the mothers of their own sons, and then they understand their mothers, finally. The twins also decide to start their business, right there, in the flat.

The brothers live and work side by side. Danny works all day with Liam and finishes his degree at night. Liam stops working for other people and puts all his time into the business. They eat tinned beans for weeks at a time, but they don't mind because they know why they're doing it. Danny sees his brother's eyes change, the resentment disappears.

Liam puts off his plans with Kate.

'I've got to look after Danny,' he says to her, which in the immediate aftermath of Doreen's passing she understands.

'No, love, not yet, I promise, soon, but you know, I've got Danny,' he says a year later when her patience starts to run thin.

'There's nothing I want more, really, Katie girl, it's just, my life is so complicated, with the business, and looking after Danny, it's not fair to you, I understand that, you need to move on,' he says six months after that, when she is unsure whether he ended it with her or she ended it with him.

FIVE

'Sad – ab – out – Kate?' Danny asks Liam at dinner one night.

'Not really, we've got so much on, and we're growing so fast, I don't have time for it, and I lost interest to be honest, so I let her down easy. She's a good girl, but not right now,' Liam says.

'How – did – you – do – it?' Danny asks.

'I just said the business and, of course, with looking after you my life was too complicated and she shouldn't wait around and she should just go,' Liam says.

'Me?' Danny asks.

'Yeah, you, of course,' Liam says. 'You're an iron-clad excuse. She can't even be that mad at me if I say I've got you, for fuck's sake, what's she going to say? And it's the truth, anyway, isn't it?' Liam says, as he clears their plates.

Iron-clad excuse. Danny absorbs the impact of each word as it hits him. He reaches for his crutches and walks across the flat with his distinctive gait, each step swinging out in turn from his inverted knees that knock each other slightly as he slowly, haltingly reaches the chair where his mother died, next to the window with its old curtains. He looks out onto the street where they have lived all their lives, and thinks of Liam's blackened fingernails, his aching back, his debt to God. Liam taking him everywhere with him when they were boys, until they grew up, and then he didn't any more. He thinks about the business plan, the structure he laid out, the presentations and pitches he wrote for Liam to deliver to investors, the money that his ideas – no, his brilliance – was bringing in. As far as the business goes, Danny doesn't need Liam. He works hard, certainly, but Liam isn't exceptional. He could be replaced, although Danny would never do that. He would never abandon the brother who needs him so much.

Except, Liam prefers telling the story that the world wants to hear, of Danny as the disabled, dependent brother and Liam as the selfless hero. And worse than everyone accepting that version of events is that Liam does too.

All right, then, Danny thinks. Let Liam live on in his myth if that's what will keep him – them – going. And he puts his brother's words away in the place where he keeps Doreen's words and the 'drink of kings', although he's starting to run out of space. And patience.

The business grows and expands. The brothers are at the forefront of designing cutting-edge assistive equipment. They are leaders in speech-generating devices and adaptive keyboards. Their biggest success comes in 2000 with the production of a voice-activated device allowing the user to control appliances with verbal commands, helping many people with disabilities gain greater independence in their own homes.

Public relations play a role in their early success. Liam learns quickly about the power of the combination of his gap-tooth smile, his strong arms and his accent, especially when they accompany Danny onto a stage. They become media darlings. It is more than just the classic tale of rags to riches via the pulling up of bootstraps that the public devours, it is the photos, the optics that they love. They love to seek out resemblance between the twins. They try to find the thread

FIVE

of similarity that binds the Grecian god-like looks of Liam to the thin figure of Danny in a wheelchair or leaning on his crutches, and marvel at the lottery of birth, and say things like 'Can you imagine' and 'How is it possible' and 'The big one must thank his lucky stars.'

They are interviewed on *Parkinson* and *Good Morning Britain,* and they even make an appearance on *The Oprah Winfrey Show* in America. Liam talks about the fake seizures and getting into the cinema for free when they were kids. How Danny has always been the brains in the family, how he helped Liam with his homework, how their mother worked two jobs to pay for Danny's tutors. 'He were that clever,' he says, knowing the authenticity that his errant grammar lends to the story. He puts a hand on his brother's knee, nudges Danny with an elbow playfully if they're sitting side by side.

Danny says little in the interviews. The interviewers simply don't have the time or patience to wait for him to speak. When they do turn to him, it is usually for the last question, when they say slowly and loudly, 'What would your mother think of your success?' and Danny says, 'She – would – say – well – done – you – cunts,' and everyone leans forward just a little and thinks they must have misheard, that he must have actually said, 'She would say well done *to us*,' of course that's what he said. His speech is just a bit slurred, that's all, and some people giggle at their mistake, and some feel ashamed that they even thought it.

And then the camera pans to the audience, where more than one woman is brushing away a tear, imagining herself as Doreen, and the interviewer, slightly flushed, says something like, 'Yes, she would be so proud of you both indeed,' and only Danny and Liam know that Danny did actually say 'cunts', because that's what he thought of everyone who interviewed him this way, with the exception of Oprah, who started the interview with a question for Danny, and held his hand and shed a tear when he spoke of the death of Doreen, and paid little attention to Liam, knowing exactly what he was about the minute she shook his hand and saw the gap in his smile.

Danny tolerates the interviews, the photos in *Hello!* and the Sunday newspaper magazines. He tolerates the tone people use with him, speaking to him as they would a child, the condescension, the talk of miracles that someone like him could have built what he did with Liam. He tolerates it because he knows that D-Tech products transform people's lives, but also because Danny is an entrepreneur, and he is wealthy. He likes money. And he wants more of it.

So when it's time to grow D-Tech, to take it to the next level, to diversify the product, to get into research and artificial intelligence, to make not just specialised products but products for everyone's homes, to go public, to really raise its profile and leave its mark and create a legacy, the brothers look for a new chief financial officer.

Emma interviews with them at their offices. She is the youngest candidate. Her rise to this position happened rather quickly, and there are rumours about how she achieved so much in her career so fast, but the brothers soon understand how she has set herself apart from the rest.

As Danny describes his vision of a future accessible to

FIVE

everyone, of leading the world in innovation and creativity, breaking down barriers, extending their reach to schools and governments, Emma looks at him directly with her piercing eyes, perched on the edge of her chair, legs crossed, left arm folded over right resting on her knees, back straight, like a praying mantis prepared for battle. She says, 'Sure, Danny, that's great, but to be honest, I don't really give a fuck. I'm here to make you some money.'

The brothers look at each other.

'Wel – come – a – board,' Danny says. And Liam smiles.

■ ■ ■ ■ ■

He smiles because this woman is going to need him, and he can't wait to see what she wants. No, Liam knows what she wants as soon as she walks in the door. He can't wait to see how she asks for it. He knows she will.

There's no denying that Emma is impressive. Self-made, ambitious, brilliant, wealthy. He's heard the stories about her and her former colleagues. But she's thirty-seven, almost thirty-eight, single, unattached, living alone, no ex-husbands, no children. Despite the ball-busting, man-eating persona and the foul mouth, he knows she's lonely. It's all a cover for her ticking clock, her shrivelling eggs crying out under that dress that makes her look like a nun. And a whore.

Liam knows all of this, because unlike Emma, Liam can read people instantly. A lifetime of caretaking and empathising, providing, protecting his brother and supporting his mother, made him an expert in detecting the needs of others. It's a useful skill if you like to help people. Or control them.

Once Doreen was gone and Danny lived in the safety of his wealth, Liam moved on to his life with his wives. Elizabeth the First, his first wife, was a receptionist at D-Tech. When he met her she was a single mum with beautiful legs who had recently escaped an abusive marriage. Liam told her she could stop working, took on her two children, and raised them as his own, delighting in how soon they called him Dad. But once Elizabeth got a bit old and puffy, with less time to be grateful to him because she was earning a degree and starting her own small online business, Liam felt restless and bored.

Which was when he met Trisha, his second wife, a stripper, who adored him and wore lingerie all day and planned a *Pretty Woman*-themed wedding because she felt that it was the story of their lives. She gave him two more children, never gained an ounce, and wore stilettos throughout each pregnancy. Over time, with the unlimited decorating budget he gave her, Trisha developed a knack for nouveau riche interior design and soon had a client list of WAGs of overpaid football players and boxers who shared her taste for gold accessories, mirrors and white marble. Liam loved their children but found the lustre had worn off his life with Trisha once she started wearing designer suits over her negligees.

Which was when he left her for Elizabeth the Second, Beth, a cocktail waitress at an exclusive social club of which he was a member, a tough cookie with a hard-knock life who'd been on her own since she was sixteen. She had the heart of an

FIVE

early Elizabeth the First and the body of an early Trisha, but unlike her predecessors she understood that her husband did not know who he was unless he was saving someone, so she kept her ambitions to herself and played the part. She liked money, so she earned it by doing her work in the kitchen and the bedroom, raising their sons, ignoring Liam's occasional indiscretions, and thanking God for her good fortune. Beth's simple attitude towards her simple husband accounted for the longevity of their marriage.

So when Liam meets Emma, he is intrigued by her performance of independence and achievement, but he is experienced in the desperation of women, and he feels hers right away. Even if she doesn't know that's what it is. When Emma meets Liam, she mistakes his interest in her and she thinks it is like looking at her own reflection. She sees his drive, ambition, grit, self-sufficiency, the kind of self-belief a person is born with who is sure of their exceptional destiny, and thinks he is like her. He has an intangible quality the dating apps and sperm bank websites could not find for Emma. He is the one for what she has in mind. So when the time is right, she makes him her offer.

'I just want your genetics,' she says, sitting behind her desk, late one night at the office, several months into her new role at D-Tech.

'I don't need your money, and I'm not interested in snatching you away from your wife or your kids. My child will not knock on your door eighteen years from now, asking to join you for Christmas dinner. If I do this right, he'll never care about you at all. He'll be too busy running things.'

'You're strange, Emma,' Liam says, coming around to her side of the desk, leaning against the edge, leaning into her. He moves a strand of golden hair behind her ear.

'What's that got to do with it?' she asks, lifting her eyes to his.

'Everything,' he says, leaning down, kissing her, forcefully, so she will feel it.

And she does feel it, but she does not feel what he feels. Emma is not very good at feelings. She lacks the internal voice that should warn her to beware the narcissism of the saviour, to look out for the man who wants to rescue her, who wants to protect her, whether she needs him to or not.

And one morning, several months after the first encounter, when she has fallen for him but refuses to admit that there is anything more to this arrangement, she says, 'Well, our work here is done,' as they rise from her silk sheets to start the day.

'What are you on about?' he says, sleepily, one eye open, gazing admiringly at the curve of her bare back as she sits on the edge of the bed.

'I'm pregnant,' she says.

'Nice one, congratulations,' he says, pulling her towards him. 'Who's the father?'

'Now, don't get sentimental,' she says, 'We had a deal. This one's mine.'

'Yes, boss,' Liam says. He will let her think it is all going according to her plan because it's easier for her than the truth, which is that he's her hero. She said she didn't want him involved, and he'll sign her little paper, but soon she'll see. She'll need

FIVE

him to save her from what she thinks she wants. Women always think they know what they want until they get it.

'Hey, I'll always be here for you, you know, if you need anything,' he says, because he knows it works, as he runs a finger from her shoulder to her wrist.

'OK,' she says, closing her eyes, to keep from feeling.

■ ■ ■ ■ ■

D-Tech grows and Emma helps the brothers reach the next level. And as Liam distracts himself with Emma, Danny also finds new ways to occupy himself. He buys an old stately home that once belonged to a baron whose disappointing son managed to lose control of the family fortune within a generation. Danny has it modernised and refurbished, equipped with ramps, lifts and adaptations, some of them experimental prototypes for machines D-Tech will someday produce. He fills the house with art and rare books. He hires a chef, a personal assistant, a gardener, a housekeeper.

He hires Brendon, a personal physiotherapist, who comes to the estate three times a week, and then every day, and then stays, and never leaves.

Danny and Brendon talk about life and the things they love and the things they hate, and they take walks around the grounds, and do exercises and therapies which make Danny stronger. To show his gratitude Danny buys Brendon an expensive watch, a bespoke suit, a carbon-fibre racing bike. They fly to Rome, to Berlin, to New York. They stay in the best hotels, they eat beautiful food. They talk and have sex and laugh, and for the first time since the death of Doreen, someone understands Danny in his entirety and sees all of him all at once.

'Are you sure about him, mate, you're sure he's not taking advantage?' Liam asks, not for the first time since their relationship began.

'We – are – in – love,' Danny answers him, again.

'If you say so,' Liam says, 'but something's off,' by which he means, there is only room for one hero in our story.

'Not sure I should trust you, mate,' Liam says to Brendon on another visit when they have a moment alone in the kitchen while Brendon mixes cocktails.

'You should, because I love him,' Brendon answers. 'You can take your time, though.' Brendon smiles as he brushes an eyelash off Liam's cheek.

Brendon holds out Liam's eyelash on the tip of his finger and says, 'Make a wish. Give it a blow.'

Liam walks away, but not before looking Brendon in the eye, not before feeling a ripple through him that is jealousy, that is fear of losing Danny, but that Liam mistakes for something else.

'There's something I don't like about this,' Liam says to Danny, on an evening when Brendon is away seeing his mum.

'You – do – not – have – to – like – it,' Danny says.

'I worry about you,' Liam says, stopping short of saying what he is thinking. *I am your protector, I'm the leading man, remember?*

'I worry that he's playing a game with you,' Liam says instead.

'So – stop,' Danny says, and he means exactly that.

FIVE

∎ ∎ ∎ ∎ ∎

'I love you,' Brendon says, as he does up the buttons on Danny's shirt for him. It is their wedding day, the five-year anniversary of the day they met. They are having a small, private ceremony on Danny's estate. Only Danny's other trusted staff will be present – the chef, the housekeeper, the gardener – and Liam and his third wife and their two sons.

Though it takes more effort, Danny chooses to stand today with Brendon to receive their guests. They position themselves on either side of the antique ornate alabaster table in the centre of the foyer, in their wedding suits, smiling, and Danny's heart is so full and proud. Above them, the hundreds of glass crystals on the enormous Edwardian chandelier reflect the sunlight from the windows of the cupola above it, casting tiny rainbows everywhere. A huge vase filled with dozens of peonies, Doreen's favourite, stands on the alabaster table.

Danny had hoped to have a moment with his brother before the ceremony with a cheeky glass of Dubonnet by the peonies to toast their mother on this important day. But Liam arrives alone and bursts into the grand entryway, the heels of his bespoke loafers ringing out on the highly polished marble floor. Before Danny can even say his name, Liam lurches toward them, red-faced, shouting, 'I knew it, I knew it, you thieving bastard, look, look at this!' clutching a sheaf of papers in his hand.

They are bank records, obtained by a private detective, which Liam believes are the proof that Brendon has been stealing from Danny all this time, small incremental amounts, then larger and larger ones, adding up to half a million pounds over three years, transferred to an account in Brendon's name.

'What are you on about, ma—' Brendon starts to say but cannot finish the sentence because Liam's fist makes contact with Brendon's face. He is stunned for a moment but regains his balance and says, bleeding from the nose, 'Liam, we're getting married—'

'The hell you are! Half a million? What, you thought he wouldn't miss it?'

'I – gave – it—' Danny tries to say he gave it to him, but he cannot get the words out fast enough.

'Danny gave it to me, to help my mum and sister, look – look at where the payments go, mate, to the care home for my mum, to pay for my nieces' sch—'

'I—' Danny starts to say but stops, he knows the other two men are not listening.

'Liar!' Liam shouts. He punches Brendon again and stumbles into the heavy stone table, where both men struggle with each other until they fall onto the ground.

Liam gets on top of Brendon and punches and punches, and Brendon can't find his breath, and Liam gets lost in his anger. The rest of their lives are determined in the next few moments.

John, the gardener and Max, the chef, run to pull Liam off Brendon and tussle and roll on the floor, fending off Liam's blows.

Danny panics, in shock, at a loss for what to do. He cannot get too close to them, he'll lose his balance, he'll get hurt, he cannot get in and stop the fight.

FIVE

Or a different truth: they do not know how to fight like he does.

Danny leans on his crutches on the other side of the table; his eyes dart around the room for a way to stop the chaos. He can yell and shout but the fighting men are too distracted to hear him.

Or a different truth: his brother just never listens.

Danny scans the room. His eyes fall on his mother's flowers, on his brother, the man who was once a boy who took him everywhere, did everything for him. Danny cannot overpower the fighting men.

Or a different truth: Danny has always had the power, the kind that matters.

Danny walks with his crutches, moves as quickly as he can to the opposite wall and hits the emergency call button. He has one in every room of the house. The alarm sounds. He casts his crutches aside. Using the wall for support, he slides down it, sinking to the ground.

John the gardener, attuned to the emergency call sound, pulls away from the fray, looks around, and sees Danny on the ground, his crutches beside him, askew, and yells, 'Danny! It's Danny! Get help!' and he runs to Danny's side. Max the chef finally manages to pull Liam from Brendon by yelling in his ear, 'Your brother! It's Danny!'

'What?' Liam gasps to himself, jumping away from Brendon suddenly, as though he has seen a ghost, as though he has re-entered his body and is not sure where he has been, the spell of the violence that overtook him now broken. He looks around the room, sees Danny's body limp in the corner.

'Call an ambulance!' John yells.

'On it!' Max replies, pulling out his phone.

'Danny! Can you hear me!' a bloody Liam shouts, and then cries as he gets to the floor, hooks his arms under his brother's body, cradles his head. 'Danny?' he almost whimpers. 'What have I done, what have I done,' he almost whispers, smoothing Danny's hair across his forehead, like their mother used to do.

It is at this moment, when only the tone of the medical alarm and the heavy breathing of winded men can be heard, that Liam knows he has made a fatal error, that Danny opens wide his alert, hardened, angry eyes, looks into his brother's worried face, and says, 'You – should – know – me – bet – ter – than – that.'

■ ■ ■ ■ ■

Soon we will reach the meeting of Liam and Emma in her kitchen in her house of evening gowns and bare walls and desperation. Soon we will get to Emma asking, on behalf of Danny, for Liam to sign the documents that will give him his half of the business to walk away from D-Tech and sever his connection to his brother forever. Brendon will agree not to press criminal charges, despite the week he spent in hospital for his injuries. Danny will agree not to release a statement accusing Liam of a hate crime, committing a homophobic assault and attempted murder of Brendon on the couple's wedding day. All Liam has to do is agree to leave with his share and not look back.

FIVE

Danny knows Liam's assault on Brendon was not homophobic. But if he released it, that's how it will play to the press. He will be believed. He knows how the public have always seen him and Liam, he has always known how to manipulate their prejudice in his favour, and he will do it now if Liam doesn't get out of his life. He knows that Liam knows that no matter how he tries to defend himself, the press will believe Danny, and Liam's muscles and height, the gap between his teeth that women love and his working-class charm will suddenly seem aggressive and creepy and bullying. The story will ruin him.

The brothers have agreed, via messages sent through Emma, not to involve lawyers. The details of Danny's disastrous wedding day are so potentially damaging, not just to Liam and his family but to the company, and neither of the brothers trusts that even with attorney-client privilege the story won't get out, through a secretary or a paralegal or an assistant who could make a mint on selling it online and to the tabloids.

Emma is the perfect choice because she has something to lose. Danny has seen how she started disappearing when she came back from maternity leave, how colourless her eyes became by the time she resigned. He's kept tabs on her because he knows something about difficult births. He knows something about mothers coping alone. He knows she has secrets she wants to keep, that her life with Gideon is hard, and that mothers, even strange mothers like her, will do extraordinary things for their children, even children that they can't love. So Emma could be useful to him one day. And the day has arrived.

She will handle this for Danny because a simple anonymous

call to social services is all it would take to make things much harder for her and Gideon than they already are. In exchange, Danny will pay her enough to cover Gideon's therapeutic school.

Despite how it seems, Danny's aim is not to hurt Liam. He is acting from self-preservation. He makes the threat, not out of hatred for his brother, but out of love for Brendon, to show Brendon that his love is real, so real that he will choose their found love over the love that bound him to his brother even before their birth.

But first, before the documents, before the blackmail, there is Liam sitting in Danny's grand reception room, several days after the fight, looking at the bottle of unopened Dubonnet that is kept there in homage to Doreen. The swelling has gone down in his face from the few punches Brendon landed, but his knuckles are still cracked and swollen.

'I didn't think, I was just so angry that he was stealing from you—' Liam says.

'No. – You – did – not – think – he – could – love – me,' Danny says.

'Love? I love you, Mum loved you, not that fucker – me, your brother, me, who's always been here, always looked after you, I love you,' Liam tries not to shout.

'You – do – not – think – some – one – could – love – me – how – I – am—'

'That's not true, of course that's not true, but I'm not going to let some arsehole steal from you and pretend he's doing it because he *loves* you,' Liam argues.

FIVE

'He – does – love – me.'

'He fooled you, Danny. You know it, deep down, you know I'm protecting you, like always—'

'You – want – to – show – me – no – one – can – love – me!'

'No, that's not it, not at all, I don't think it's cos you're disabled, I think it's cos you're *rich* and disabled, and he hit the jackpot with you, didn't he—'

'Why – did – I – do – it?'

'To stop us, to make it stop, look, I get it—'

But Danny will not be spoken over, not this time. He pounds the table next to him. 'No! – To – make – *you* – stop. – You! – So – you – would – not – kill – him. – To – save – *you!* – If – he – dies – what – hap – pens – to – you – to – your – kids? – The – com – pa – ny? – I – did – it – to – save – *your* – life. – And – his. – But – you — first.'

Many truths can be true.

Many loves can be loved.

Danny will always love the toddler Liam who slept curled around him, and the boy Liam who pushed his chair, and the teenage Liam who tarred roofs to help pay the rent, and the young man Liam who built a fortune with him, and he even loves this Liam, now, who has only ever used Danny to make himself the centre of their story, to be the man of the house even though Danny was also there, in that same house with him, and also a man. But Liam could not see Danny that way then, and he still can't do it now.

Danny triggered the alarm, he pretended to collapse, he caused a scene on top of the scene already caused and saved

Brendon. But Danny also saved Liam from going too far, from making a worse mistake. Danny chooses Brendon over Liam, but Danny will always love his brother because 'I love you' and 'Goodbye' can both mean the same thing.

'I lost control, it was a mistake, it's just, can't you see I'm trying to protect you?' Liam says.

'I – do – not – need – you – to.'

'Oh, don't be stupid,' Liam says in the flat, impotent way of someone who cannot admit defeat. He stands up and walks to the window overlooking the century-old hedge maze in Danny's garden and leans one arm against the wooden frame.

'I – do – not – need – you.'

There is silence between the brothers. Danny's words settle on the room. A nerve struck, a truth told, words spoken that cannot be unsaid.

▮ ▮ ▮ ▮ ▮

Liam picks up Emma's gown off the floor, gets in front of her in the doorway so she can't pass. He will not let her walk away. He hands her the gown, unnerved by her vulnerability. 'Cover yourself,' he says. 'What do you mean, what you did to the boy? Where is my son?' he says.

'*Your* son?' Emma laughs, surprised. 'Oh, Daddy, aren't you cute,' she says, slyly, stroking his face with the back of her hand. He bats her away. She is again two women in one. The bitch and the lunatic. But she has miscalculated.

He turns and bolts down the hall, runs up the stairs.

FIVE

'What are you doing?' she yells frantically, panicked, behind him. 'You signed your rights away, remember?' she says impotently to his back as he darts from room to room. 'Gideon is none of your business!' she shouts, wedging herself in her bedroom doorway, trying to keep him out of it. He notices how the skin stretches over her upper ribs.

'He is now,' Liam says, pushing open doors, turning on lights, scanning the mostly dark and empty rooms, the blinds drawn, all the furniture sold, to pay for years of spending on clothes and cars and her beautiful things, and years of spending on Gideon.

'You can't do this! You can't go in there!' she screams as he approaches the door to Gideon's room. She jumps on him, beats on his shoulders, uncertain how this has all turned around so fast and got out of her grasp.

He unbolts the top bolt. 'What the fuck, Emma,' he says, 'bolts?' unbolting the bottom one.

'I'll do what you want!' she screams, desperate to get in front of him, to stop him opening the door. 'Whatever you want!' But she cannot stop the inevitable.

'Where is he?' Liam shouts as he opens the door. The television, on mute, flashes cartoons in the corner. He stops short. He can't walk into the room because the floor is covered in precise, straight lines of Gideon's belongings. The first is a line of toy cars and trucks, in size order, according to colour, each parked behind the other, exactly half an inch apart. The second is a line of Cheerios, impossibly straight, each one touching the next, more than a hundred of them, not one out of place.

The third, a line of children's books laid flat, face down, their bindings touching, straight as a ruler. The bare mattress smells faintly of urine.

'I was just washing his sheets, it's not normally like this,' she says, quietly, as if this explains everything.

Liam picks up a book at his feet, a Dr Seuss. 'I hate you' is written over and over on each page, each word perfectly formed.

'He has beautiful handwriting,' Emma says. 'Much better than most kids his age.'

'So is he a genius or is he disturbed, Emma, which one is it?' Liam says, putting the book carefully back in its place in the line.

'I'm not signing that contract. You tell Danny to drop all this nonsense and to go with me to that meeting and make the investment with me tomorrow. It's big, he won't regret it, and you get him to do it, or I take Gideon.'

'Take him? Take him where?' she says, disbelieving.

'I'll make a call, they'll take him away from this,' Liam says.

'I didn't do this! This is Gideon, this is who he is, look what he's done to me, this is what he's like, this isn't me,' Emma says, panicked, aghast.

'I don't know what this is,' Liam says, pushing past her, leaving the room. 'Or what you're doing, but I won't let it go on.'

'You think I can't make a call too!' she calls out to Liam, as he descends the stairs. 'I'll call the *Daily Mail* right now, I'll tell them what you did! Attempted murder of a gay man, you're a bully! And a monster!'

Liam turns around. 'And I'll tell them about you,' he shouts at her from the bottom of the stairs. 'SINGLE PSYCHO MUM

FIVE

LOCKS CHILD IN HOUSE OF HORRORS. Who do you think they'll believe? Just *look* at the state of you.' Disgusted, he scans her from head to toe. Then he slams the front door behind him, leaving Emma alone.

She shivers in her slip. She forgot that's all she was wearing. She goes to the bathroom to wash her face, and a sudden soreness reminds her of her wounded eyebrow. She looks in the mirror over the sink. A red patch of blood is spreading through the bandage. Her hair is stringy, her teeth are red wine stained. Her collarbones jut out at hungry angles.

'Are you there?' she whispers to her reflection.

She considers her position. One brother uses her child as bait to get her to do his bidding. The other uses her child as a threat, to get her to do the same. But what these men have forgotten is that Gideon is hers. *Hers.* He frightens her, he hurts her, he is not well, he is not happy, but he is hers. She made him and she would do anything for him. It is hard to love him, but she is also hard to love. These men have forgotten who she is.

Emma sits on the edge of the bath and places a call. While it rings, her foot touches an old lipstick near the leg of the tub. She takes off the lid. It's blunted and misshapen, another victim of Gideon.

'Hello?' a voice answers.

'Hello, I need to speak to . . . hello?' Emma says when the line suddenly goes quiet, the reception dipping in and out.

'Are you still there?' the voice comes back.

'Yes,' Emma says, as she runs the dark red around her lips. 'I think so.'

Time	Destination	Expected
1st 7:06	London Victoria	7:08
South London Service formed of 8 coaches.		
2nd 7:13	Bedford	7:16

07:08

And so here we are.

The child, the mother, the businessman, the old woman and the gambler. One of them will die despite your attachment to them, regardless of your judgement of their behaviours or your empathy with their situation. There is probably one that you're OK with getting rid of. Of course there is. You've chosen your favourite. You don't have to admit to anyone who it is. But perhaps you should ask yourself why, what makes them worthy of surviving in the internal universe of your brain where you are God.

Let us review their positions, just this one last time.

Sonny is standing on the tracks as the train approaches.

Liam is on the platform, between the edge and the yellow line, on all fours, struggling to stand due to concussion.

Mrs Worth remains in her position on the ground, breathing with difficulty, wheezing 'Man on the tracks,' into the mobile phone next to her.

Emma is running from Mrs Worth's side to Medical Student at the platform edge to inform him that Sonny wants to die.

Gideon is looking at his tablet while he balance-walks on the concrete lip of the platform, occasionally raising his eyes, taking note of the adults' positions.

'The train's right there!' Medical Student warns and pleads to Sonny, reaching his hand out to him from the platform edge. As soon as he says this, the train lets out a warning blast of its horn. To Do List and Bad Back, standing behind him, flinch when they hear it.

'He's trying to kill himself!' Emma calls, running towards the trio, passing on Mrs Worth's message.

And then she shouts, 'Liam? Liam!' when she sees him a bit apart from them, trying to stand up.

'Danny,' he groans, hands on his head. 'Hold on, I'm coming.'

'Emma! Emma!' Gideon, who has now reached his mother, shouts, tugging at her trouser leg. 'I want a different show! This is a baby show.'

'Not now!' she scolds Gideon. Then, pleading with Medical Student, she says, 'She said he wants to die, you have to get him!' and then, pleading with Sonny, 'Please!'

The train gets closer. Sonny stays still. Gideon steps back from his mother and watches.

'Should we get him?' Bad Back asks Medical Student, who cannot think.

'Um, hey, c'mon, hey!' Bad Back shouts, uncertainly and without conviction, waving a hand at Sonny.

Gideon homes in on Liam, who has finally stood up, a few steps away from the group that is focused on Sonny.

FIVE

'Liam, Biam, new show, please, this one's for babies,' Gideon says, holding out his tablet to Liam, who is dizzy and unsteady but upright. Liam's back is to the tracks, his feet on the yellow line, close to the edge. He looks at Gideon, who is so small. Liam tries to focus his eyes, he knows the child, but he can only say, 'Danny?'

Sonny, despite the pleas of Medical Student, Emma and Bad Back, is paralysed by a second blast of the train horn. The train is so close now, they can all feel the rumble under their feet, the vibration of the horn's volume reverberating in their chests. With every second the wheels on the track are closer, the hum and puff of the engine are louder, the face of the terrified driver through the windscreen is clearer.

This is it, thinks Sonny, dropping to his knees.

The train driver has been on trains that have hit people before, he has comforted his friends who have left the job because of these events, but so far it's never been him driving, until today. He looks at the people he can see up ahead and issues another blast from the train after triggering the emergency brake. He knows from his training that it will take at least thirty seconds to stop and that this will not save the young man in front of his train. There is nothing else he can do as a single tear runs down his face but pray, '*Zdrowaś Maryjo, łaski pełna,*' Hail Mary, full of grace.

Seeing what is about to happen, Emma whips around, finds Gideon, and shouts, 'C'mon!' grabbing his arm roughly.

'You're hurting me!' Gideon whines, throwing his tablet to the concrete, struggling against her.

'C'mon!' she says, pulling Liam's hand, pulling him from the platform edge. If you took their photo, they would look, for just this one second, like a family holding hands.

'That hurts!' Gideon complains, suddenly hysterical. Emma lets go of Liam's hand and grasps her son from behind, under his arms, pulling his back to her, restraining him. But his legs are still free. Gideon kicks her once. Twice.

Liam stands in front of them. 'You're hurting Danny!' he says, confused, concussed, as he tries to unclasp Emma's arms from around her child. Now that Liam's close enough, Gideon kicks again, getting him in the thigh. The boy hears the train, the people shouting on the platform. He wants to see. He lands a fourth kick to Emma's knee.

'Fuck!' she swears, and unable to hold him any longer, she lets go of him. Liam, unbalanced by Gideon's escape from his mother, sways backward. He stumbles towards the yellow line, a step beyond it, a step closer to the platform edge, his back to the oncoming train.

The train lets out a blast. And then another. And another.

The person about to die thinks, *Wait, not yet—*

'Stop!' Emma shouts at Gideon, a few feet away from her, standing on the yellow line, then stepping past it.

'Oh my God!' To Do List shrieks, her hands over her bloody face. 'C'mon, c'mon!' Bad Back calls out nervously to Sonny. 'Man on the tracks!' Gideon mimics and points.

'Don't do that!' Liam warns, and reaches for Gideon.

The person about to die thinks, *Now? No—*

Ten.

FIVE

'God help us,' Mrs Worth – the daughter, the doctor, the old woman – lying alone, whispers to herself.

Nine.

'Move!' Bad Back pleads with Sonny.

'I can't,' Sonny – the fuck-up, the lover, the gambler – says, listening for his mother.

Eight.

The person about to die thinks, *Please, God—*

Seven.

'Get off me!' Gideon – the psycho, the genius, the child – shouts as Liam grasps his arm.

Six.

'Danny!' Liam – the saviour, the narcissist, the businessman – calls to Gideon, seeing his brother but reaching for his son.

Five.

'Don't do this!' Medical Student begs Sonny, and jumps.

Four.

The person about to die thinks, *I can't go, please—*

Three.

'Get off of him!' Emma – the Rich Bitch, the lunatic, the mother – roars at Liam, her palm against her son's chest.

Two.

'Oh fuck,' Liam says, letting go of the child.

One.

Fear has a sound. It is hard to recognise because we only hear it once or twice in our lives. We may have a feeling that we think is fear more often than that, when we travel to foreign countries and need medical attention or have a near miss in a car or get into a fight in a bar with a big stranger or come home to a house that's been burgled. But it isn't until we hear the fear of life ending, the fear of seeing it end in front of us, that we know the difference. The guttural cry or wailing scream, the shrill call of succumbing to disaster, the whispered prayer of a last breath – the sounds of fear are worse, sometimes, than the sights.

'Gideon!'

Emma's cry for her son is the last word uttered before the train finally stops. And the sound that none of them will ever forget.

Time	Destination	Expected
1st 7:06	London Victoria	Cancelled
2nd 7:13	Bedford	Cancelled
3rd 7:20	London Victoria	Cancelled

Gideon

Emma and Gideon are driving home in silence. He sits in the passenger seat, leaning on his elbow staring out the window. She picked him up from the facility for youth offenders about an hour ago.

When she first saw him in the visitors' room there, he was a young thirteen, just on the cusp of puberty. He looked tiny and fragile next to the hulking man-boys at the adjacent tables, all of them taller and bigger than their haggard, exhausted, tear-stained mothers. Emma hated the room's banana-yellow and pea-green walls, the sticky chairs, hated being searched every time by the guards, hated standing in the queue of terrible mothers waiting to see their wayward sons.

All of the visitors were women. She was envious of the ones who weren't mothers, who were aunts or grandmothers or older sisters who had taken the place of mothers, because no one deemed them directly responsible for the crimes of their boys. But the mothers, even if they were good mothers, even if they had sacrificed for and loved their boys, even if they had given them good homes, were still and always would be the bad mothers of terrible sons. Even if the sons were led to their mistakes by their fathers, even if the fathers showed them how to make those mistakes. It was still the fault of the mothers, for choosing such poor fathers for their children.

Emma knew, however, that this prejudice was not a silent injustice in her case. She was not a victim of sexism, or Freudian views of motherhood, or society's casual dismissal of mothering as work until it failed and children grew into criminals. And then police and social workers and lawyers and the public needed someone to blame.

Emma knew that everything about Gideon was entirely her fault. She had brought him into the world through spite, to prove her superiority, to harm the women – her mother, her sister, her cousin, all the women like them – who should have loved her but didn't. Who should have protected her, helped her, brought her in instead of keeping her out. But Gideon has done much more harm than she ever did and the blame for his crimes, of course, is hers.

Now, at fifteen, almost sixteen, Gideon is taller than her, broader, handsome features emerging beneath the angry acne and greasy black hair. The gap between his teeth has closed somewhat, like the dentist said it would, but not entirely. She wonders when he will learn to use it to his advantage. It crosses her mind that despite how thin he is, he is physically much stronger than her now and she suppresses the thought of what this might mean. They have said almost nothing to each other since she picked him up this morning. Neither knows where to begin. They don't have much to say. They have too much to say.

FIVE

'Are you hungry?' she asks, both hands on the wheel, staring straight ahead at the road.

'Not really,' he says. Loss of appetite, she knows, is a side effect of his new medication.

She does not push beyond this, she does not say 'Oh nonsense, you must be' or 'My goodness, you must want some real food after whatever they gave you in there' or any of the things another mother in her position might say. She does not press. She will give it time. Although she is worried about how unhealthy he looks, the gauntness of his shoulders, the sharpness of his cheekbones, she will let him acclimatise at his own pace.

The turn-off after the university campus on the right side of the road is approaching. It is the turn they always took to get to Anne and Ollie's house, only five minutes from here.

'What does it look like now?' Gideon asks, with a deeper voice than he had the last time they were in a car together.

'It's gone, it's just an empty space,' she says, knowing what he is asking.

'Can we go there?' Gideon asks.

'Maybe after you've been home for a while,' she says.

'I want to see it,' Gideon says.

'There's nothing there,' she says.

'I need to see it, Emma,' Gideon says.

'All right,' she says, and makes the turn.

A few minutes later, they get out of the car and stand on what was once the gravel driveway of Anne and Ollie's house, now overgrown, weedy, abandoned. A chain-link fence stands along the perimeter of where the house used to be before Gideon burned it down, with Anne, Ollie, Louise and the dog sleeping inside. They had the charred remnants of the house cleared and a fence put around the footprint to discourage squatters and vagrants and feral cats. To make it seem less like an empty lot and more like a work in progress until a decision is made about selling or rebuilding, a decision Anne and Ollie still can't bring themselves to think about. Morning glories creep up the links of the fence, bursting with blooms, impervious to the crime that took place here and to the young man who committed it, standing before their bright heads, bobbing in the breeze.

'Where are they?' he asks, hands pushed deep into the front pocket of the new hoodie she bought him, his right foot unconsciously sweeping across the gravel. The hoodie is far too big because she didn't know his size. It has been so long since she bought him any clothing, since she has been familiar with the contours of his physical presence. He notices that the sign that says PRIVATE PROPERTY, KEEP OUT is rusting in the corners where it attaches to the fence.

'They left,' Emma says. 'They don't want us to contact them. They didn't say where they were going. Remember, I told you?'

These are lies. She knows that Anne, Ollie and Louise moved to Cardiff, to be near Ollie's family, to start over, to forget. They all survived the fire, except for the dog. Anne miscarried from the shock and the smoke inhalation. Ollie sustained significant burns to his torso from shielding Louise with his body as he ran through the blaze to save her. Louise

FIVE

was unharmed, physically, but psychological scars will appear later in her life from a childhood of dealing with her mother's years of depression and her father's suffocating, anxious love and the sense that she can never do enough to ease her parents' mourning for their children who did not live and their children who were only dreams.

'Do they hate me?' Gideon asks.

'No. They're sad for you. And afraid of you,' she says, lying and telling the truth in the same breath.

'Are you afraid of me?' he asks, not looking at her, but looking in the distance through the fence to the back garden beyond, remembering how Ollie used to let him put the dog in a kiddie pool to give her a bath in the sunshine. Ollie was nice to him. He knows he was.

'No,' she says, as quickly as possible, because it is the right thing to say, even though it isn't true.

Wordlessly, they slowly walk around the plot. She waits for him to say something. She does not expect remorse or regret from him. She does not chastise or rehash the past or lecture him about how he will have to behave in future. She does not lay ground rules. She does not say that this is a fresh start. She does not mention a blank slate. She does not say she hopes he learned his lesson. She knows that he does not understand the rules that govern the lives of other people. Even other people who have done bad things. His conscience is weak and mute, if it is there at all. Right and wrong will have to be explained to him as facts, because they are missing as his instincts.

They stand for a long while in front of the fenced-in

overgrown weeds. The sun comes out from behind a cloud. Gideon closes his eyes and turns his face to it. It is the most tender thing she has ever seen him do.

Eyes still closed, he says, 'I wasn't trying to kill them. I wasn't thinking about them, not really.'

'I know,' she says.

'I don't feel things,' he says.

'No,' she says. 'I know,' she says.

'I don't want to be bad,' he says.

'No?' she says, a slight question, a slight hope in her voice.

'Because I don't want to go back there,' he finishes the thought, 'ever again.'

A different mother would say something here about the goodness inside of him, that it has always been there, that she believes in him, even if he doesn't believe in himself. That she will do the believing for him. She's read that true psychopaths aren't deterred by punishment. That he doesn't want to go back to prison gives her a small shred of hope, the smallest. She hangs onto it.

She says, 'Well, that's enough of a reason.'

'Other people feel things,' he says.

'Yes, but we're not like other people, I don't feel what other people do,' she says.

'What happened on that day with the train? Was it because you couldn't feel? Were you trying to feel?' he asks. He has asked her about this episode in their lives many times, and each time the question is different.

FIVE

'No. I was trying to save you,' she says. 'You were so close to the edge of the platform.'

'Yeah,' he says, through glimpses of memory. He is a little boy. *Paw Patrol* on his tablet. People yelling. An alarm. The big man holding his head. An old lady on the ground, sleeping. Emma grabbing him, kicking her until she lets him go. The train is coming. He kicks the big man. Another man on his knees on the tracks. That's his chance. When the adults all look at the train and the kneeling man. A blast of sound. He pushes, but he's not strong enough. He's pushed back. The rush of air from the train passing. A big hand on his chest. Falling backwards, landing hard.

That is what he remembers. But that is not the story his mother tells.

'It was all so fast,' she says. 'And so loud. The alarm, the train, the screaming. So much was happening. I've told you this, an old lady had a heart attack, a man was on the tracks, two guys tried to help him, another lady was bleeding. I was trying to hold you but you struggled against me, you were close to the edge and I was afraid you would fall.' She does not mention how he kicked her. She has always been too afraid of what she saw her son do, whether she did actually see it, to speak it out loud. In case Gideon remembers. In case he tells her that it's true. In case he remembers what she did. And didn't do.

'We fell. I remember. Why? How?' he asks.

'I grabbed you and someone grabbed me,' she says. 'A man,

and he pushed us away from the train.' She does not say which man.

'Did you want to die?' Gideon asks as he has asked before.

She avoids that question. She says, 'We don't feel things, Gideon. Love is different for us—'

'Love?' he says, with slight derision, slight disdain in his voice.

'Yes, love. I would jump in front of a train to save you. That's love,' she says.

'That's crazy. I wouldn't do that for you,' he says, shaking his head.

'That's because you're not my mother,' she says.

Gideon laughs. It is unexpected, the sound of it. It surprises him, and her. He has not laughed for a long time.

'That would be fucked-up if I was, Emma,' he says, a chuckle in his voice.

'I know,' Emma says, looking at her son. 'We're fucked-up, Gideon, aren't we?'

07:28

@OfficialBritishRailways It is with great sadness that we report a person hit by a train on the South London line. All trains between West Woodard and East Croydon are blocked while emergency services attend the scene. Expect delays. We apologise for the disruption to your journey.

@Sophiesoph79 So sad for the family. Poor train driver. How awful. 😳

@alice57895 I'm eight months pregnant on the train that hit the person. Theres no toilets. sorry for the family but how long will we be here?

@BritishRailways to **@alice5789** We apologise for the inconvenience. Delays of 60 minutes or more are expected. We will endeavour to keep you updated.

@johnnyrightwings72 I'd get to London faster in a migrant boat.

@Debbuchan7879 Awful for the family and staff involved. So sad 😳 How do I apply for a ticket refund?

@crustykingrichard Bloody British railways, it's always something. Sorry, bloody is a poor choice of words, considering. LOL

@everyanon5 Poor train conductor. Poor bloke. RIP whoever you are.

The young officer ties the yellow caution tape to a parking sign and pulls it taut between all of the available signposts to cordon off the entrance to the station. The local police and paramedics arrived about ten minutes after Medical Student placed the call. The railway's mobile operations manager and the British Transport Police soon followed. Of course, by the time they all arrived, everything had already happened. But they are here now, and their presence in the aftermath is a relief.

The officer is posted at the station entrance to close it off and redirect the public while the situation is stabilised. As he is new to policing, he has not learned to leave enough slack

FIVE

in the tape as he weaves it between the signposts, so as soon as he ties the end to the final post, the tape snaps at the first post, and the end flutters to the ground in the breeze.

He feels a flush rising up his neck as he tries to pick the tape up off the ground to begin again, with more and more commuters and students arriving, unsure from his movements as to whether he is putting the caution tape up or taking it down. A teenager on his way to school, headphones on, only half-paying attention, proceeds to the entrance.

'Back up, back up, please, station closed,' the officer says with as much authority as he can muster, shooing the teen away with one hand while he tries to reattach the tape to the first post. However, somehow the tape is now not long enough to reach the final post. So he must find another place to anchor it.

Impatient office workers and sleepy students gather in front of the station. People begin pulling out their phones and saying things into them like 'Some sort of delay' and 'Of course, useless, bloody police aren't saying anything' and 'So sorry, I'm going to be late.'

A group of older women arrive dressed in floral blouses and sensible shoes, with rarely used expensive handbags, ready for their day out in the city. They're supposed to have a champagne brunch at a five-star hotel and then catch a matinee in the West End today. Their leader says, 'This simply won't do,' and emerges from the steadily building crowd and says to the officer, 'Constable, excuse me, excuse me,' waving a manicured hand at him, but he doesn't look up. He has now tied the caution tape to a post and woven it through a few others, and he thinks he might be able to make this work if he just doesn't stretch it to the last one, when the tape slips through his fingers and flutters to the ground. Again.

A mischievous breeze lifts the end of the tape off the pavement, then lowers it again just out of reach of the officer, then lifts it again, as he hobbles about trying to catch it. He is starting to sweat. He finally does catch the end with a bit of a skip and a hop and a lunge, his belly wobbling over his belt. As he finally, triumphantly, grasps at the end of the caution tape, his police hat, new and stiff with its glittering shield, falls off and hits the ground.

'Excuse me, constable,' trills the leader of the older women.

'Mum, can you pick me up and drive me to school,' says a teenager on the phone to his mother.

'Damn it, Sarah, it's not my fault,' says a man on the phone to his wife, whom he will soon divorce.

But there is a sudden hush in the small crowd when the first of the five gurneys emerges from the station.

'Hey! Can you cut this tape? We can't get by,' one of the paramedics says. The young officer had not realised that in his determination to cordon off the area he has, in fact, blocked the paramedics' pathway to their ambulance. *Oh God,* he says to himself, internally slapping his forehead. 'Of course, sorry, lads,' even though the paramedic speaking is a woman. He rushes to break the tape and let them through.

Pause here, for a moment.

Consider what you know and what you don't about the child, the mother, the businessman, the old woman, and the gambler.

FIVE

You know now that Gideon and Emma survive. Perhaps that is a relief. Perhaps not.

Parts of the child and the mother die, of course, metaphorically speaking, if you like those kinds of metaphors. Metaphors about life and death, or the death of the spirit versus the death of the body, or the death of the past to enable the birth of the future, these are always good topics to raise in book club when the conversation lags.

Especially because it is too uncomfortable to talk about how, privately, you may think that Gideon should have been the one to die because he is a psychopath who ruins three lives. Four if you count his mother. Or five if you count the dog. And that's before he's even old enough to drive.

It's hard to admit that you feel that way because, after all, he is only a child. And he is still a child when he commits his crimes and still a child once he has served his sentence. Surely, he can't be entirely lost at such a young age, surely, we must believe in his redemption.

And yet.

You can't get away from the feeling, because his recollection of today, which is ten years old by the time you have read it, is so disturbing. So, to avoid an awkward conversation over the charcuterie board and chardonnay, raise the point about the metaphors instead. You can steer things away from the fact you think Gideon should have been condemned to death even though he is only a child and even though you know that after ten years, memory, especially a childhood memory, is a flaky, fleeting thing.

And the point is, you don't believe in the condemnation and execution of children. Not really.

When everyone gives the British Transport Police their statements, they refer to Emma as 'that mother', 'that pale woman' and 'that one who couldn't handle her kid'. They recount her jumping on the tracks this morning and her struggles with her rambunctious son. She is the first one taken off the platform on a gurney. She has a concussion. She is not sure if that is what is making her cry so hard, or if it is the death, or if it is the future with Gideon stretching out in front of her.

The crowd outside the station parts and gives the paramedics a wide berth when they see her and hear her hysterical crying, followed by a solemn Gideon wearing a silver emergency blanket because his coat was lost in the melee that surrounded the saving of his life. When the crowd see the screaming woman and the silent boy, they understand that something terrible has happened this morning.

A video of Emma is posted on TikTok: *POV Monday morning.*

Another video is posted to a private group on WhatsApp: *My first day back after mat leave and this is how it starts. I know how she feels but FML.*

At every station down the line towards London, announcements are made over loudspeakers: *Due to a person hit by a train, all trains to London Victoria are cancelled. We apologise for the disruption to your journey.* A few station staff cannot bring themselves to say the words 'person hit by a train' and refer instead to 'a customer incident'. A few others

FIVE

do say them, because they know the truth usually makes the public less volatile on a morning like this. A few others think about the train driver, and feel awful for him, and listen in on walkie-talkies to hear if it is one of their friends who will now be changed forever.

To Do List was watching as Emma was handled by the paramedics on the platform and then taken away. When it is her turn to be checked, she asks whether she too could be taken out on a stretcher because of her ankle and bloody nose and her mental distress. After all she did and witnessed, she really feels that she deserves hospital admission. She thinks how wonderful it would be to lie in a bed and have everything done for her, and how her husband and sons would rush to see her and be so worried.

But her nose has stopped bleeding and she can walk, so the paramedics tell her that she is fine and let her go. She gives the transport officers her contact details and a brief statement, skipping over the part about triggering the alarm. With her purse and laptop bag in hand, she leaves the station to find a cab. All of the taxis in the local area have now lined up outside the entrance because news of the station closure has been on local morning TV and radio, and there is a mad dash for them. But when the waiting commuters see the bedraggled To Do List emerge, they grant her the respect of taking the first taxi.

The driver has to say to her, 'Your belt, please, love,' when the seat belt indicator bell in the car goes off, because she has not put it on yet. But he drives off anyway to make space for the queue of cars behind him.

'I'm almost done,' To Do List says, referring to the fact that she is almost done pulling off her restrictive high-waisted tummy control undergarment. She would not ordinarily do this in front of a man, but she no longer cares what anyone thinks of her. She just wants to breathe and restore circulation to her abdomen.

'Oh, thank God,' she groans in relief, when she finally shimmies the body-contouring undershorts down to her swollen ankle. 'That's better,' she says, as she presses the button to lower her window, throws her oppressor onto the side of the road, and fastens her seat belt. And then she stares out the window for the rest of the ride, wondering what it means that she wants to go anywhere but home.

Later, after she gives her presentation to a colleague to deliver for her at work, she goes for a drink at the bar in the luxury hotel next door to her office. She will meet a silver-haired gentleman, allow him to buy her several drinks, and then go upstairs with him to his room. She will feel appreciated and adored. She will feel free now that she has escaped the prison of her shapewear, and she will be in the arms of a stranger who will find it far more alluring that she is wearing no undergarments at all.

To Do List will arrive home the next morning, hungover and tearful, grateful to have forgotten the morning on the platform for a while but hit with the wrecking-ball memory of it when she enters her house. She will be home in time for her grocery delivery. She will remember the silver fox she bedded, and the alarm she set off, Emma's scream and trying to help and, of

FIVE

course, the death, the awful death, and she will insist to the grocery delivery man that she ordered Pink Lady apples and she will be devastated to learn that she did not.

Bad Back, unfortunately, does not, like To Do List, simply walk away from the platform to have liberating sex with a stranger. He is taken out of the station on a gurney. All he can hear as he stares blankly at the sky is an argument between what sounds like an older lady and a police officer.

'But we have a brunch! At a five-star hotel!' he hears.

'Sorry, madam, there's nothing I can do, take a taxi like everyone else, or go home,' he hears.

Bad Back can't lift his head to see who's speaking. It even hurts to close his eyes, so he tries to focus on the clouds and sees a bird fly overhead before he is lifted into the ambulance.

He was injured when he ran behind Emma and Gideon, who were struggling with Liam, and he broke their fall. Bad Back remembers grabbing them both, pulling them away from Liam and the edge of the platform. And no one was more surprised than he was. But when they all fell backward onto the concrete, he threw out his back in a very real way. He finally did something to help someone but then found himself on the ground in spasms of paralysing pain.

As he looks at the bird flying free, Bad Back knows there is an important lesson for him in the irony of this moment, but he decides to put off learning it until the muscle relaxers kick in. Later, he will feel embarrassed by his pretence of pain on the platform, his inertia and cowardice until the last moment, but he will also remember that he helped. He will tell his wife that he almost died saving a mother and child, and she will postpone filing for divorce, in case the experience has made him a changed man. And it has, though not the man that either of them had hoped for.

For a while, with his marriage on the mend, he will start to feel better about himself and life in general, because he has proof now that he is a good person, or at least not as shit as he thought he was.

But when the prescription painkillers they give him that make him feel this way run out, he will put one hand on his lower back and limp and overstate his pain and get another prescription, just to tide him over, just until he feels better. And then he'll change doctors to get the next prescription. And then he'll find other ways to get it because he needs it for his pain, which will no longer be in his back but in a place inside himself that he doesn't know the name for.

As word spreads through the suburb that the station is closed, the crowd begins to recede behind the yellow caution tape as people find alternate routes to their destinations. Groups of teenagers meander towards the bus stop to get to school. They are young, and as they take their detours to the corner shop or the café for hot chocolate and let the first few buses pass, they do not realise the human cost of their morning's unexpected leisure and enjoy the luxury of their youth.

The middle-aged commuters lined up for taxis outside the station at the taxi stand are annoyed and tired and acutely alert to any queue jumping. There are natural problem solvers

FIVE

among them who try to organise the group to share rides according to destination. There are solitary souls among them who would rather poke their own eyes out than have to share a taxi with a stranger, so they stand aside to wait. They pass the time by mentally reconfiguring their schedules, sending texts about being late, and asking for favours from other parents to pick up their children later. A few of them check the morning's news on *Metro* and the *Evening Standard* online and the railway website for live updates.

They read, 'Severe disruption due to person hit by a train,' which they already knew. A few of them shudder, a few think, *Bloody hell*, a few imagine the body parts strewn on the track and try to banish the thought. A recent widow gives up on the taxi queue and heads for the bus stop, wondering about the people who love the person who died, and how they may not yet know their love is now in the past tense.

But unlike you, the middle-aged commuters are unfamiliar with the travellers on Platform 1. They don't know them as well as you do. They do not know what you know.

So they do not appreciate the gravity of Mrs Worth's survival as they see her taken out on the next gurney, this time with the paramedics yelling and running. Mrs Worth's endurance means, of course, that we have only two more possibilities. Although she did come close to dying today. She was dead enough to need CPR when the paramedics arrived and she was lucky they were in time and able to whisk her off and bring her back to life.

Several months later, long after the news has moved on to

other tragedies around the country and the train station has reopened and is functioning as normal, Medical Student will stop in the local café on his way to work.

In the corner booth by the window, he will see Mrs Worth, much diminished physically but not in spirit. It will take him a moment to place her. He will not know why she is so familiar to him until he turns to leave, and then he will remember. He will stand at the cream and sugar station and stir his coffee while he looks at her surreptitiously from the side of his eye. He will see pride and loneliness in her face, and regret, so common in the faces of the elderly that he knows from his work.

He will walk over to her booth and politely, with a smile, say, 'Excuse me, madam, may I sit down with you?'

Mrs Worth will be uncertain at first. Her memories of the day are hazy, but she will recognise his voice, his precise pronunciation, and then she will know right away who he is.

'If you like,' she will say, and she will try not to purse her lips when she says it, but she won't be able to help it.

'I remember you from the station. You are up and about. That is good. How are you feeling?' Medical Student will say and take a sip of his drink.

Mrs Worth will be taken aback by the familiarity with which Medical Student speaks to her, but she will say, in spite of herself, 'Yes, I'm fine. I'm better.' And then, because she will realise that no one but her son has asked her how she is since it all happened, she will say, 'Thank you for asking.'

'What a terrible day? No?' Medical Student will say. 'I'm glad you're all right.'

FIVE

'Yes, it was awful,' Mrs Worth will say. Then, after a pause she will surprise herself and ask, 'Are you all right?'

'I am, thank you,' Medical Student will say. And then, after they each sip their drinks in silence he will say, 'I suppose we are the lucky ones. I must be getting to work now. Nice to see you. I'm glad you are well. Have a blessed day,' and he will turn to leave.

'Wait,' Mrs Worth will croak, and adjust her neckerchief and swallow a lump in her throat, and shed something that is not quite a tear, but that also is, and then she will reach for Medical Student's hand and say, 'Thank you.'

After finishing her tea she will take the train to London. She never made it to Livvie's funeral because of the other death and almost dying herself. But she will do today what she meant to do then.

When she gets to Nicholas and Livvie's house on the corner of a leafy, quiet road in Wimbledon, she will hear Rafi and Robi's voices carry out to the street. She will follow the sound, through the front gate, round the path at the side of the house, to the garden in back. She will see Horatio, old and bony and grey, lying on a dog pillow under a tree, his head on his paws.

'Hello, old chap,' she will say, scratching his head.

The boys will be throwing pieces of gravel at a wooden crate, assigning points in some indecipherable way that only children understand.

'Excuse me, boys?' They'll turn around and look at her, quizzically.

'I'm not sure if you remember me, I'm your grandmother,

Matilda,' Mrs Worth will say, putting out her hand awkwardly to shake with each of her grandsons. They will look like different versions of Nicholas.

'We have a grandmother,' Robi will say, unsure of why this strange old woman is in their garden applying for a vacancy already filled and wondering whether this is an example of stranger danger and whether he is supposed to start shouting for help.

'Yes, I know. Florence. She's – well, she's your mother's mother,' Mrs Worth will say, keeping a promise to herself not to say anything unkind while still remaining truthful.

'I'm your dad's mum. The last time I saw you, you were very young, probably four and six, I should think,' Mrs Worth will say.

'Yeah, I remember,' Rafi will say, unimpressed. 'You showed us how to do surgery on Robi and then you ran over our dog—'

'Oh, you're *that* lady,' Robi will say.

'Yeah, Dr Gran. Mum didn't like you,' Rafi will say, loyally.

'No, she didn't. And she was right not to,' Mrs Worth will say.

'Why?' Robi will ask.

'We didn't get along and it was stupid of me not to fix that. And I'm sorry because it meant I didn't get to see you grow up, and now here you are.' And then a silence will lie between them.

Then Mrs Worth will say, 'I won't bother you any more, I just wanted to see you, and you are very handsome, nice

FIVE

young men. That's good,' and she will turn to go when Rafi will ask, pointedly, 'Do you still cut up dead people?'

'You *cut up* dead people?' Robi will say, in astonished disgust.

'I'm retired. But, yes, I did, and the appropriate term is *autopsy*, which I did in hospital, to help people find out why someone died,' she will say by way of explanation to Robi.

'Do their fingernails keep growing? Because when I said Mummy was dying Oscar said that people's fingernails keep growing after they die and she was going to have really, really long nails,' Robi will say, shivering very slightly from the thought.

'No. They just look that way, because the skin shrinks a little when someone dies, so it makes hair and nails look longer, but they're not actually growing,' she will say.

'Can dead people still hear, because Oscar said she could hear everything we were saying even when she was asleep? And I tried asking her but she couldn't answer, so I don't know if she heard me or not,' Robi will say.

'There is some research to suggest that as people move towards death their sense of touch and hearing are the last things that stop working,' she will say.

'So she heard us say "Bye" in the morning?' Robi will ask. 'Before she died? That's true?'

'Yes, she did,' Mrs Worth will say as her heart breaks for her grandsons. And for Livvie.

'OK, good,' Robi will say.

She will notice that Rafi is quiet but she will not press him.

There is another, longer silence, and she will start to say, 'Why don't I go find your dad now,' when Rafi will ask, 'Is it true about heaven?' accusingly, not looking at her, throwing another pebble at the crate.

Mrs Worth will consider this, carefully, and then say, 'We can't know for sure because they don't come back to tell us. But I've spent time with thousands of dead people in my life, in the quiet, in the morgue. I think they go to the memory of the time where they were the happiest they'd ever been, and they stay there. I'm pretty sure your mum has gone to a day with you two and your dad and Horatio, laughing on a beach, or at Christmas.'

'And she's buying dog clothes?' Robi will add.

'Most likely,' Mrs Worth will say.

'And drinking white wine?' Rafi will say.

'Hopefully not too much, but she's allowed,' Mrs Worth will say.

'And a half-caf cappuccino with almond milk?' Robi will say.

'And then telling the waiter she doesn't want the chips that come with her food but then eating all of Dad's?' Rafi will say.

'And doing the laundry?' Robi will add.

'I'm not sure about that,' Mrs Worth will say, uncertainly.

'No, I mean the laundry from when we were babies, because our socks were so cute she said, she told me once, it's true,' Robi will say, suddenly worried, desperate to be right that his mother is holding his baby socks, wherever she is.

'Yeah, she's got a whole pile of baby socks next to her, and

FIVE

those brownies you made her that time,' Rafi will say, and rub his little brother's head. 'Don't worry.'

'OK,' Robi will say, and walk off to gather more gravel to throw.

'Is what you're saying true, or is that some crap like Santa because he's little?' Rafi will whisper to her quietly, behind his hand, his other hand curled in a tight fist.

'How old are you?' Mrs Worth will ask.

'Eleven,' Rafi will say.

'Ah. You're very astute. I suppose you're old enough now to know. The truth is, I haven't seen any studies that contradict my theory, and while I can't prove it empirically, I believe it, because I died for a few minutes three months ago when I had my heart attack and that was my observation,' she will whisper back to him.

'OK,' Rafi will say, suspicious, but deciding to accept her reply.

'May I have some of those?' she will ask, and the boys will give her some pebbles, and the three of them will throw them against the crate for a bit.

And then she will hear, 'Hello, Mum,' behind her. Both boys will rush to their father at the sound of Nicholas's voice, and he will hold one under each arm.

There is so much to say, but he knows she needs time, and he needs time, and they have already wasted too much.

'Why don't you come inside?' Nicholas will offer.

And as the four of them turn to walk up the garden path to the house, Livvie will be watching them from high above on a pink cloud, her highlights done, her gels topped up, two pairs of baby socks and a doggie tuxedo on her lap. She will see them enter her house, as she takes a sip of her half-caf cappuccino and smiles.

And so, a tidy resolution, a mother and son reunited, an old woman's hardened heart (remember how hardened it was from her childhood trauma?) softened by a near-death experience and the presence of young, motherless children (*motherless*, don't forget, *so* moving) who have helped her see the error of her ways so that she could learn to forgive. And be forgiven. Complete with a whimsical view of a happy, rose-coloured afterlife. Isn't that lovely?

Later tonight, Officer Tempest of the British Transport Police, who is currently standing on the tracks with her colleagues, preparing to remove a man's severed forearm from where it fell after the train hit him, will watch a late-night film with a similar plot to Mrs Worth's story, while she drinks a large quantity of vodka. She's been on the job for five months, seen four dead sheep, investigated three near fatalities and two separate cases of elderly people who died in their sleep on a train, and has now attended her first dismemberment.

It's not the gore of the stiff, detached limb, the weight of it, that has left her numb and unblinking in front of the TV, as much as the absurdity of the fact that the wrist of the arm was still wearing a watch. And that the watch was still working and telling the right time. The dead man's arm, the watch that read twenty past nine. That's the picture she won't be able to get out of her head.

FIVE

While Officer Tempest is dealing with the arm that will haunt her for years to come, her colleague, Officer Chubb, who somehow got out of body recovery on the tracks and is taking statements in the ticket office, is speaking with Medical Student.

'So, I understand you're the hero here. I'd like to ask you a few questions,' Chubb says to Medical Student.

'Sorry?' Medical Student says, confused.

'That young guy, everyone says you pulled him out of the way. Well done, amazing work,' the officer says, as Sonny is rolled by on a gurney.

Medical Student says, 'Excuse me, please, I must speak to him,' and runs to his side.

Sonny's right arm is extended at a bizarre angle from his body. His shoulder was dislocated by the force of Medical Student pulling him away from the oncoming train and into the crawl space under the platform and being forced to lie awkwardly on it for an hour until they were both pulled out from between the platform and the train.

'Peace be with you, brother. I will pray for you. You pray too. It will help. I am glad you are still with us,' are the words that come to Medical Student.

Sonny, unable to find any words, says only, 'It hurts,' and Medical Student knows the kind of hurt he means.

'You are stronger than the pain, remember that,' Medical Student says, as they wheel Sonny away. And Sonny knows the kind of pain he means.

Later, Sonny will be asked many questions by well-meaning

professionals about his behaviour on the tracks. It will not be clear to them whether he intentionally did not move from the path of the oncoming train or whether he was simply paralysed with fear. They will read the witness statements collated by the police. They say that Sonny helped the old woman, that he rescued Liam the first time he fell and was bleeding. They say that he seemed concerned with making everyone safe, but also that he seemed to want to die. Some will say that he knelt in front of the train on purpose. Some will say he seemed to freeze, which was also plausible.

Sonny will not be sure how to answer and so for several days he won't. He will take painkillers and barely touch the hospital food and lie awake most of the night and sleep most of the day. He will ask Gabriela and Valentina to leave when they arrive to see him, even though their tears will pain him. He will think about the events and people that intervened to keep him alive when he thought he wanted to die. He will wonder about helping the old woman, but he won't be sure if he did it because he wanted to or if he did it because it would have looked weird if he hadn't and would have made him look suspicious or if he did it because his mother never would have forgiven him if he hadn't helped an elderly woman on the ground and he knew his mother was always around somewhere, watching.

He will think about running to get that big bald bloke off the tracks, and he won't be sure if he did it because it was the perfect cover for getting onto the tracks or if he did it because he didn't want that guy to die, or if he even cared about that

FIVE

guy dying. The best outcome would have been for him to save the big bald bloke and then for him to die accidentally in the act of saving, and so die a hero. But then he would have died in a lie. And he was always living in one and that was the problem. Death surely is preferable to this, lying in pain, rescuing someone who died anyway, who died the way he intended to die himself.

He will think about the people on the platform, strangers, who stopped him. Who insisted that he live. That weird old mum screaming at him and that weird young mum with that weird kid screaming at him, even the old lady falling down in front of him. And, of course, the doctor guy who was like Black Panther, saving everyone everywhere all at once. They knew nothing about his life, what a mess he had made of it, but they all wanted him to live. They risked their lives so he would live. He will marvel at how extraordinary ordinary people are. So loyal to life that they demand living from everyone. Even him.

He will not know how to express all of this to the well-meaning professionals. He will not know how to explain his contradictions and juxtapositions and the crossroads of his thoughts and actions. He will not know how to describe the relief he felt when he learned it was Liam who had died and it was him who had survived.

You start at the beginning.

Sonny will stare straight ahead at the mint-green wall of his hospital room and push away the voice he hears.

You start at the start. They will help you, but only if they know.

He will close his eyes. Having never been able to hear her in all these years, he will at first deny it, he will blame the voice on painkillers and exhaustion.

Are you listening to me?

He will be afraid to say her name out loud. But, as she would have in life, she will persist. And finally he will say, 'Mama?'

I'm here.

And Sonny will tell his mother everything, but unlike what she would have done in life, she will listen. She will not try to fix it. She will say only, *I trust you,* which he never heard her say before.

For a long time, Sonny will struggle through his problems, he will lean on Gabriela and Valentina, he will fail sometimes, many times, but he will also succeed. Every day something small will change, until all the small changes will become his new life: imperfect, challenging, sometimes very hard and very painful, but also extremely beautiful. And one day he and Valentina will have a son, whom he will sit on his shoulders, and for a second he will remember the day he almost died, and then his boy will say, reaching upward, 'Touch the sky!' and they both will feel a feeling like flying. And Sonny will be grateful for this joy, and hold onto it, and keep it close, and wrap himself in it for the times that he will still feel pain, though his pain will no longer be coupled with hopelessness because he will know that he can survive it. And he will.

Medical Student returns, reluctantly, to Officer Chubb, who says, 'I have a few more questions for you, I know you've had a rough morning, but—'

FIVE

Medical Student agrees to sit with the officer but gives only very short answers and pretends not to understand English well, although his English is perfect. He gives a brief statement. He says he left his ID at home. When asked for his contact details, he swaps two of the numbers around in his phone number and gives an old address. He wants no further interaction with police at all because it will lead to questions about his status in this country and he knows those conversations rarely have good outcomes, even when the police are patting him on the back, even when they are calling him 'hero'.

As he leaves the station he remembers, fleetingly, news footage of a man from Mali who scaled a building in Paris to save a child who was dangling off a balcony, four storeys up, out of reach of his shrieking parents. And that the French government gave him citizenship for his bravery. But Medical Student knows what country he is living in and he doubts he will be rewarded for saving a man who wanted to die but not saving the one who didn't.

Who, as you know by now, is Liam. You may have guessed it earlier, during the countdown. You may have ranked him as your first-choice candidate because of the bullying, the misogyny and his membership in the one per cent (with Gideon ranked a close second, even though we know you really wanted to put him first), and you are pleased that you have solved today's mystery. Perhaps you could take a poll at book club to see how many people knew it was Liam before the last platform scene. Or thought they knew it, or knew they knew it but rejected their instinct and thought it must be one of the others because it's too improbable, too convenient, similarly to the earlier train delay, to have a character fall on the tracks once, be rescued and then die anyway. What are the chances of that *really* happening?

Well, quite high, actually, if you've been paying attention. For surely, you have learned by now from the lives of our five passengers that life and death happen because they do. In the way that they do. Life and death happen regardless of what you think or guess or put in your online review or dream of or work for or choose or want. Or deserve.

Remember Anne, Ollie, Louise? Graham? Luna and Doreen? Brendon? Jo and Gerald? Remember little Rusty?

Did they deserve what they got?

Did you?

Yesterday, when Liam left Emma's house, she called a tabloid to leak the story about Danny's wedding and Liam's violence. Or Emma called a celebrity gossip podcast host to leak the story about Liam's love child and how he would not support her as a single mother of his bastard son. Or Emma called Danny to do what Liam had asked her to so he wouldn't take Gideon away from her. Or Emma called a hit man to kill Liam, but the train got him first.

Liam came to the station this morning to apologise to Emma for threatening her. Or he came to the station to suggest they go see Danny together to resolve their conflict. Or he came to the station to make sure Gideon was all right. Or he came to the station to take Gideon away from his mother.

FIVE

Liam's story can be told any number of ways, and we will never know why he really came to the station this morning, but we will always know that at the end he died. Because no matter what Emma and Liam did or didn't do, no matter why they did it or why they did not, the result is Liam's death. And Gideon's life.

Because our passengers were too busy with other events on the platform to see what Liam, with his blurred vision and throbbing head, saw. There was too much happening for them to see Emma moving closer to the edge of the platform with her son struggling against her. To see Gideon kicking to get away from his mother as she brought him nearer to the tracks and the train. To see Liam stepping in between Emma and Gideon and pulling Emma away from her son and pushing Gideon back to safety. Mother and child falling into the arms of a man with a bad back behind them, and Liam losing his balance, and falling in front of the train, believing, because of the blow to his head, that Gideon was Danny, the brother he loved from before he even took his first breath, for whom he would have always given his life if asked. Always.

Wait, not yet, Liam thought in the chaos on the platform. He had so much more to do.

Now? No, he thought, as he reached for Danny. Liam was not used to not getting his way.

Please, God, he thought, just before it happened. Liam, like many others, didn't believe in God, not until the end. Not until he had to.

I can't go, please, Liam thought, and then he did not think again.

After Liam's death, Danny makes the investment in the project with lifesaving potential on a world-changing scale after Emma tells him about her last meeting with his brother. Danny gives Emma back her old job, and she earns the money to send Gideon to a therapeutic school where he does well and gets better for several years. And so, Liam keeps his promise, in the end, to take care of Gideon and Emma, although he had to die to make it happen.

Unfortunately, Liam's phone is crushed by the train. He saw the email but had not yet responded. It said, *The data is off. Can't make those claims yet. Something's not right. Hold your fire at the meeting. Don't put the money in, not yet.*

Liam's widow, his third wife, Elizabeth the Second, drops her boys at school and is on her way to Pilates when her Waze flags heavy traffic around the train station. 'Ugh,' she groans. The cars in front of her slow. She hears an ambulance in the distance that she does not know is for her husband's body, and a cute emergency vehicle icon pops up on the map on her screen. Her phone rings over the car's console. Danny. She doesn't answer and lets it go to voicemail. Weird. They haven't spoken since his and Brendon's nonwedding. She can't deal with him now, it's too early, she'll call him back after class when she's feeling more Zen.

The cars in front of her stop. 'Ugh,' she groans again, as she runs her forefinger over the smooth red gel on her thumbnail, an unconscious habit she adopts when she's stressed, or bored,

FIVE

or both. She will forget to cancel her next nail appointment three weeks from now, as by that time she will be locked in battle with Elizabeth the First and Trisha and their children over funeral arrangements and, of course, Liam's estate.

While still in the chaos of grief and greed, she will get into Liam's email and his phone records but keep them to herself. She will have no idea who the last email is from or what it means, so she will ignore it and forget it. She will be relieved that there is no email or record of a call from that woman, the thin strange blonde he used to fuck.

Five years later, when the two young people Liam was convinced had a life-changing, world-saving idea are arrested for committing fraud on a global scale, the stock plummets and Danny loses almost everything, as does Emma, and Gideon is pulled out of his school and starts setting fires. Because no matter what anyone did or didn't do, or how the story is told, Gideon becomes who he is meant to be.

At the train station and afterwards in the hospital, the police ask Gideon only a few questions because they don't want to inflict more trauma after an already-traumatic event. As Emma has carefully avoided the involvement of social services to this point in Gideon's life, and because they are white and Emma's shoes and handbag indicate affluence, and because this station is in a quiet suburb with a low crime rate and Gideon attends private school, they are not on anyone's radar. Emma is not questioned very much about her son or why they were at the station that morning or why they were so close to the tracks.

Everyone who was there, except for Mrs Worth, who does

not remember much, reiterates the same story. Emma struggled with her son, her phone fell on the tracks, she went after it, then she climbed up onto the platform, there was an alarm, then Liam fell on the tracks the first time, but no one saw it happen, then Sonny saved him, then Sonny wouldn't move, Medical Student jumped, and when it was all over, Liam was hit by the train. It happened so fast. In the blink of an eye. What more could Gideon add?

He could have added that Liam's last word before his last words was 'Danny' but he doesn't know who Danny is. And he won't until he's twenty-two and comes across an article in the prison library about how Danny, with Brendon's help, rebuilt his former empire from scratch after losing everything, with an old photo of a young Danny with his brother, Liam, a tall, handsome man with a gap between his teeth that Gideon sees whenever he looks in a mirror.

When Gideon is paroled, he will find his Uncle Danny, much older, a recent widower, but affable, sitting in his library, sipping a Dubonnet on the rocks. He will have gained entrance to the house as the apprentice of the electrician, hired to fix the stair lift. Gideon will find the library and he will see in Danny's eyes that he knows who he is right away. Of course he does.

'You were his last word, just so you know. Well, actually, "Oh fuck" were his last words, but you were the word before that,' Gideon will say.

Danny, with the spirit of Doreen in his glass and the second coming of the brother he loved standing in front of him, will say, 'Sounds – a – bout – right.' And Gideon will smile Liam's

FIVE

smile and Danny will smile too and something lost will be regained.

The train must be checked for damage, so its passengers are moved through a controlled evacuation procedure to Platform 2. They do not consider themselves lucky, although they should, because they weren't on the platform, they didn't witness the death, and they are free to think of it only as a sad detached thing that happened to an unknown person in the distance. Some of them give up on the day, go home, and consider their unexpected day off a cosmic gift, and don't give a single thought to the person who died. Some of them give up on the day, go home, and weep for the people they've lost, long ago and not so long ago. But others wait and eventually board a replacement bus service which takes them to a larger urban station where they get on another train, which finally pulls into London Victoria at 12:30.

They arrive in London, exhausted, frustrated and hungry. And late. They are late for work and doctor's appointments and job interviews and university lectures. They are late for five-star brunch reservations and memorial services and meetings with literary agents and apartment viewings and connecting trains to other destinations.

A few are relieved to have missed their appointments, as they were not looking forward to them. A few caught up on their emails and their reading while the train stood still on the track. A few got in a little nap during the delay. One or two passengers exchanged numbers with the people seated next to them who they got talking to and thought were kind of cute and thought what a good story this would be to tell someday at their wedding or to their friends about how they met on a delayed train (they will skip the part about the death because it's a downer until their tenth wedding anniversaries, when they will start to make dark jokes about it) and how the hours felt like minutes and just flew by in each other's company on that fateful morning. They will say things like, 'When you know, you just know.'

The train that eventually replaced the 7:06 now stands empty on the track in Victoria. Its delayed passengers have spilled onto the platform and scattered in all directions to continue living.

A mouse, a distant cousin of the one who tended to Liam when he fell, scurries across the platform, taking advantage of the communal distraction and self-absorption of the commuters as they look down at phones and up at the arrival and departure boards. They do not notice the mouse as it sits, for a moment, on a folded, discarded newspaper that has been left under a bench next to a crumpled lottery ticket, a half-empty Coke bottle and a half-eaten packet of mini-cheddar crackers, a real windfall for the mouse. Waiting for the platform to clear, it nibbles on a cracker and rests on the headline. It scurries off to see what lies under the next bench. The edge of the folded newspaper lifts just slightly in an air current. Another train is on its way. It will be here soon.

Acknowledgements

Many brilliant, forward-looking, creative, and talented people have been involved in the making of *Five*. Writing a story is a solitary undertaking, but making it a book is a team endeavour, and I am so very grateful to my extraordinary team.

My unending thanks to my thoughtful, wise, and ingenious editors, Manpreet Grewal, Amy Einhorn, and Lori Kusatzky, for elevating this story and inspiring me to give you the best writing I can give. My thanks also to your teams, who have done a million things behind the scenes to create this book.

I am fortunate to be represented by two fierce and fearless agents. Thank you, Alice Lutyens, for your straightforward honesty and incredible eye and editorial skill which shaped this manuscript. Rebecca Gradinger, thank you for your guidance, calm and coolness under pressure, and overall coolness in general.

My forever gratitude to my writing group, the writer-mother-genius-woman-warriors who have cheered me on and kept me going: Sarah Asante Gregory, Caro Giles, Hannah Loy, Nicola Washington, and Penny Wincer.

Infinite thanks and love to my trusted early readers for your friendship and your time: Jessica Alexander, Lesley Bourns, Elaine Davenport, Crescent Maaz, Mariah Pizzano, and Jen Rachman. With special thanks to Barry O'Leary, for his continuous support from the beginning of my career. Every writer needs a friend like Barry.

My love and thanks to Tim, Leo and Rex, without whom there is nothing, and for whom I would do anything and everything. And for whom I do actually do everything as it turns out, so you guys got a pretty good deal with me. I love you.

To make the platform scenes in *Five* as plausible as possible, I rode many British trains, waited on many platforms, and did in-depth online research, and I found the website www.railforums.co.uk, where UK railway staff give insights and explanations about their work, very helpful. My sincerest thanks to the many unsung, unseen heroes of the railways and stations who work hard, day after day, in stressful and ever-changing conditions to keep the public safe and moving in the UK.

And, in case you want to check, the BBC did in fact say that only fifty-six per cent of British trains were on time in 2023, as reported in the article, 'Rail disruption: Train cancellations as high as 13% in 2023', by Jonathan Fagg and Emily Unia, https://www.bbc.co.uk/news/uk-england-66664323, 4 September 2023.

For the stories of Gideon and Emma, I researched sociopathy and psychopathy and was influenced by: the articles,

FIVE

'Life as a nonviolent psychopath', by Judith Ohikuare, *The Atlantic,* January 21, 2014; and 'When your child is a psychopath', by Barbara Bradley Hagerty, *The Atlantic*, June 2017; the films, *The Family I Had* (2017, Investigation Discovery Films, Katie Green, Carlye Rubin, Tina Grapenthin, producers, Katie Green, Carlye Rubin, directors) and *We Need to Talk About Kevin* (2011, Paramount Pictures, Jennifer Fox, Luc Roeg, Robert Salerno, producers, Lynne Ramsay, director), especially the performance of Tilda Swinton; and the books, *Sociopath, A Memoir*, by Patric Gagne and *We Need to Talk About Kevin*, by Lionel Shriver.

For the story of Mrs Worth, I researched PTSD in war veterans, animal necropsy, and forensic pathology, and I was influenced by: the articles, 'The long echo of WW2 trauma', by Stephen Mulvey, https://www.bbc.co.uk/news/stories-48528841, 8 June 2019; 'The family that wouldn't let PTSD drive them apart', by Matthew Green, https://www.bbc.co.uk/news/magazine-39152095, 6 March 2017; and the books, *Color Atlas of Small Animal Necropsy*, by Richard E. Moreland, and the truly incredible *Unnatural Causes*, by Dr Richard Shepherd.

For the story of Liam and Danny I watched many online videos and talks by people with cerebral palsy, and I researched societal attitudes towards people with disabilities in Britain in the 1980s and 90s. I was also influenced by the following: *Down All the Days* and *My Left Foot*, by Christy Brown; *Stairs for Breakfast: An Inspiring Memoir by a Man with Cerebral Palsy Who Doesn't Let Anything Stand in His Way*, by Patrick

Souiljaert; and, 'Attitudes towards disability in the 80s made my life hell, but things are changing', by Darren, https://www.scope.org.uk/news-and-stories/attitudes-towards-disability-in-the-80s-made-my-life-hell, 25 May 2022. Special thanks to Athena Stevens for her thorough feedback and insights on the character and life of Danny.

For the story of Sonny, I researched gambling addiction and drew from gambling recovery podcasts and TED Talks, as well as spending time on online gambling websites. I was also influenced by many articles including, 'I stole £70,000 to feed my addiction', by Rachel Stonehouse, https://www.bbc.co.uk/news/newsbeat-56997362, 7 May 2022; 'Female gambling addicts: I lost £50,000 in six days', BBC East Midlands, https://www.bbc.co.uk/news/uk-england-derbyshire-56675466, 11 April 2021.

I spent time researching passenger injuries and deaths by suicide involving trains in the UK. I came across many sad stories of loss, as well as stories of hope, and both are a testament to the depth of the human spirit. I was influenced by Mackenzie J, Borrill J, Hawkins E, *et al*, 'Behaviours preceding suicides at railway and underground locations: a multimethodological qualitative approach', *BMJ Open* 2018.

Additionally, for Sonny's story, I drew courage from the raw, beautiful, and honest writing of my friend and colleague, Caro Giles, and her unflinching memoir, *Unschooled*, which should be required reading for any education professional who works with neurodiverse children.

I am the mother of two brilliant, talented, funny, and

FIVE

spirited neurodiverse children. I took my kids to the Balham Pizza Express for many years and my son did once throw a blue glass across the restaurant just to see what would happen and the staff were nothing but kind and gracious. It is kindness without judgement that mothers always remember.

But we remember the judgement too. Because it wears away at our children, day after day, and it clings until they become adults, and it sticks until they do something, like Sonny, that very nearly can't be undone. And we, like Luna, would even come back from the dead to undo it, if only we could. For those who judge the children like Sonny, the mothers like Luna, you know who you are, and we know who you are, and I want you to know that your judgement causes damage that lasts forever. So, if you cannot see neurodiversity as a harbinger of limitless human potential; if you use only the narrowest, tiniest little ruler for measuring achievement; if you cannot be kind or even decent, you are free to be so. But please understand that we are not seeking your approval. We are just asking you, respectfully, to get the hell out of our way. We have extraordinary children to raise.

Juniper

Fiction to think about.

Juniper strives to reimagine what literary fiction can achieve. Our novels will resonate across generations, transcend genres, and break convention. Like the juniper tree and its berries, every story we publish embodies a spirit of wisdom, strength, resilience, and hope, and will stand the test of time.

Every Juniper author brings an undefinable spark of fearless creativity to their writing, which will surprise and inspire readers around the world.

Follow us
@readingjuniper